Changeling Press LLC

ChangelingPress.com

Rebel (Devil's Boneyard MC 14)
A Dixie Reapers Bad Boys Romance
Harley Wylde

Rebel (Devil's Boneyard MC 14)
A Dixie Reapers Bad Boys Romance
Harley Wylde

ISBN: 978-1-60521-955-4

Publisher:
Changeling Press LLC
315 N. Centre St.
Martinsburg, WV 25404
ChangelingPress.com

Printed in the U.S.A.

Editor: Crystal Esau
Cover Artist: Bryan Keller

The individual stories in this anthology have been previously released in E-Book format.

Table of Contents

Rebel (Devil's Boneyard MC 14)
A Dixie Reapers Bad Boys Romance
Harley Wylde

Are you ready to dive into a world where love and vengeance intertwine?

Rio -- I thought I had my future mapped out with the Army until two men shattered that dream, leaving me medically discharged and lost. I journeyed west then returned east after a call from my superior, urging me to testify against those who hurt me. When I stepped into a biker clubhouse along the way, I never expected to find a place I could truly call home. Rebel makes me want to trust again. He's charming, bold, protective, and understanding. I started my journey as a way to escape my past. I ended up finding a family -- and possibly love.

Rebel -- The moment Rio walked into the clubhouse, she had my attention. Proud, confident, and armed, she's a storm ready to be unleashed. When her past comes looking for her, I know I'll do whatever it takes to keep her safe. Those men have made a fatal mistake. They thought they were hunters. What they don't know is that *I'm* the predator, and they aren't walking out of my town alive.

Love isn't just a feeling. It's a battle worth fighting for.

Chapter One

Rio

The fluorescent lights buzzed overhead, making my skin crawl. I stood at parade rest, and stared at the blank wall behind Lt. Col. Harrison's empty chair. Two minutes till the meeting. Two minutes of pretending I wasn't about to shatter into a million fucking pieces. The office smelled like pine cleaner and stale coffee. Military efficiency. No room for mess. No room for the mess they'd made of me.

The door opened with a metallic *click*. I snapped to attention, keeping my eyes fixed on a spot on the wall, listening to the soft squeak of polished shoes against linoleum. A chair scraped back.

"At ease, Private Taylor."

I shifted my stance, feet shoulder-width apart, hands clasped behind my back. Not quite at ease. Not quite anything, anymore. Harrison shuffled papers on his desk. He was a small man with wire-rimmed glasses and a permanent frown. Twenty-five years in the Army had filed him down to the essentials -- no excess fat on his body, no excess emotion in his voice.

"The two men who assaulted you are in custody," he said without preamble.

My jaw locked tight. Assault. A sanitized word. Clinical. What they had done wasn't assault. It was destruction.

"Private Ellis and Sergeant Denton will face court-martial proceedings for sexual assault, administering a controlled substance without consent, and conduct unbecoming."

I stared at the wall. Blinked. Tried to match his detached tone with dispassionate thoughts. Fragments of memory hit me hard -- hands holding me down, the taste of something bitter, the ceiling spinning.

"Do you understand what I'm saying, Private?"

"Yes, sir." My voice sounded strange, like it was coming from somewhere else. Some other woman's mouth.

He glanced up at me, then back down at his papers. "Good. Now, regarding your status."

Here it came. The real reason for this meeting. Not justice for me -- bureaucracy for them.

"The medical board has reviewed your case," he continued, flipping to another page. "Based on the evaluation by Dr. Hayes and the subsequent psychological assessment, they've recommended a medical discharge."

The bubble in the paint seemed to grow larger, swelling until it was all I could see. Medical discharge. Two words that erased my years of service. Years of busting my ass, of being the best fucking soldier I could be.

"Sir, with respect --" My voice cracked like glass.

"This isn't a negotiation, Private." He looked up, his expression softening for just a second before hardening again. "The board's decision is final."

I swallowed the argument rising in my throat. What would I say anyway? *Please let me stay in this place where I was drugged and raped? Please let me walk past the barracks every day where it happened? Please let me salute men who think what happened to me was just a party that got out of hand?*

"The discharge will be processed as honorable," Harrison continued. "You'll retain all benefits associated with your service, including education benefits and VA healthcare."

His words filled me with bitterness. I'd worked so hard for it to fall apart like this. He made a note on his paper. "You're required to meet with a counselor before separation. I've scheduled your appointment for tomorrow at 0900."

My eyes narrowed. "I don't need a counselor."

"It's not optional, Private." His tone left no room for argument. "It's part of the discharge protocol in cases like... yours."

Cases like mine. Like I was a file to be processed and shelved away. A problem to solve. I wondered how many other women had stood where I was standing, hearing the same clinical words, feeling the same rage burning in their bellies.

"How long?" I asked.

"For the discharge? Two weeks, give or take. You'll be placed on convalescent leave effective immediately. Your CO has already been informed."

Two weeks. Fourteen days, and I'd be a civilian again. The thought should have brought relief. Instead, it felt like one more thing being taken from me without my consent.

"And them?" The question slipped out before I could stop it.

Harrison paused, pen hovering over his papers. "Private?"

"Ellis and Denton. What happens to them?"

He removed his glasses, pinched the bridge of his nose. For the first time, he looked directly at me. "That's not your concern anymore, Private."

Something inside me snapped like a rubber band pulled too tight. "Not my concern? They drugged me. They --" I stopped, throat closing around the words I couldn't say aloud. "And it's not my concern?"

"I understand you're upset --"

"Upset?" I laughed, a harsh sound that scraped my throat raw. "No, sir. Upset is what you feel when the mess runs out of chocolate milk. This isn't upset."

"Private, you need to control yourself." His voice hardened again, the momentary glimpse of humanity gone.

"Or what? You'll discharge me?" I took a step forward, fingers uncurling from behind my back. "Too late."

Harrison stood, placing both palms on his desk. "That's enough. I understand this is difficult, but this behavior only confirms the board's decision."

I felt it then -- the rage I'd been holding back for weeks, rising like floodwater, threatening to drown me. My hands shook. My chest heaved with each breath. For a horrible moment, I thought I might lunge across the desk and show him exactly how "upset" I was.

Instead, I forced myself back into parade rest. Stared at the wall.

"The counselor will help you process these emotions," he said, sitting back down. "Dr. Winters is very experienced with… trauma cases."

Trauma cases. Another neat little box to put me in. I didn't respond.

Harrison sighed, shuffling his papers again. "You have an exemplary service record, Private. Before this… incident. It's a shame to lose a soldier with your potential."

The compliment hit like a slap. My potential. Like it was something I had misplaced, not something that had been stolen from me while I was unconscious.

"What if I refuse the discharge?" The question was hollow, and we both knew it.

"You can appeal, but I wouldn't recommend it." He slid a folder across the desk toward me. "The process would extend your time here by months, and given the circumstances, the outcome would likely be the same."

Given the circumstances. More soft words for a hard truth; no one wanted damaged goods around. I was a reminder of something ugly, something that wasn't supposed to happen in today's Army.

"Take the folder, Private."

I stepped forward, picked it up. It was heavier than it looked. Inside would be forms to sign, benefits to claim, a neat paper trail documenting the end of everything I'd worked for.

"Report to Building C, Room 112 tomorrow at 0900 for your counseling session." He made one final note in his file. "After that, you'll meet with Sergeant Mills to begin out-processing."

"Yes, sir." The words were automatic, empty.

"You're dismissed."

I snapped to attention, saluted, and executed an about face, my movements wooden and precise. Military training was good for something at least -- it taught you how to keep moving when everything inside you had stopped.

"Taylor." His voice halted me at the door. I didn't turn around. "For what it's worth, I'm sorry this happened to you."

For what it's worth. Nothing. It was worth nothing.

"Is that all, sir?"

A pause. "Yes. That's all."

I closed the door behind me with a soft *click*, stepped into the hallway, and kept walking. One foot in front of the other. Left, right, left. Simple. Mechanical. My body remembered how to move even if my mind had fractured into a thousand sharp-edged pieces.

Two weeks. Then I would never have to see this place again. Never have to walk these halls, salute these officers, pretend I still belonged in this world of order and discipline that had failed to protect me when it mattered most.

Two weeks to figure out what the hell came next when everything I'd planned for was suddenly gone.

Two weeks to become someone else. Someone who hadn't been broken.

I made it to the women's restroom before I threw up, my knees hitting the cold tile floor, my breakfast burning its way back up my throat. When there was nothing left, I sat back against the stall door, wiped my mouth with the back of my hand, and stared at the ceiling.

The fluorescent lights buzzed overhead, just like in Harrison's office. The same sterile white light everywhere in this place. No shadows allowed. No place to hide.

I laughed until I cried, then cried until I couldn't anymore. Then I got up, washed my face in the sink, smoothed my uniform, and walked out with my spine straight and my chin up.

Just another day in the United States Army.

Just another soldier following orders.

Just another woman learning justice was never meant for people like me.

* * *

The counseling room looked exactly how I expected. Beige walls. Generic landscape print that someone had ordered from an office supply catalog. Two chairs facing each other, close enough for "connection" but far enough apart to avoid discomfort. A box of tissues positioned within easy reach. I'd been in this room before, even if I'd never set foot in

Building C, Room 112. The Army loved its templates --
same layout, different base. Same bullshit, different
day.

I arrived fifteen minutes early, military habits
dying hard. The door was unlocked, so I went in and
chose the chair facing the exit. Always have an escape
route. That was something the Army had taught me,
something I actually planned to keep.

The overhead light hummed. The constant drone
set my teeth on edge. I crossed my ankles, uncrossed
them, then crossed them again. My uniform felt too
tight across my shoulders, even though I knew it fit
perfectly. Everything felt wrong these days, like my
skin didn't belong to me anymore.

The door opened at precisely 0900. Military
punctuality. The counselor walked in carrying a leather
portfolio and a coffee mug with the Army logo. Of
course.

"Private Taylor?" He extended his hand. "I'm Dr.
Winters."

I stood briefly, shook his hand with the exact
pressure and duration that was socially acceptable,
then sat back down. "Sir."

"You don't need to call me sir." He smiled,
settling into the chair across from me. "Doctor is fine,
or James if you prefer."

I didn't respond to that. Kept my expression
neutral as he flipped open his portfolio and clicked his
pen. Another bureaucrat with forms to fill. Another
box to check before they could wash their hands of me.

"I understand you're being processed for
medical discharge," he said, glancing at what I
assumed was my file. "How do you feel about that?"

Straight to the point. No warm up. No gentle
lead in.

"Fine."

He looked up, studied my face. "*Fine* is a word people use when they don't want to say how they're really feeling."

I shrugged. "It's a word people use when their feelings aren't relevant to the situation."

"Your feelings are very relevant here, Private Taylor." He glanced down. "May I call you Rio?"

"It's my name."

He smiled again, patient and professional. I hated it. Hated the way he looked at me, like I was a puzzle to solve in the fifty minutes we had together.

"Let me explain the purpose of this session," he said, setting his pen down. "This isn't therapy, though I would recommend ongoing therapeutic support after your discharge. This is an exit assessment to help determine what resources might benefit you as you transition to civilian life."

I tapped my foot against the floor, a quick staccato rhythm. "I know what resources I need."

"And what are those?"

"My discharge papers and my last paycheck."

Dr. Winters leaned back slightly. "I understand your frustration with the system --"

"Do you?" The words came out sharper than I intended. "Because I don't think you do."

"Why don't you tell me about it?" His voice remained even, professional. Like he heard women like me every day. Maybe he did.

I shifted my gaze to the corner of the room, focused on the place where the walls met the ceiling. A tiny crack had formed there. Something structural giving way under pressure. I knew the feeling.

"There's nothing to tell that isn't in your file." My muscles coiled tight, ready to flee even though I hadn't moved. "Two soldiers drugged me. They raped me. They're in custody. I'm getting discharged. End of story."

"That's the event," he said softly. "I'm asking about your frustration."

My jaw clenched so hard I thought my teeth might crack. "My frustration?" I let out a humorless laugh. "My frustration is that I'm sitting here having to explain my frustration when it should be fucking obvious."

He didn't flinch at my language. Just nodded like I'd said something profound instead of cursing in his pristine little office.

"It should be obvious," he agreed. "And it is, to anyone who's paying attention. You've had your career taken from you because of someone else's criminal actions. That's a profound injustice."

I hadn't expected him to say that. The acknowledgment knocked something loose in my chest, something I'd been holding tight. I reeled it back in quickly.

"Yeah, well." I shrugged again. "The Army's gonna Army."

"What does that mean to you?"

I sighed, the sound harsh in the quiet room. "It means the machine keeps moving. People get ground up, spat out, and the gears keep turning. I'm just another cog that didn't fit right."

Dr. Winters made a note. I wanted to snatch the pen from his hand, see what he was writing about me. What box he was putting me in.

"Let's talk about your plans after discharge," he said, looking up from his notes. "Do you have somewhere to go? Family? Friends?"

"I've got plans."

"Would you share them with me?"

I tapped my foot faster, shifted in my seat. "I'm going to travel. See the country. Figure things out."

"That sounds very open-ended."

"That's the point."

He nodded, made another note. "Do you have a support system in place? People you can reach out to if things get difficult?"

"I don't need a support system." The words came out automatically, defensive. "I've been taking care of myself since I was sixteen."

"Everyone needs support sometimes, Rio."

"Not me." I shook my head, dismissive. "I'm good on my own."

Dr. Winters took a sip of his coffee, watching me over the rim of his mug. His eyes were kind in a way that made me want to look away. I didn't want kindness. Kindness made things harder.

"The trauma you experienced --"

"Don't." I cut him off, my voice hard. "Don't call it that."

"What would you prefer I call it?"

I blinked, caught off guard by the question. No one had asked me that before. "I don't know. Just... not that."

"Okay." He set his mug down. "We can find different words."

An uncomfortable silence settled between us. The humming light seemed louder suddenly. My foot kept tapping, tapping, tapping. A physical outlet for the anxiety crawling through my veins.

"You said you're going to travel," he said finally. "Any particular destination in mind?"

Safe territory. I relaxed a fraction. "Heading west first. Maybe California. Then wherever I feel like going."

"How will you support yourself?"

"I've got savings. And my discharge benefits. I don't need much."

He nodded. "It can be helpful to have a routine after leaving military service. Many veterans struggle with the lack of structure in civilian life."

"I'm not most veterans." I shook my head. "Structure is the last thing I want right now."

"What do you want?"

The question caught me off guard again. What did I want? Freedom. Space. Distance from everything that reminded me of what happened. But deeper than that -- what did I really want?

"I want…" I hesitated, uncertain. "I want to feel safe in my own skin again."

The admission hung in the air between us. I hadn't meant to say it out loud. Hadn't even known I was thinking it until the words were already out.

Dr. Winters didn't rush to respond. He let the statement exist, giving it weight.

"That's a good goal," he said finally. "And a challenging one."

I looked away again, uncomfortable with having revealed too much. My gaze drifted back to that crack in the corner. "Yeah, well. One day at a time, right? Isn't that what you people always say?"

"Sometimes clichés become clichés because they contain truth." He reached into his portfolio and pulled out a pamphlet. "This has information about VA services, including counseling options across the country. Wherever you end up, there will be resources available to you."

I took the pamphlet without looking at it, folded it, and tucked it into my pocket. I'd probably throw it away later, but refusing it would just prolong this conversation.

"I also want to give you this." He handed me a business card. "My direct line. If you find yourself needing to talk, I'm available."

"You do this for all your exit assessments?" I raised an eyebrow, skeptical.

"No." His honesty was surprising. "But I think you're at a particularly vulnerable juncture, whether you want to acknowledge that or not."

I stiffened. "I'm not vulnerable."

"Everyone is vulnerable at some point, Rio. There's no shame in it."

"Save the greeting card wisdom for someone who cares." I regretted the words immediately but couldn't take them back. Couldn't soften them.

Dr. Winters didn't seem offended. "Anger is a normal response to trauma --" He caught himself. "To what you experienced. It's protective. It keeps the deeper pain at bay."

"Are we done here?" I sat forward, ready to leave. "You've assessed me. I'm fine. Can you sign whatever you need to sign so I can go?"

He studied me for a long moment, then nodded. "I can sign off on your assessment. But I want you to consider something."

I waited, impatient.

"Running from place to place won't help you outrun what happened. Eventually, you'll have to stand still long enough to face it."

"Is that your professional opinion, Doctor?" My voice dripped with sarcasm.

"It's my human experience." He closed his portfolio. "And yes, also my professional opinion."

I stood, smoothing the front of my uniform out of

habit. "Well, thanks for the assessment. And the life advice."

He stood as well, extending his hand again. "Take care of yourself, Rio. And remember, reaching out for help is a sign of strength, not weakness."

I shook his hand briefly. "I'll keep that in mind."

I wouldn't. Or at least, I told myself I wouldn't. But I took his card anyway, slipping it into the same pocket as the pamphlet.

At the door, I paused. Something made me turn back, though I couldn't have said what. "When does it stop?"

Dr. Winters looked up from gathering his things. "When does what stop?"

"The feeling that they're still…" I couldn't finish the sentence.

His expression softened with understanding. "It changes. With time, with support, with work. It doesn't disappear, but it transforms into something you can carry without it crushing you."

I nodded once, a sharp dip of my chin. Not a thank you, not quite an acknowledgment. Just a motion to end the conversation.

I left Building C with my discharge paperwork signed and my head high. The Georgia sun hit my face, warm and bright, a stark contrast to the cold fluorescent lighting inside. The air smelled like pine trees and diesel fuel -- the familiar scent of an Army base that had once felt like home.

Two weeks, and I'd never smell it again. Two weeks, and I'd be free. Free to run as far and as fast as I wanted.

Dr. Winters was wrong. I could outrun this. I could outrun anything if I just kept moving.

I had to believe that.

Chapter Two

Rio

The room looked emptier than it had any right to. Two years in the Army, and I'd accumulated almost nothing that mattered. A few clothes. A laptop. Some books I never had time to read. Everything I owned would fit in a duffel bag. Twenty minutes to pack, then I'd be gone, like I'd never existed here at all.

The bed was already stripped, sheets washed and folded in a neat stack on the bare mattress. The closet held my uniforms -- two sets of ACUs, one service uniform. I took them off their hangers one by one, folding and rolling them with crisp, precise movements, muscle memory from countless inspections guiding my hands.

My fingers lingered on the sleeve of my service uniform. I'd worn it exactly three times. Basic graduation. The promotion ceremony when I made E-3. The memorial service for a soldier in my unit who died in a training accident. I'd never wear it again. Another life, discarded like a snake shedding its skin.

I packed my civilian clothes next. Jeans. T-shirts. The one dress I owned for occasions that never seemed to happen. Everything folded and rolled to the exact same dimensions, arranged in the duffel bag like pieces of a puzzle.

Everything except the Army shirts. I lifted my faded PT shirt, held it between my hands. The fabric was soft from countless washes, the letters cracked and peeling. *Army*. Such a simple word for something that had defined my whole existence. Something I'd believed in.

"Fuck you," I whispered to the shirt, then packed it anyway. Precise corners. Exact creases. I stuffed it down the side of bag. I wasn't taking it because I wanted to remember. I was taking it because I didn't want to forget what happens when you trust too much, believe too deeply.

The nightstand drawer contained the few personal items I'd kept. A photo of my mom from before she got sick. The last birthday card she'd given me before cancer took her when I was sixteen. A smooth stone I'd picked up from the lake where we'd scattered her ashes. A silver necklace with a small pendant -- her gift for my eighteenth birthday, the day I'd enlisted. Even though Mom had died before that, she'd made arrangements for it to be delivered to me. I hadn't worn it since the night it happened. Couldn't bear to, knowing they'd touched it when they'd…

My hands froze mid-motion. *Breathe. Just breathe through it.* I tucked the necklace into the side pocket of the duffel bag, wrapped in tissue paper like something precious and breakable.

Like me.

I caught my reflection in the mirror as I zipped my toiletry bag closed. Strawberry blonde hair pulled back in a severe ponytail. Blue eyes that used to spark with humor, now watchful and guarded. Freckles scattered across pale skin that hadn't seen much sun lately. I hardly recognized myself.

"Rio Taylor," I said to the reflection, testing the name like it belonged to someone else. In a way, it did. The Rio who had enlisted -- eager, idealistic, desperate to belong somewhere after years of foster homes and group housing -- that girl was gone. I didn't know who was taking her place yet. Just that she was harder. Angrier. Less trusting.

Maybe that was better.

Back in the bedroom, I pulled my laptop from

the desk and wrapped the cord around it neatly before sliding it into its case. The desk drawer held my discharge paperwork, the pamphlets from Dr. Winters, and the plain white business card with his direct line. I almost left them behind, a symbolic rejection of everything the Army wanted me to do -- get help, get better, move on quietly. Instead, I tucked them into the laptop case. Not because I planned to use them, but because part of me -- a small, scared part I didn't want to acknowledge -- was afraid I might need them someday.

Everything essential was packed in twenty minutes flat. Military efficiency, turned toward escape rather than duty. I stood in the center of the room again, duffel bag at my feet, and took one last look around.

My gaze fell on the car keys lying beside a map of the United States I'd bought yesterday at the PX. I picked it up and unfolded it. I'd already marked my route with a red pen -- Georgia to Tennessee to Arkansas to Oklahoma, then straight west through the Texas panhandle to New Mexico, Arizona, finally California. No timeline. No reservations. Just the open road and as much distance as I could put between me and this place.

I traced the line with my finger, imagining empty highways and anonymous motel rooms. Different towns every night. Different faces. Places where no one knew my name or what had happened to me. Places where I could be anyone I wanted.

"One month max in any place," I said aloud, making the rule real by speaking it. "First sign of trouble, move on."

Trouble meant different things now. Men who looked at me too long. Rooms with only one exit.

People who asked too many questions about my past. Anyone in uniform. I had a mental list of triggers a mile long, things that made my heart race and my palms sweat. Easier to run than face them. Easier to keep moving than to risk getting trapped again.

I folded the map along its creases, tucked it into my pocket, and picked up my keys. The metal was cool against my palm, the weight familiar and comforting. Freedom, right there in my hand.

At the door, I paused for one final sweep of the place. Two years of military service, all ended in one night by two men who saw me as nothing but a body to use. My jaw tightened. My fingers curled into a fist at my side. The anger was always there now, simmering just below the surface, ready to boil over at the slightest provocation. The counselor had said it was normal, protective. But it felt dangerous, like a live wire inside me that might burn everything it touched.

I picked up the duffel bag and stepped into the hallway. Didn't look back as I walked down the stairs to the parking lot, to my truck. I tossed my bag in the passenger seat, climbed in, started the engine.

The truck rumbled to life, faithful as always. I'd bought it used when I first got stationed here, saved up from my meager Army pay for months. It wasn't pretty -- faded blue paint, a few dings in the fenders -- but it was solid. Reliable. Like I used to be.

I pulled out of the parking space, navigated through the base housing area toward the main gate. MPs checked my ID one last time, waved me through. Just like that, I was off base. A civilian again. The weight of that reality settled over me as I merged onto the highway, heading west.

The late afternoon sun slanted through the windshield, warm on my skin. I rolled down the window, let the wind tangle my hair. Reached over and turned on the radio, found a station playing something loud and angry that matched the feeling in my chest. Turned it up until I couldn't hear myself think.

Everything I'd planned, everything I'd worked for, wiped away in a single night. But I was still here. Still breathing. Still moving forward, even if I had no idea where I was really going.

One day at a time. One mile at a time. One state after another until I found a place that didn't hurt to exist in.

I pressed my foot harder on the accelerator, watched the speedometer climb. The road unfurled before me like a promise. Not of safety -- I knew better than to expect that now. But of possibility. Of space to breathe, to rage, to become whoever I needed to be to survive this.

It would have to be enough.

I drove until the stars came out, until Georgia was nothing but a memory in my rearview mirror. Tennessee welcomed me with a sign that barely registered as I blew past it. My shoulders ached from tension. My eyes burned from staring at the endless ribbon of highway. But I didn't stop. Couldn't stop. Movement was survival now.

The gas gauge finally forced me to pull off at a truck stop somewhere near Nashville. The place was all harsh fluorescent lights and bleary-eyed travelers. I pumped gas with one hand, the other hovering near the pepper spray in my pocket. Old habits from basic training -- always be aware, always have a weapon within reach. New habits from *trauma* -- trust no one, especially men who look at you too long. I still didn't like that word, but counselors sure seemed to love it.

Inside, I grabbed coffee and a shrink-wrapped sandwich. The cashier barely glanced up as I paid. Perfect. Invisibility was my new superpower.

"Heading far?" he asked, ruining my moment of anonymity.

I shrugged. "California, maybe."

"Long drive for a pretty girl alone."

My spine stiffened. My fingers tightened around my change. "I can handle myself."

He raised his hands, placating. "No doubt. Just making conversation."

I nodded, already backing toward the door. "Have a good night."

Outside, the air was cooler. I leaned against my truck, sandwich forgotten, coffee scalding my palm through the thin paper cup. The interaction shouldn't have rattled me. It was nothing -- less than nothing. Just a bored cashier making small talk with a customer.

But my heart hammered in my chest like I'd narrowly escaped danger. Like threat lurked behind every casual question, every glance, every smile from a stranger.

"Get it together, Rio," I muttered, forcing myself to take a bite of the sandwich. Tasteless. Mechanical. Fuel for the body, nothing more.

My phone buzzed in my pocket. I fished it out, squinted at the screen. Unknown number. Georgia area code. My thumb hovered over the reject button, then curiosity won. I answered without speaking.

"Rio? It's James Winters."

The counselor. My jaw tightened. "How'd you get this number?"

"Your file." No apology in his tone. "I wanted to check in, see how you're doing."

"I'm fine." The default answer. The lie. "Just

stopped for gas."

"So you left already." Not a question.

I took another bite of sandwich, chewed deliberately before answering. "Yep."

"Where are you headed?"

"West." I wasn't giving him specifics. Wasn't giving anyone specifics. "Look, I appreciate the call, but I'm good. Really."

A pause on the line. I could almost see him making notes in that leather portfolio of his. Classifying me. Diagnosing me from hundreds of miles away.

"I understand you want space," he said finally. "But trauma doesn't just disappear because you've crossed state lines."

"Thanks for the bulletin." I crushed the sandwich wrapper in my fist. "Anything else?"

"The offer stands. If you need to talk --"

"I won't." I cut him off, throat tight with something I refused to name. "But thanks." I ended the call before he could say anything else, before whatever emotion was building in my chest could escape. Shoved the phone deep in my pocket like I could bury the conversation along with it.

Back on the highway, long past dark, the roads emptied. Just me and the occasional semi-truck, all of us running from or toward something. The miles slipped by one after another. The dashboard clock ticked past 2 AM before my eyelids grew too heavy to ignore.

I pulled into a rest stop, parked under a bright security light near the bathroom building. Locked all the doors. Reclined my seat just enough to be horizontal without losing visibility through the windows. Kept my hand on the knife I'd tucked between the seat and the console.

Sleep came in fractured pieces, broken by every sound -- doors slamming, engines starting, distant voices. Each time I jolted awake, heart racing, sweat beading on my forehead despite the cool night air. Each time I forced my breathing to slow, reminded myself where I was. Not in that barracks room. Not helpless. Armed. Alert. Free.

Dawn broke gray and misty over the Arkansas hills. I splashed water on my face in the rest stop bathroom, brushed my teeth, pulled my hair into a fresh ponytail. The woman in the mirror looked exhausted, shadows under her eyes like bruises. I stared her down.

"One day at a time," I told her. She didn't look convinced.

Back on the road, it wasn't long before Oklahoma came in a blur of flat farmland and small towns. The state stretched endlessly. I stopped only for gas and coffee, eating from the stash of protein bars I'd picked up along the way. Avoiding conversations. Avoiding eye contact. Avoiding everything but the asphalt ribbon unwinding before me.

Within hours, I'd reached the Texas panhandle. The land flattened further, horizons stretching so far they seemed impossible. I felt exposed here, visible for miles in any direction. No place to hide. But also nothing to run from except memories, and those followed no matter how fast I drove.

I pulled into a motel outside Amarillo just as my vision began to blur from fatigue. The neon vacancy sign buzzed and flickered, casting red shadows across the cracked asphalt parking lot. Not fancy, but cheap and anonymous. Perfect.

The night clerk barely looked up from his phone

as I paid cash for one night. No ID required. Another point in the place's favor.

"Room 17," he muttered, sliding a key across the counter. An actual key, not a card. Old school. Harder to track. I liked it.

The room smelled like cheap cleaner and cigarettes, despite the no smoking sign on the door. One double bed with a faded floral comforter. A TV that probably got three channels on a good day. A bathroom with rust stains in the shower. Home for the night.

I threw the deadbolt, then wedged a chair under the doorknob for good measure. I checked the window -- painted shut. Good for security, bad if I needed a quick exit. The bathroom window was too small for anything bigger than a cat.

One way in, one way out. The thought made my skin crawl.

I laid my knife on the nightstand, positioned so I could grab it in one motion. Put my pepper spray under the pillow. Kept my boots on as I stretched out on top of the covers, too exhausted to care about comfort, too wired to truly sleep.

The ceiling had water stains that looked like continents on a map. I traced them with my eyes, making up names for these imaginary lands. Anything to avoid closing my eyes. Anything to avoid the dreams that waited there.

My phone buzzed again. Not the counselor this time, but a number I recognized -- Sergeant Mills from the out-processing office. I let it go to voicemail. Whatever paperwork issue they had could wait until morning.

The voicemail notification dinged a minute later. I hesitated, then played it.

"Private Taylor, this is Sergeant Mills. Just calling to inform you that the court-martial date has been set for Private Ellis and Sergeant Denton. The JAG office requested I notify you, as you'll be called to testify. Please contact Lt. Col. Harrison at your earliest convenience for details."

The phone slipped from my fingers, bounced on the mattress. Testify. They wanted me to come back. To sit in a courtroom and tell strangers exactly what had happened. To look at those men again. To relive every moment while lawyers picked apart my story, my character, my behavior that night. Why the fuck hadn't I considered all that before now?

"No fucking way," I whispered to the empty room. "No way in hell."

I grabbed the phone, deleted the voicemail with shaking fingers. Then I turned the phone off completely. They couldn't make me come back. I was discharged. Civilian. Free.

The lie tasted bitter on my tongue. I wasn't free. Wouldn't be free until those men were out of my head, out of my nightmares. Maybe not even then.

I rolled onto my side, curled my knees to my chest, made myself small in the center of the sagging mattress. The knife glinted in the dim light filtering through the thin curtains. I focused on it, on the promise of protection it offered. On the cold comfort of knowing I'd never be defenseless again.

Sleep came eventually, dragging me under despite my resistance. And with it, the dreams. Always the same.

Chapter Three

Rebel
One Month Later

I leaned against the wall near the bar, nursing my whiskey and watching the usual Friday night chaos unfold. The Devil's Boneyard clubhouse pulsed with life around me -- half-naked women draping themselves over patched members, Prospects hustling drinks, the bass from the speakers vibrating through the floorboards. Then she walked in, pushing the door open with more force than necessary, like she needed everyone to know she wasn't sneaking in. The metal hinges had protested with a squeal that somehow cut through the roar of Guns N' Roses blasting from the speakers. For a split second, a few heads turned -- then most went back to their business. Not mine. I kept watching.

Strawberry-blonde hair, fierce blue eyes, and a don't-fuck-with-me stride that parted the crowd like Moses and the Red Sea. Something electric snapped in the air, and I knew my quiet night had just gotten a hell of a lot more interesting.

She stood there in worn jeans, combat boots, and a leather jacket that had seen better days. Not trying to show skin like the club girls but somehow commanding more attention. Her eyes scanned the room with military precision, taking stock of every exit, every threat. I recognized that look. Had worn it myself once.

The clubhouse wasn't much to look at. Worn hardwood floors bearing cigarette burns and knife marks that told stories of parties past. The walls were covered in a collection of road signs, license plates, and probably a bit too much Harley-Davidson memorabilia. The lighting was shit -- dim yellow bulbs -- but it hid the stains well enough.

She wrinkled her nose, probably at the cocktail of smells -- stale beer, motor oil, leather, sweat, and the unmistakable scent of sex. Her shoulders tensed as two hang-arounds brushed past her, but she stood her ground. Didn't flinch. Interesting.

Charming sat at his usual table in the corner, silver-threaded hair catching the light as he nodded at something Havoc was saying. Even from across the room, you could feel his presence. His years as president had that effect. Men unconsciously straightened when he looked their way, women's voices dropped to deferential tones. Not out of fear -- though plenty feared him -- but out of the kind of respect that can't be demanded, only earned.

I watched her clock him immediately. Smart girl. In a room full of predators, she'd identified the alpha in seconds. Her eyes narrowed slightly, assessing, calculating. But she didn't approach. Instead, she made her way to the bar, keeping her back to the wall, ordering something I couldn't hear over the music.

"Who's the new blood?" Chaos appeared beside me, beer in hand, voice unnecessarily loud as usual.

"Don't know yet," I said, not taking my eyes off her. "But I'm about to find out."

"She looks like she'd cut your dick off for saying hello wrong." He grinned, obviously considering this a challenge rather than a warning.

"Then I better say it right." I drained my whiskey and set the glass down with a decisive *clink*.

Across the room, one of the club girls -- a blonde with tits that defied gravity and the IQ of a doorknob -- was trying to chat her up. Probably recruiting for the stable, or assessing if she would be a rival. The strawberry blonde's expression had gone from cautious to thunderous. Time to intervene before something ugly happened.

I crossed the floor in long strides, noticing how several of the brothers were now watching with idle interest. New female faces always drew attention, especially ones that didn't fit the typical groupie mold.

"Tiffany," I said to the blonde, not bothering with pleasantries, "I think Java's looking for you."

She pouted, those silicone lips forming a perfect bow. "I'm just being friendly, Rebel."

"Be friendly elsewhere." My tone left no room for argument.

She huffed but retreated, her six-inch heels clicking against the hardwood. I turned to the newcomer, close enough now to see the freckles scattered across her face and the tension in her jaw.

"The recruitment pitch gets old fast," I said, not bothering with introductions yet. "You looking for someone specific, or just lost?"

Her eyes -- startlingly blue up close -- locked onto mine. "Do I look like the type that gets lost?"

Southern accent. Georgia, maybe. And an attitude I could feel from three feet away.

I smirked. "No, you look like the type that walks into a biker clubhouse alone on purpose. Which means you're either crazy or have a death wish."

"Or I can handle myself." Her hand shifted slightly, drawing my attention to the slight bulge under her jacket. Carrying. Interesting.

"I don't doubt it." I gestured to the bartender for two more drinks. "But even the best fighters might think twice about a thirty-to-one ratio."

The corner of her mouth twitched -- not quite a smile, but close. "Thirty? I counted fourteen, and half of them are too drunk to stand straight."

I laughed, genuinely surprised. "You military?"

Something darkened in her expression. "Was."

The bartender slid two whiskeys toward us. I pushed one her way. "I'm Rebel."

She eyed the drink suspiciously. "Original."

"Says the girl who hasn't given her name at all."

She picked up the glass, sniffed it, then took a small sip. Testing. "Rio."

"Like the city?"

"Like the river. It flows where it wants to."

I raised my glass in acknowledgment and took a swallow, feeling the burn hit my throat. "So what brings you to our humble establishment, Rio who flows where she wants to?"

Her eyes flicked around the room again, lingering on a group of Prospects playing pool. "Just passing through. Heard this was where the action is in this shithole town."

"And what kind of action are you looking for?" I kept my tone neutral, but we both knew what the question implied in a place like this.

She met my gaze head-on, challenge sparking. "Not the kind you're thinking."

"You'd be surprised what I'm thinking."

A commotion near the door drew our attention. Two Prospects escorting a belligerent drunk outside, his protests lost in the music. Rio's hand had drifted back toward her concealed weapon, her body tensing for trouble.

"Relax," I said, stepping slightly closer. "Just the usual Friday night housekeeping."

"I don't relax in places I don't know with people I don't trust," she said, but her hand dropped back to her side.

I studied her for a moment -- the way she held herself, alert but not skittish. Dangerous but controlled. "Smart policy."

Across the room, Charming's gaze connected with mine, one silver eyebrow raised in silent question. I gave a subtle nod. Nothing to worry about. Yet.

"Your President's watching," Rio said without turning around. The observation impressed me -- she'd maintained awareness of the room without being obvious about it.

"He notices everything," I confirmed. "Especially strangers with hidden weapons."

She took another sip of whiskey, longer this time. "Should I be worried?"

"Depends on why you're really here."

The lights caught the angles of her face, highlighting then shadowing the determination etched there. Up close, I could see the faded bruise near her temple, almost healed but still telling a story she probably wouldn't share. Of course, with the attitude she seemed to carry with her, it wouldn't surprise me to discover she'd been in a bar fight.

"Maybe I just needed a drink and a break from the road," she said, but we both knew there was more to it.

I leaned against the bar, deliberately relaxing my posture. "We both know there are easier places to get a drink."

"Easier isn't always better."

"No," I agreed, feeling something shift between us -- not quite trust, but a mutual recognition. "It rarely is."

The music changed, something with a heavy beat that vibrated through the floorboards and rattled the glasses behind the bar. Around us, the party atmosphere intensified -- women grinding against leather-clad men, voices growing louder to compete with the music, the smell of weed joining the already complex bouquet of the room.

Rio didn't flinch, but her fingers tightened around her glass. Not comfortable, but determined not to show it. Interesting woman.

"You have somewhere to stay tonight?" I asked, surprising myself with the question.

Her eyes narrowed. "Why?"

"Because it's going to get a lot louder and a lot drunker in here as the night goes on. And while I'm sure you can handle yourself, even rivers need to rest somewhere."

For a moment, I thought she might tell me to fuck off. Instead, she finished her whiskey and set the glass down. "I've got my truck outside. I'll find a motel."

"The only motel in town with openings rents by the hour and has a bedbug problem." I straightened up from the bar. "I've got a spare room. Clean sheets. Door locks from the inside."

"Why would you offer that to someone you just met? Someone carrying a gun, no less."

I shrugged. "Call it professional courtesy. Or maybe I'm just tired of watching you calculate escape routes instead of enjoying your drink."

Something like surprise flickered across her face, quickly masked. "That obvious, huh?"

"Only to someone who's done the same." I set my empty glass down. "No strings. You can leave whenever. But at least you'll get some sleep without one eye open."

She studied me for what felt like a full minute, those blue eyes seeing more than I was comfortable with. Finally, she nodded. "If I agree and you try anything, I'll put a bullet in you before you clear your zipper."

I grinned, strangely delighted by the threat. "Noted. Just need to make a stop first."

I steered Rio through the thickening crowd, my hand hovering near the small of her back but never touching. The party had kicked into high gear -- shots flowing, music cranked, inhibitions dropping with every passing minute. She moved like a soldier behind enemy lines, hyperaware and tightly wound. The brothers we passed gave us space, curious eyes following but mouths staying shut. They knew better than to push when I had that look on my face. And I definitely had that look.

"Where are we going?" Rio asked, her voice just loud enough to carry over the heavy bass.

"To meet the President." I nodded toward Charming's corner. "Protocol."

She stiffened slightly. "I don't need an audience."

"Not an audience. A courtesy." I leaned closer, speaking near her ear to be heard. "You're carrying in his house. He deserves to know who you are."

The back half of the clubhouse was marginally quieter, the thrum of conversations replacing the worst of the music's assault. The lighting was better too.

Charming watched our approach with those penetrating eyes that had assessed threats and opportunities for longer than I'd been alive. At sixty-three, he might have been going silver, but nothing about him suggested weakness or decline. Beside him, Havoc stood sentinel, the Sergeant-at-Arms' weathered face and vigilant posture broadcasting his role without a word needed.

"Charming," I said, stopping at a respectful

distance from the table. "This is Rio. She's passing through."

Charming's gaze shifted from me to her, taking in everything from her stance to the concealed weapon in one practiced sweep. "Armed visitors usually introduce themselves first." His tone wasn't accusatory -- more amused than anything.

"Wasn't planning on a meet and greet," Rio said, chin lifting slightly. "Just a drink."

Havoc's eyebrow ticked up at her direct response. Most people showed more deference their first time in front of the club's leadership.

Charming's mouth curved into a half-smile. "Yet here you are." He extended his hand across the table. "Welcome to the Devil's Boneyard, Rio."

She hesitated only a moment before shaking it, her grip firm. "Thanks for the hospitality."

"Rebel showing you around?" Charming asked, though his eyes flicked to me with the real question.

"I offered her my spare room for the night," I said. "The Cherry Bomb Motel isn't fit for rats, let alone guests."

Havoc snorted. "That dump should've been condemned a decade ago."

Rio glanced between the three of us, clearly assessing the dynamic. "I appreciate the offer, but I don't want to impose."

"No imposition," I said, then added for Charming's benefit, "She's military. Former."

Something in Charming's expression shifted -- a subtle recognition. Many of our members had military backgrounds. It created an unspoken bond, regardless of which branch or when you served.

"Marines myself," Havoc said. "Long time ago now."

Rio nodded but didn't elaborate on her own service. The tension in her shoulders spoke volumes though.

"How long you planning to stay in town?" Charming asked, signaling to a Prospect who materialized with fresh drinks for everyone.

"Just passing through," Rio said, accepting the whiskey but not drinking yet. "Heading east."

"No destination in particular?" His tone was conversational, but I knew Charming never asked casual questions.

Rio's eyes narrowed slightly. "Does it matter?"

"Only if you want it to." Charming leaned back, completely at ease despite the edge in her voice. "We're particular about who passes through our territory. Especially those carrying."

"I'm not looking for trouble," she said. "Or business. Just a place to rest before moving on."

Havoc and Charming exchanged a look I couldn't quite interpret.

"Rebel's vouching for you," Charming finally said. "That counts for something. Enjoy your stay, however brief."

The dismissal was polite but clear. Rio seemed to relax marginally, taking her first sip of the whiskey -- much better quality than we'd had at the main bar.

I guided her away from the President's table toward a quieter alcove near the back, where the music was muffled enough for conversation without having to shout. A couple of the older members nodded as we passed, their expressions neutral but observant.

"That seemed important," Rio said once we were relatively private.

I shrugged. "Just how things work. Territory, respect, chain of command."

"Military without the uniforms." Her voice had a bitter edge.

"Something like that." I studied her over the rim of my glass. "You didn't stay in long."

Her expression shut down instantly. "No."

"Bad discharge?"

"Medical." The word sounded like it had thorns.

I let the silence stretch, giving her space to elaborate if she wanted to. When she didn't, I nodded. "None of my business anyway."

"That's right, it's not." She took another drink, then sighed. "Sorry. Touchy subject."

"Figured that much." I leaned against the wall, deliberately casual. "Look, I didn't bring you here for any other reason -- I'm impressed by you. Not trying to recruit you, sleep with you, or pump you for information."

She tilted her head slightly, those blue eyes searching my face for deception. "Why are you impressed? You don't know me."

"I know you walked into a biker clubhouse alone, armed but not threatening, and didn't back down when challenged. That says something about your character."

"Or my stupidity," she muttered.

I chuckled. "Maybe both."

Around us, the party continued. I'd had every intention of just introducing her and walking out. Hadn't counted on the conversation lasting as long as it had. Across the room, Chaos was entertaining a group with some wild story, his arms gesturing broadly as his audience laughed. The club girls circulated, some working the room for potential customers, others already paired off with members or hang-arounds. Through the doorway to the main bar, I could see more Prospects keeping order, ensuring the growing rowdiness didn't evolve into actual problems.

Rio watched it all with the same careful attention she'd shown earlier, though her posture had relaxed somewhat. The whiskey probably helped.

"How long were you in?" I asked, steering back to safer ground. As much as I wanted to get her out of here, I wondered if she needed this bit of chaos a little longer.

"Two years." She stared into her glass. "Signed up at eighteen. Out by twenty."

I nodded, not pushing for details. "Army?"

She stared at me, but didn't deny it.

"They taught you to handle yourself?"

"Some." Her mouth tightened. "Life taught me the rest."

From the corner of my eye, I noticed Havoc watching us, his conversation with Charming continuing but his attention divided. The Sergeant-at-Arms didn't miss much, especially potential security concerns. But his expression wasn't hostile -- more evaluating than anything else.

"Your club seems... organized," Rio observed. "Different than what I expected."

"What did you expect?"

"More chaos. Less discipline." She nodded toward where a Prospect was quietly removing an overly intoxicated hang-around. "You run a tight ship."

"Charming does," I corrected.

A loud crash from the main room drew both our attention. Someone had knocked over a table of drinks, and the resulting commotion had a few tempers flaring. Rio's hand instinctively moved toward her weapon again, her body tensing for trouble.

"Easy," I said quietly. "Happens every Friday. No one's shooting up the place."

Sure enough, Havoc was already moving in that direction, his presence alone enough to defuse the situation before it escalated. The guilty parties began cleaning up, chastened looks on their faces.

Rio exhaled slowly, but the wariness hadn't left her eyes. "I should go."

"Because of a spilled drink?"

"Because I don't belong here," she said bluntly. "This is your world, not mine."

I studied her face -- the weariness beneath the defiance, the shadows under her eyes suggesting she hadn't slept properly in days, maybe weeks.

"The offer of my spare room still stands," I said. "Clean sheets, and like I said, door locks from inside and no questions asked."

She frowned. "Why would you do that for a stranger?"

"Because you look like you haven't had a decent night's sleep in weeks. And because we take care of our own."

"I'm not one of yours," she countered.

"Military," I reminded her. "Different branches, different wars maybe, but same foundation."

Something in her expression cracked, just for a second -- a glimpse of raw vulnerability quickly masked. "It wasn't combat that got me discharged."

I waited, giving her space to continue or retreat.

She drained her glass and set it down. "Two men in my unit thought a female soldier was fair game. Drugged me. Did what they wanted." Her voice was flat, clinical, like she was reading a report. "By the time the dust settled, they ended up in the custody of the MPs while waiting for a hearing, and I had a medical discharge."

The anger that flashed through me was immediate and visceral. Not pity -- she wouldn't want that -- but the kind of cold fury that demanded retribution. I kept my expression neutral with effort.

"Those men still breathing?" I asked, my tone matching her matter-of-factness.

A ghost of a smile touched her lips. "Last I checked. Military justice isn't always just, but it's also not always swift. I don't know if they're dragging things on for a reason, or they're just backlogged."

I nodded, understanding more than she probably realized. "The spare room comes with no expectations, Rio. Just a secure door and a night of peace."

She looked around the clubhouse once more, her gaze lingering on the various members and women, the exits, the potential threats. I could almost see her weighing her options, calculating risks against her obvious exhaustion.

"One night," she finally said. "I'm leaving at first light."

"Your call." I straightened from the wall. "My place is down the road from here. You can follow me."

"If this is a trap --"

"It's not," I cut her off. "But you can keep your weapon, your suspicions, and whatever else makes you feel safe. I'm offering a room, not demanding your trust."

Something shifted in her expression -- not quite relief, but perhaps the closest thing to it she could manage. She nodded once, decisively.

"All right."

As we moved through the crowd toward the door, I caught Chaos watching us, his eyebrows waggling suggestively. I shot him a look that promised retribution later. Havoc nodded slightly as we passed his table -- acknowledging the situation but trusting my judgment.

Outside, the cool night air was a relief after the hot press of bodies inside. Rio took a deep breath, some of the tension visibly leaving her shoulders.

"Better?" I asked.

"Different," she corrected. "Not necessarily better."

I laughed. Something told me Rio didn't find many things "better" -- just different kinds of challenging. As she followed me toward my bike, I couldn't shake the feeling that whatever storm had blown her into our clubhouse was just getting started.

And for reasons I couldn't quite name, I was looking forward to the thunder.

Chapter Four

Rio

I jolted awake to the sound of my own ragged breathing. The guest room was barely lit, the light of dawn beginning to creep around the edges of the curtains. For a moment, I didn't remember where I was -- only that it wasn't my place, wasn't anywhere I'd called home. Safety was a concept I'd stopped believing in weeks ago. The digital clock on the nightstand read 5:13, and the compound was still quiet. Too quiet.

When I first began my journey back east, I'd had every intention of going to the trial. But somewhere along the way, I'd decided to take a detour, go see the ocean. Or maybe I just really didn't want to face those fuckers again. From my point of view, I'd been discharged. Why the fuck did they think they could still tell me what to do?

A month ago, I'd have never stopped at a biker compound. Things had changed. I had. I'd become tougher. At first, I'd avoided men like the plague. Then I'd realized what I was doing and forced myself to go to bars and face my fear. Gotten into a few fights. I'd always won. The "incident" had taught me a tough lesson. No one touched my fucking drink. I watched it being poured, kept my hand over the top of it when I wasn't paying attention, and never went anywhere isolated by myself. Coming here had been a challenge for myself.

Two nights here, and I still couldn't sleep through the night. Every creak, every shadow set my nerves on edge. It was only supposed to be one night, but when I'd walked into Rebel's kitchen the next morning, looking more like a haggard raccoon than a human, he'd said I could stay another night.

My phone vibrated against the wooden nightstand, the sound unnaturally loud in the stillness. I reached for it, my fingers trembling slightly. The bright screen burned my eyes, but it was the message that made my blood turn to ice.

I gripped the phone so tightly my knuckles turned white. *Your attackers have escaped. They may be coming for you.*

The words refused to make sense at first, like they were written in some foreign language my brain couldn't process. Then they hit me all at once, a physical blow that knocked the air from my lungs.

They were coming for me.

The men who had --

My breath caught in my throat, turning into a strangled gasp. The room swayed, and I closed my eyes against the sudden dizziness. Bad move. The darkness behind my eyelids became a canvas for memories I'd been trying to bury.

Rough hands.

The smell of cheap cologne and cheaper liquor.

My own protests, muffled by a calloused palm.

I forced my eyes open, but the flashbacks kept coming in jagged bursts.

The tearing of fabric.

Pain, white-hot and searing.

Blood on my thighs.

A voice whispering that nobody would believe me anyway.

"Stop," I whispered to the empty room, pressing my palms against my temples. "Stop it."

My heartbeat thundered in my ears. Sweat slicked my skin despite the chill in the air. I needed to move, to do something, but my limbs felt like they were filled with concrete. The phone slipped from my fingers, landing on the rumpled sheets.

I focused on my breathing, the way my therapist had taught me. I'd hated going to one, but Dr. Winters had called me several times and finally convinced me to talk to someone. I'd only had a few appointments before I'd moved on, but I used those lessons now. Four seconds in. Hold for seven. Out for eight. It wasn't working. The panic clawed at my throat, threatening to drag me under.

Two days of hiding here. Of pretending everything would be fine. Since I'd missed the original hearing date, they'd moved it. That was the real reason I'd been traveling this way. Heading back to base. I'd convinced myself everything would be fine. But now, I didn't think I could go through with it. Didn't want to. I'd tried so hard to move on with my life. Why did they want to drag me back?

What a fucking joke.

I swung my legs over the side of the bed. The floor was cold against my bare feet, the sensation grounding me for a moment. I grabbed my phone again, reading the message a second time, hoping I'd somehow misunderstood.

No such luck.

I needed to tell someone. The thought came with surprising clarity, cutting through the fog of panic. I couldn't handle this alone. Not again.

I pulled on a pair of sweatpants under the oversized T-shirt I'd slept in. My hands shook so badly I could barely manage the simple task. I caught a glimpse of myself in the mirror over the dresser -- pale face, dark circles under my eyes, hair a tangled mess. I looked haunted. I was.

The hallway outside the guest room was dimly

lit by a single bulb at the far end. I padded down the hall, my bare feet silent on the wood boards. Each step sent fragments of memory ricocheting through my mind.

The crack of my head against concrete.

Laughter, low and menacing.

I stumbled, catching myself against the wall. My breathing was too fast, too shallow. Black spots danced at the edges of my vision. I couldn't pass out here. I forced myself to straighten, to keep moving.

The sound of male voices up ahead made me freeze. For a heart-stopping minute, I was back in that moment, surrounded and outnumbered, drugged and barely standing. My fingers dug into my palms, the sharp pain bringing me back to reality. These weren't my attackers. These were the men of the Devil's Boneyard, men who'd offered protection, a safe place to crash while I figured out my next move.

Not that I fully trusted them either. I wasn't that naive.

I recognized one of the voices now -- Rebel's distinctive cadence, cocky even at this ungodly hour. Relief washed over me, followed immediately by a fresh wave of dread. How was I supposed to explain why I looked terrified?

The metallic taste of fear coated my tongue. Another memory surfaced -- blood in my mouth from biting my cheek to try and bring clarity to my drug-addled brain. I swallowed hard, trying to force it back down where it belonged.

The living area came into view, a spacious room with mismatched furniture that somehow worked together. A couple of low lamps cast pools of yellow light, illuminating Rebel's tall frame as he leaned against the kitchenette counter that separated the two rooms, coffee mug in hand.

He wasn't alone. Two other club members whose names I didn't know lounged on the threadbare couch, cleaning what looked like gun parts spread across the coffee table. They all looked up when I appeared in the doorway.

"Well, look who's up with the birds," Rebel said, his smile fading as he got a better look at my face. "Jesus, Rio. You look like shit."

I opened my mouth to respond, but no words came out. Instead, a sob broke free, shocking me as much as it did them. I hadn't cried since it happened. Not during the rape kit. Not during the interview with the MPs. Not during any of it, not even my discharge.

But now, standing in a biker compound at five in the morning, I finally broke.

"They're out," I managed to say between ragged breaths. "They escaped."

The room went deadly silent. Even from across the space, I could see Rebel's knuckles whiten around his coffee mug. The other two men exchanged glances, then quietly gathered the gun parts and quickly walked out of the front door, leaving us alone.

"How do you know?" Rebel asked, his voice low and controlled in a way that somehow scared me more than if he'd shouted.

I held out my phone, the screen still displaying the damning message. My hand was shaking so badly the words blurred. Rebel crossed the room in three long strides and took the phone from me, his eyes narrowing as he read.

Another memory hit me -- their promise that they'd find me if I talked. That I'd beg for death before they were done.

My legs gave out. I would have hit the floor if

Rebel hadn't caught me, his grip firm but not painful. He lowered me to the couch, then crouched in front of me.

"I need you to breathe, darlin'," he said. "In and out. Nice and slow."

I tried, but the air kept catching in my chest. Black spots expanded across my vision.

"Rio." His voice cut through the roar in my ears. "Look at me. Right here."

I forced my eyes to focus on his face. The lines around his eyes were tight with concern, but his expression was steady.

"They are not getting to you," he said, each word precise and weighted with conviction. "Not while you're under my roof. You understand me?"

I nodded, not trusting my voice. Some of the tension eased from my shoulders.

"Good," he said. "Now, I need to talk to Charming about this. You stay put."

"No," I said, the word tearing from my throat. "Don't leave me alone."

Rebel's eyes softened for a fraction of a second before his cocky demeanor slipped back into place. "All right, sweetheart. You can come with me. But let me do the talking, yeah?"

I nodded again, letting him pull me to my feet. My legs felt steadier now, but the fear remained, coiled in my gut like a venomous snake. As we moved toward the door, I caught a glimpse of my reflection in a window -- pale, disheveled, but standing. Still standing.

They hadn't broken me.

I wouldn't let them break me now.

"Um. Maybe I should change. And shower," I murmured.

He nodded. "I'll wait. Take your time."

I turned and went back to the guest room, grabbing clean clothes, before heading for the hall bathroom.

* * *

The club's common area was more like a war zone this early in the morning. The aftermath of last night's party lay scattered everywhere. I even saw a thong hanging off the back of a chair.

I clutched my phone in my hand as Rebel guided me through the narrow space, his body a buffer between me and the few club members who were already up. Their gazes followed us -- curious, assessing, and in a few cases, suspicious. I wasn't one of them. I was an outsider allowed here on Charming's orders, nothing more.

"Wait here," Rebel said, depositing me on a battered leather couch that had seen better days.

My hand shot out, grabbing his wrist. "No."

His eyebrows rose, a flicker of surprise crossing his face before his usual cocky expression returned. "You got a death grip there, darlin'. Something you want to say?"

"I'm coming with you." My voice sounded stronger than I felt, the words clipped and certain despite the chaos inside my head.

Rebel studied me for a long moment, his gaze unreadable. "Fine. But you stay quiet while I handle this."

I nodded, releasing his wrist.

I followed him down a hall to some rooms at the back. We stopped outside what looked like an office. Rebel didn't knock. He pushed the door open wider, revealing a cramped space dominated by a corkboard covered in photos, newspaper clippings, and handwritten notes connected by red string, as well as a desk with a computer and overflowing with papers. Charming sat behind the desk and another man, one I didn't recognize, stood beside him.

"Got a situation," Rebel announced without preamble.

Both men focused on us. The stranger -- tall, with a neck tattoo peeking above his collar -- gave me a once-over that made my skin crawl. Not lecherous, but calculating, like he was assessing a potential threat. I lifted my chin, refusing to be cowed.

"This is a private meeting," the stranger said, his voice carrying the faint hint of an accent I couldn't place.

"It'll keep," Charming responded, his eyes shifting between Rebel and me. "What's the problem?"

Rebel jerked his head in my direction. "Show him."

My hands trembled as I unlocked my phone and held it out to Charming, the damning message displayed on the screen. "I got this twenty minutes ago."

Charming took the phone. His brow furrowed. "And what's this about?"

I swallowed hard. "I was medically discharged from the Army, after two of the men in my unit drugged and raped me."

His expression hardened as he read the text again. "Who sent this?"

"My old supervisor. He's been keeping tabs on the case."

"And you trust his information?" The stranger had moved closer, reading over Charming's shoulder.

"Yes." The response was automatic. He wouldn't have warned me if he didn't think they posed a real threat to me.

"How did they get out?" Rebel asked, arms folded across his chest.

"Does it matter?" I countered, a flare of anger cutting through the fear. "They're out. They're coming for me, just like they said they would if I told anyone what happened."

"It matters," Charming said, his voice deceptively calm. "We need to know if someone helped them escape, or if this was some bureaucratic fuckup. I doubt they escaped because they were just that good."

"I need to check with my sources," the stranger said, already moving toward the door. "I'll be in touch."

He slipped out without another word, leaving the three of us in a silence that felt heavy with unspoken questions.

Rebel broke it first. "We need to move her. If he thinks they're coming for her, that means they have a way of tracking her. This location could be compromised."

"No," I said, the word sharper than I intended. Both men looked at me with surprise. "I won't run and hide."

"This isn't about your pride, sweetheart," Rebel said, his tone patronizing.

"It's not about pride." I stepped closer to him, close enough to see the flecks of gold in his hazel eyes. "It's about survival. I've spent weeks looking over my shoulder, jumping at shadows. I can't keep living like this."

Actually, it was closer to four to five weeks since I'd left the base and headed west. But I didn't think he really cared about exact dates. A generalization seemed good enough in this situation.

"So, what? You want to make yourself bait?" Rebel's voice rose slightly, his cocky facade slipping to reveal genuine concern.

"I want to end this," I replied, my voice steady despite the fear churning in my gut. "One way or another."

Charming handed my phone back to me, his expression thoughtful. "It's not that simple."

"It never is," I agreed, pocketing the device.

"I need to make some calls," Charming said after a moment. "Rebel, stay with her. Don't let her out of your sight."

Rebel nodded, his jaw tight.

"And, Rio," Charming added, his gaze locking with mine. "No heroics. You're under our protection."

I didn't respond. I wasn't sure what I could say that wouldn't sound like a lie. The truth was, I didn't want to be protected. I was tired of being a victim. The men who attacked me had taken enough from me already -- my sense of safety, my peace of mind, my job.

Charming seemed to read some of this in my expression. His eyes narrowed slightly, but he didn't press the issue. "Give me five minutes."

Rebel guided me back to the common area, his hand a steady pressure at the small of my back. The space had filled with more club members in the short time we'd been gone, their conversations creating a low hum that set my teeth on edge. Too many people. Too many unknown variables.

"Breathe," Rebel murmured close to my ear. "You're safe here."

"Am I?" The question wasn't entirely rhetorical.

Rebel's expression hardened. "No one gets to

you without going through me first. And trust me, darlin', I'm not easy to get through."

Despite everything, a small smile tugged at my lips. "Always the cocky one, aren't you?"

"Only because I can back it up." He winked, but the humor didn't reach his eyes. "Stay here while I talk to Charming. I mean it this time."

I sank onto the couch, suddenly exhausted despite the adrenaline still coursing through my system. Rebel hesitated for a moment, looking like he wanted to say something else, then turned and strode back toward Charming's office, even though it hadn't been five minutes.

Left alone, I became acutely aware of the glances cast my way. Some curious, some wary, a few openly hostile, but those were from the women. I was an outsider, a complication they hadn't asked for. I couldn't blame them for their suspicion.

Fifteen minutes stretched into twenty. The waiting was almost worse than the fear. My mind conjured a dozen scenarios, each more catastrophic than the last. What if Charming decided I wasn't worth the risk? What if they handed me over to the police for "proper protection" -- or worse, back to the Army, the same people who had failed me before?

"You look like you're planning a murder."

I started, head snapping up to find a club member I'd seen but never spoken to standing in front of me. Tall, with a beard that couldn't quite hide the scar on his chin.

"Sorry," he said, holding up his hands. "Bad joke. You just looked… intense."

I forced a tight smile. "Just thinking."

"Dangerous pastime." He glanced toward the door Rebel had disappeared through. "They've been in there a while."

"Yeah." I didn't elaborate, unsure how much this man knew about my situation.

"For what it's worth," he said, lowering his voice, "Rebel's a good man to have in your corner. Charming too. If they're taking their time, it's because they're making sure all the angles are covered."

Before I could respond, Rebel emerged from the hallway, his expression unreadable as he scanned the room. When his eyes landed on me, he jerked his head in a silent command to join him.

I rose from the couch, my legs surprisingly steady as I crossed the room. The bearded club member stepped aside, giving me a small nod that might have been encouragement.

Rebel led me to a quieter corner of the common area, his back to the room, shielding our conversation from curious ears.

"Well?" I prompted when he didn't immediately speak.

"Charming's making arrangements." Rebel's voice was low, his usual swagger muted. "We've got three days to figure this out."

"Three days until what?" The question came out sharper than I intended.

Rebel's eyes met mine, serious in a way I wasn't used to seeing. "Until we have to make a big decision."

Another flash of memory -- my attackers' faces, contorted with a mixture of rage and satisfaction as they left me bleeding.

"And in the meantime?" I asked, pushing the images away.

"In the meantime, you don't leave my sight." Rebel's tone left no room for argument. "We'll set up surveillance, reach out to contacts, see if we can figure out where these bastards are holed up."

"I should call my old superior, see if he has more information."

Rebel nodded. "Do it. But speakerphone. I need to hear what he says."

I bristled at the implication. "You think I'm going to lie to you?"

"I think you're scared, angry, and looking for payback." His voice was surprisingly gentle. "And that makes people do stupid things."

He wasn't wrong. The rage that had been simmering beneath my fear was dangerously close to boiling over. Part of me wanted to hunt them down myself, to make them feel a fraction of the terror they'd inflicted on me.

"I'm not stupid," I said finally. "I know I can't take them on alone."

"Good." Rebel's customary smirk returned. "Because you've got a whole MC who will gladly turn those fuckers into roadkill."

The promise of violence should have disturbed me. Instead, it sent a surge of something like relief through my chest. My attackers thought I was alone, vulnerable. They had no idea what was waiting for them.

I met Rebel's gaze, my own hardening with resolve. "Three days."

"Three days," he confirmed, his expression mirroring mine. "And then... Well, we'll discuss it more later."

In that moment, standing in the heart of a motorcycle club's compound, I felt something I hadn't felt since the attack -- powerful. Not because I was stronger or faster or meaner than the men who had hurt me, but because I wasn't facing them alone anymore.

My hands stopped trembling. My breathing steadied. The flashbacks receded, at least for now.

Three days.

I could survive anything for three more days.

Chapter Five

Rebel

I should have told Rio why we had three days. I'd had all night to say something. Now it was the next afternoon, and I still hadn't said shit. She entered the living room, dressed and ready to go.

I cleared my throat. "Um, there's something you need to hear before we go anywhere."

"What?" She folded her arms, staring at me.

"The three days I mentioned yesterday. Charming said I had three days to either convince you to be my old lady, or you'd have to go. I did make it clear to him I wouldn't send you off on your own. If you have to leave, I'm going with you. At least until those assholes are found and dealt with."

"Old lady?" Her brow furrowed.

"You may have noticed some of the women around here also wear a cut like mine," I said, tugging on the leather. "Except theirs say *Property of* and whichever of my brothers they belong to. For instance, Havoc's woman has one that says *Property of Havoc*. If you agreed to be mine, you'd get one too and it would say *Property of Rebel*."

She opened and shut her mouth a few times, clearly at a loss for words.

"I know, it's a lot to process." I sighed. "It wouldn't mean I own you. Think of it like a marriage, without divorce. Once you agree, that's it. We're together for life."

"What the fuck, Rebel? I don't even know you!" She took a step back, looking seconds away from running.

"I know, and I tried asking Charming for time. Three days is all he gave me. As for his reason, a lot goes down here. If you aren't one of us, then you're a liability. People from town are only allowed here to party, and there's surveillance in the clubhouse. Cameras and audio."

"Three days to decide something that will last the rest of my life?" she asked.

I nodded. "Yeah. It's… well, you probably think it's insane. But like I said, if that's not something you want, I'll go with you when you leave. Help watch your six until those men are caught. Or buried. I personally prefer option two."

Her lips twitched like she might smile. "Fine. But I need the full three days to think it over, and I want to know more about what I'm getting myself into."

"And that's why we're on our way to the clubhouse. About this time, two of the old ladies should be setting out lunch for the single guys."

She followed me outside and climbed onto the back of my bike. We rode over to the clubhouse and parked at the end of a line of bikes. Looked like quite a few people were here already.

I guided Rio through the main doors of the Devil's Boneyard clubhouse, my hand hovering near the small of her back without actually touching her. She'd made it clear she didn't like being handled, and I respected that boundary. Rio's gaze darted around, taking in every exit, every person, cataloging threats. Even after being with us a few days, she hadn't broken the habit. I wondered if she ever would, or if she'd be on edge the rest of her life. It went beyond her military training. Because of what happened to her, she was in constant survival mode.

"You good?" I asked, keeping my voice low.

She nodded once, sharp and quick. "Fine."

The main room buzzed with activity. A few

brothers played pool in the corner, the crack of balls against each other punctuating the rumble of conversation. Behind the bar, bottles clinked as one of the Prospects restocked the shelves. Music thumped from speakers mounted on the walls, just loud enough to fill the space without drowning out conversation.

I spotted Jordan and Josie near the long wooden table that had seen more than a decade of club celebrations, and the occasional brawl. The scars in the dark wood told stories of their own. Today, they were laying out food -- burgers, wings, and sides that steamed in aluminum trays. It was something the old ladies had started doing a while back, making sure all the single men were fed.

"This way," I said, nodding toward them. Rio followed, her stride confident but her body tense, like a spring coiled tight and ready to snap.

Jordan looked up as we approached, her eyes quickly assessing Rio before she offered a small smile. Josie continued arranging food containers, her movements efficient.

"Jordan, Josie, this is Rio," I said. "Rio, these ladies have been with the club for a while. They know the score."

Rio crossed her arms over her chest, chin tilted up slightly. "Hey."

"Heard you know how to handle yourself," Jordan said, wiping her hands on a towel.

Rio's eyebrow quirked up. "Yeah, I guess."

I moved toward the food. "You hungry? Josie makes the best pulled pork this side of the Mississippi."

"Not really." Rio stayed where she was, still scanning the room.

Jordan leaned forward, elbows on the table.

"We've all been there, fighting our own demons." Her voice dropped, intimate and knowing. "Every woman connected to this club has a story that would curl your toes. We've all had to prove ourselves, usually *to* ourselves, one way or another."

Rio's eyes narrowed. "I'm not trying to prove anything to anyone."

"Aren't you?" Jordan tilted her head. "Then why are you still here? You could have left town this morning."

I watched Rio's jaw clench, a muscle jumping beneath her skin. She didn't answer.

Josie set down a stack of plates with a clatter. "Club life isn't easy. There are long nights when you don't know if they're coming home. There are rivals who think targeting us is easier than targeting the men. There are law enforcement assholes who think we're all criminals or whores or both."

"So why stay?" Rio asked, her eyes fixed on Josie now.

"Because once you earn your place, you've got family for life," Josie said. "Not the kind that shares your blood, but the kind that would spill theirs for you. This club has taken down rapists, murderers, human traffickers, drug dealers, and more."

"What Josie's saying is that it's not just about the men. We look out for each other too." Jordan pointed at Rio's hands. "Those scars on your knuckles tell me you've been fighting alone for a long time. That gets exhausting."

Rio's hands unconsciously curled into fists at her sides. "I manage."

"Sure you do," Jordan said. "But there's a difference between surviving and living."

I could almost see Rio's defenses climbing

higher, her eyes hardening. Time to step in.

"I brought you here because I was impressed, and I could see you had something in common with women like Jordan," I said, placing a steady hand on her shoulder, making sure she could see it coming. I locked eyes with her. "Not for any other reason. And despite what you might think about MCs, character matters here. We don't let just anyone stick around."

Rio studied my face, most likely looking for lies or manipulation. "So what, this is a recruitment pitch?"

"No." I shook my head. "This is me introducing you to people who might understand what you've been through better than most. People who won't ask questions you don't want to answer, but who'll have your back if you need it. Even if you decide to walk out of here tomorrow, I'm sure Jordan would be willing to swap numbers and listen if you ever needed someone to talk to."

The distant roar of motorcycles filtered in from outside as a few more brothers returned to the clubhouse. Ice clinked in glasses at the bar as the Prospect poured drinks. Through it all, Rio stood still, absorbing, evaluating.

"How do you know what I've been through? Just because I told you about one event..." Her voice was quiet but sharp.

"I don't," I admitted. "But I recognize the look. The way you check exits. How you position yourself in a room. The way you flinch when someone moves too fast near you. We've all got ghosts, Rio. Some of us just hide them better than others. And I have a feeling you may have more than the one you've told me about."

"You're not wrong, exactly. But some of it is just my Army training. Always observe your surroundings and be prepared for anything."

Josie picked up a plate and loaded it with food. "Eat something. You're too skinny."

For a moment, I thought Rio would refuse again. Then, surprisingly, she reached out and took the plate.

"Thanks," she muttered.

Jordan smiled. "There's beer in the cooler or soda if you prefer."

"Water's fine." Rio's posture had relaxed just a fraction, her shoulders dropping an almost imperceptible amount.

I grabbed a beer for myself and a bottled water for Rio. As I handed it to her, our fingers brushed briefly. She didn't pull away immediately, which felt like progress.

"So what happens now?" Rio asked, looking between the three of us. "Is there some kind of club initiation I should know about?"

Jordan laughed, a genuine sound that lightened the mood. "Honey, you already passed the first test by not backing down from us. Most women run for the hills after five minutes with me. I'm with Havoc for a reason. He's the only one who could handle me."

"She can be intimidating," Josie agreed with a small smile. "But it's necessary. Too many women come around thinking they want the MC lifestyle until they actually see what it entails. Or they're the type to stick a knife in your back if they think it will profit them in some way."

Rio took a bite of pulled pork, chewing thoughtfully. "And what does it entail, exactly?"

"Loyalty," I answered before the others could. "Above all else. To the club, to your brothers and sisters. It means having each other's backs, no questions asked sometimes. And especially to the man you've let claim you."

Josie snorted. "*Let*. Better not let some of your brothers hear that word. They think they laid down the law."

"As if anyone here would take a woman without their consent. I can be the first to admit we're hard as nails, but we all have a soft spot for women," I said.

"And if I'm not looking to join some family?" Rio asked, her gaze steady on mine.

"Then you eat good food, enjoy the hospitality, and leave when your three days are up," I said. "No strings. But my offer stands either way."

"What offer?" Jordan asked, raising an eyebrow at me.

I kept my eyes on Rio. "Protection. To be mine, but only when she's ready. Charming gave us three days to sort shit out. Otherwise, she has to leave. And I said I'd go with her until I know she's safe."

Josie whistled low. "That's generous, Rebel."

Rio's eyes narrowed slightly. "Why?"

It was a loaded question, and I knew my answer mattered. I took a pull from my beer, buying myself a second to find the right words.

"Because sometimes people deserve a fucking break," I finally said. "And it looks like you're due for one. I'd be lying if I said I wasn't attracted to you. Hell, you had my attention the moment you walked into this place. But I will never take a woman against her will."

Rio's face remained carefully neutral, but I noticed her posture straighten just a bit. Her gaze scanned the room again, but this time it felt different -- less like she was looking for danger and more like she was truly seeing the place for what it was.

Jordan and Josie exchanged a look that communicated volumes. Jordan had been in Rio's shoes once, wary and untrusting. And Jackal had fucked up with Josie. I was amazed he'd convinced her to give him a shot. I could see them remembering their own journeys to find peace within these walls.

"Eat," Josie urged again. "Everything looks clearer on a full stomach."

This time, Rio didn't hesitate before taking another bite. The background noise of the clubhouse continued around us -- laughter from over by the pool table, the clink of bottles, the low rumble of conversation -- but in our little circle, something had shifted. Not trust, exactly, but the possibility of it.

And for now, that was enough.

The conversation gradually softened as Rio worked her way through the plate of food. I noticed her shoulders drop another inch, her gaze scanning the room less frequently. That's when I spotted Cade making his way toward us, practically vibrating with eagerness. The kid had been prospecting for three months and still hadn't learned when to hang back. I shifted my weight, preparing to intercept him if necessary. With Rio's history, overeager puppies like Cade could be a trigger.

Jordan noticed my attention shift and followed my gaze. "Shit," she muttered, setting down her drink.

Cade maneuvered through the room, his Prospect cut still stiff and new-looking compared to our worn leather. His eyes were fixed on Rio, that hungry look men get when they see fresh meat. Not necessarily sexual -- though there was probably some of that too -- but the thrill of someone new to impress, to bring into the fold.

"Hey, is this the chick from the other night?" he called out as he approached, too loud, too familiar.

Josie shot him a warning look. "Cade --"

But he was already pushing his way into our

circle, his hand reaching toward Rio's shoulder. "I've been dying to meet you."

It happened in a blur. Rio's hand flew up, blocking his before it could make contact. Her body pivoted, stance dropping lower, more stable. Her eyes narrowed to slits, hard and cold as winter ice.

"Don't touch me," she said, voice low and lethal.

Cade froze, confusion flashing across his boyish face. "I was just --"

"Cade, back off," I cut in, stepping between them. "She's not a toy or your new best friend."

The silence that followed felt heavy. Everyone in our vicinity had clocked the confrontation, conversations pausing as their gazes turned our way. Rio's fists were clenched at her sides, knuckles white, body thrumming with fight-or-flight energy.

"I didn't mean anything by it," Cade mumbled, face flushing red.

"Doesn't matter what you meant," I said, keeping my voice even but firm. "When someone's body language says 'keep your distance,' you respect that. Especially with women you don't know."

He stumbled back a step, visibly deflating. "Sorry, I just wanted to --"

"To what?" Rio interjected, her gaze locked onto him with laser focus. "To test if I'm tough? If I'm easy to get into your bed?" Her Georgia drawl thickened with her anger. "I'm not a sideshow attraction or a pet."

The tips of Cade's ears turned crimson. A few chuckles sounded from the bar where some brothers were watching with interest.

"I think you've got Prospect duties to attend to," Jordan said pointedly, gesturing toward the bar.

Cade nodded, shooting one last apologetic look

at Rio before retreating. I watched him go, making a mental note to talk to him later. The kid needed to learn boundaries if he was going to survive here.

I turned back to Rio, studying her. She was still coiled tight, ready to spring. "You good?"

She exhaled slowly through her nose. "Fine." Her eyes followed Cade as he moved behind the bar. "Who is he?"

"Cade. Prospect," I explained. "Means he's trying to earn his way into the club. Does all the shit jobs, follows orders, proves his loyalty."

"Like a pledge at a fraternity?" Rio asked.

"Something like that, but with higher stakes." I took another pull from my beer. "He's young. Enthusiastic. Doesn't always think before he acts."

Rio's posture gradually relaxed, though her eyes remained alert. "So what happens if he fucks up? Gets kicked out?"

Josie snorted. "Depends on the fuck-up. Could be anything from cleaning toilets with a toothbrush to... well, worse."

"The club takes loyalty seriously," Jordan added. "Breaking that trust isn't something you come back from easily."

Or at all, but I left that part unsaid.

Rio seemed to consider this, her gaze drifting back to me. Something had shifted in her expression -- a flash of hesitation, contemplation. "Earlier, you said we could take things at my pace, if I agreed to be yours. What's the catch?"

I felt the weight of Jordan and Josie's attention, knew they were curious about my answer too. This wasn't my normal play. I generally kept to myself, focused on club business. Couldn't remember a time I'd ever kept a woman around.

"No catch," I said. "You'd have your own space. You can keep sleeping in the spare room until we've had time to get to know each other better. I won't make a move until you tell me you're ready."

"And in return?" Rio pressed, skepticism etched in every line of her face.

I shrugged. "You don't cause problems for the club, don't betray anyone here. That's it."

"Bullshit." Her voice was flat. "Men don't offer something for nothing."

"Then I guess I'm not most men." I set my empty bottle on the table. "Look, I've got no interest in pushing myself on you, if that's what you're worried about. You'd be under my protection, which means you're off-limits to everyone in the club."

Rio's eyes narrowed. "Under your protection? What does that mean exactly? Does it have to do with that property cut you mentioned earlier?"

I could feel Jordan and Josie watching this exchange with interest. They knew what I was offering -- what it meant in our world.

"Yeah, it's about that. It means you'd be considered mine," I said bluntly. "Not as property, but as someone I'm responsible for. No one would fuck with you without answering to me."

A tense silence stretched between us. Rio's jaw worked as she processed my words.

"And if I walk away? Decide this isn't for me?" she finally asked.

"Then you walk," I said simply. "Door's always open. Like I said, I'd have your back until your issue is settled. The club just wouldn't be standing by us."

Josie leaned forward, voice low. "It's a good offer, Rio. Better than most get. Rebel doesn't take in strays."

Rio shot her a sharp look. "I'm not a stray."

"No," I agreed. "You're not. You're a fighter who's been on her own too long. That's different. It's up to you to decide if you need us. Need me."

The silence returned, filled with the background noise of the clubhouse. The clink of glasses. Someone cranked up the music a notch.

"Why?" Rio asked finally, the single word loaded with suspicion.

I considered my answer carefully. The truth was, I wasn't entirely sure myself. Something about her had gotten under my skin from the moment I saw her. The way she moved -- efficient, deadly, but with a control that spoke of training. The hollow look in her eyes that I recognized all too well. The way she held herself apart, always ready to run or fight.

"Because we recognize our own," I said finally. "And because sometimes the universe puts people in your path for a reason."

Rio's eyebrow arched. "Didn't take you for the spiritual type."

"I'm not," I said with a half-smile. "But I've been around long enough to know coincidences are rare."

She studied me for a long moment, weighing, assessing. I could almost see the calculations running behind her eyes -- the risk assessment, the cost-benefit analysis of trusting someone after God knows what she'd been through.

"One night," she said eventually. "I'll stay one more night, and then I'll decide."

I nodded, careful not to show too much reaction. Something told me it would be longer, but I wouldn't press the issue. "Fair enough."

Jordan and Josie exchanged glances. I knew them well enough to realize they felt something was off with

Rio, as if she wasn't quite herself.

"I need some air," Rio said abruptly, setting down her barely touched drink.

"Hang a right off the porch and you'll find a picnic area," Josie offered, pointing. "Quieter out there, unless a bunch of kids are there."

Rio nodded her thanks and moved away, her stride purposeful. I watched her go, noting how the brothers made space for her as she passed, respect already forming after word spread that she was former military.

"What are you doing, Rebel?" Jordan asked once Rio was out of earshot.

I glanced at her. "Helping someone who needs it."

"Is that all?" Josie pressed, arms crossed.

I didn't answer immediately. The truth was more complicated than I was ready to admit, even to myself.

"She's running from something," I said finally. "Or someone. I'd rather she ran to us than keep going alone."

"And if she brings trouble?" Jordan asked, always the pragmatic one.

I shrugged. "Then we handle it. That's what we do. And just FYI, Charming is already aware of what's going on."

Josie studied me for a moment longer, then nodded slowly. "I'll tell Jackal to keep an ear out, see if anyone's looking for her. You know he has friends at the bars in town."

"Appreciate it," I said.

I looked toward the door where Rio had disappeared. Through the window, I could see her leaning against the railing, staring out at nothing, her posture alert even in this moment of solitude. Looked like she hadn't wanted to go over to the picnic area. She might say I was a stranger, but I got the feeling she felt safer with me nearby.

And for reasons I wasn't fully ready to examine, I liked that I made her feel safe.

Chapter Six
Rebel

Rio had been here longer than she'd planned. Not that I was going to rush her off. I liked having her in my house, which made me realize I really wouldn't mind it being a permanent thing. Ridley had taken to her and made sure she had appropriate clothes for riding a motorcycle, seeming to know Rio belonged here with us.

I spotted Rio across the parking lot before she saw me. Her focus was entirely on her riding gear, fingers testing straps and pockets with the precision of someone who trusted nothing to chance. Good. She'd need that attention to detail for what I had in mind. The sunlight was nearly blinding, but it was a great day for a ride. I only hoped she liked the surprise I had for her.

The lot was empty except for us. I stepped closer, letting my boots scuff against the ground just enough to announce my presence.

Rio's head snapped up. Her strawberry-blonde hair caught the light as it shifted around her shoulders. Those blue eyes narrowed, assessing me in a heartbeat. She didn't relax when she recognized me. Smart girl.

"Thought you'd be inside," she said, nodding toward the clubhouse behind us. Her Georgia drawl made the words sound almost friendly. Almost.

"Had something better in mind." I stepped aside and gestured to what I'd parked behind me.

The Harley-Davidson Nightster sat like a coiled beast waiting to pounce. All sleek black lines with just enough chrome to catch the afternoon light. Brand fucking new, with pipes that would wake the dead when fired up proper. Not my bike -- mine was built for power, not seduction -- but this one had a different purpose.

Rio froze, her gaze locked on the machine. Her face didn't give much away, but I caught the slight parting of her lips, the momentary pause in her breath.

"That yours?" she asked, keeping her voice flat.

"Could be yours." I took a step forward. "For today, anyway."

I ran my hand along the bike's frame, leather gloves whispering against the smooth finish. "Heard you can ride."

Her eyes flicked from the bike to me, then back again. The caution there was mixed with something else -- desire... not for me, but for what the machine represented. Freedom. Power. Control.

"Who told you that?" Her voice had an edge to it.

"Shade." I offered the name like a peace offering. "He's the club hacker. He ran across some stuff from your past while making sure the two assholes hunting you weren't closing in."

Rio scoffed. "Shade needs to keep his mouth shut."

"He also said you were good." I leaned against the bike, casual, confident. "But talk's cheap."

That got her. The corner of her mouth twitched, almost a smile but too sharp for that. She approached the bike slowly, circling it like a predator sizing up potential prey. I didn't move, just watched her. Those blue eyes missed nothing.

She crouched beside the front tire, fingers pressing against the tread. "These are new," she muttered, more to herself than to me.

"Everything's new." I folded my arms. "Bike hasn't seen fifty miles yet."

Rio stood and moved to the handlebars, her body still coiled with tension but her movements more fluid now, more focused on the machine than on keeping her distance from me. She ran her fingers over every inch of the bike, not asking permission. I liked that.

"Mind if I start her up?" she asked, not looking at me.

"Be my guest."

She swung her leg over and settled into the seat like she belonged there. No hesitation, no awkward shuffling to find her balance. Her hands gripped the bars, testing the feel while her boot nudged the kickstand up.

She started the bike like a pro, and the Nightster roared to life. The sound bounced off the clubhouse and nearby homes. Rio's body changed on that bike -- tension flowing out of her shoulders even as her focus sharpened. For a second, I caught a glimpse of who she might have been before the Army. Before whatever had put those walls up.

She revved the engine, and I felt the rumble in my chest. There was something fucking primal about that feeling, something no amount of high-tech bullshit could replace. Rio felt it too. I saw it in the slight curve of her lips, the way her thighs tightened against the machine.

After a long moment, she cut the engine. The sudden silence felt louder than the noise had been.

"Not bad," she said, but her eyes gave her away. They were brighter now, more alive.

"Wanna see what she can do?" I asked.

Rio dismounted, her movements slow and deliberate. "Why? What's in it for you?"

Direct. I appreciated that.

"Need someone who can keep up," I said with a

shrug. "Most of the guys ride like they've got something to prove. Get themselves killed trying to show off. Either that, or they ride they like they're grandpas out for a Sunday cruise."

"And I don't have anything to prove?" One eyebrow arched higher than the other.

"Do you?"

She didn't answer right away. Her fingers trailed over the seat she'd just vacated.

"Where would we go?" she finally asked.

"Coastal highway. Good roads." I paused. "Unless you've got somewhere better in mind."

"You always hand out bikes to women you barely know?"

I smiled, not bothering to soften it. "Only the ones Shade says can handle them."

"And if I wreck it?"

"Don't."

Rio laughed then, a short, sharp sound that seemed to surprise even her. "You're not big on bullshit, are you?"

"Waste of time." I pushed off from where I'd been leaning. "So is standing around talking when we could be riding."

She studied me for a long moment, like she was trying to read something written in fine print on my face. Whatever she was looking for, she must have found it, because she nodded once.

"I'll need a helmet," she said.

"Got one for you." I moved to the clubhouse porch and pulled out a matte black helmet with a tinted visor from a paper sack I'd stashed there. "Should fit."

She took it, checked the sizing with a critical eye. "You planned this."

Not a question. I didn't treat it like one.

"My bike's around back," I said instead. "Meet you at the gate in five."

I turned to go, but her voice stopped me.

"Rebel."

I looked back.

"Thanks," she said, the word awkward in her mouth, like she didn't use it often. "For the ride."

I nodded once. "Don't thank me yet. Ride's just starting."

As I walked away, I heard the Nightster's engine roar back to life behind me. The sound followed me across the parking lot, a promise of speed and freedom that made my blood hum in response. Whatever baggage Rio carried, whatever had put that wariness in her eyes, it wouldn't matter once we hit the open road.

On a bike, going fast enough, the past can't catch you. At least not for a while.

* * *

The coastal highway unraveled beneath our tires like a snake shedding its skin. Rio kept the Nightster steady beside me, neither falling behind nor pushing ahead. The ocean crashed against the surf off to our right. She rode like she had something to prove, but only to herself. No stupid risks, no showboating. Just pure skill and the kind of focus that told me more about her than words ever could.

Wind tore at my clothes, a constant battle that kept the blood pumping. Beside me, Rio leaned into a curve, her body an extension of the machine. The Nightster responded to her like they'd spent years together instead of less than an hour. Natural talent. Couldn't be taught.

The sun hung fat and low over the water, casting a golden path across the waves. The highway curved, taking us closer to the beach, then farther away, before curving back again.

Rio didn't hesitate. She took the tighter line, the Nightster's pipes echoing as she accelerated through the turn. I matched her, staying close enough to see her in my peripheral vision but giving her space to maneuver.

Rio glanced over at me, her face obscured by the helmet but her posture relaxed now, fluid. She gunned the engine, pulling ahead by a bike length. Challenge issued. I grinned inside my helmet and opened up my throttle.

We weren't racing. Not exactly. Just two predators testing each other's speed, finding a rhythm that worked between us. No words needed. The bikes spoke for us, negotiating boundaries with engine growls and tire squeals.

The highway curved inland for a stretch, cutting through a stand of palm trees. Shadows dappled the road, making it a constantly shifting puzzle. Rio had been wasted in the Army. This was where she belonged.

Twenty minutes later, the road brought us to a stretch of beach dotted with weathered buildings. One caught my attention, a wooden shack perched on stilts just above the high tide line. Smoke curled from a chimney, carrying the scent of butter and seafood.

I signaled, pointing toward it. Rio nodded and followed my lead as I turned onto the gravel lot beside the building. We parked beneath a wooden awning that creaked with each gust of wind off the water. The sign above the door simply read "CATCH" in faded red letters.

Rio dismounted first, pulling her helmet off in a smooth motion. Her hair tumbled free, tangled from the wind but somehow making her look more alive because of it. She ran her fingers through it once, a practical gesture with no vanity behind it.

"Hungry?" I asked, removing my own helmet.

"Starving." She looked at the shack with skeptical eyes. "This place actually serve food?"

"Best seafood on the coast." I hung my helmet on my handlebars. "If you don't mind eating with your hands."

The hint of a smile touched her lips. "Would think less of a place that gave me a fork for crab legs."

Inside, the shack was bigger than it looked from the road. Mismatched tables were scattered across a plank floor worn smooth by decades of salt water. The walls were covered with fishing gear, buoys, and faded photographs of men holding up their catches.

The place was mostly empty. A couple of fishermen hunched over beers at the bar, their conversation a low, indecipherable murmur. An old man in the corner mended a net, his gnarled fingers working with surprising speed. No one looked up when we entered.

I led the way to a table by the window, where we could watch our bikes and the ocean beyond. Rio took the seat with her back to the wall, eyes scanning the room before settling. Always assessing. Always ready. The stance of someone who'd learned the hard way that relaxation could be costly.

A weathered woman with sun-bleached hair approached our table, dropping two laminated menus in front of us without a word.

"What's fresh?" I asked her.

She shrugged. "Everything came off the boats this morning. Shrimp's good. Got some crab. Clams. Oysters if you're feeling brave."

"Bring us a mix," I said. "And two beers."

She nodded and disappeared toward the kitchen.

Rio raised an eyebrow. "You always order for your dates?"

"This a date?" I countered.

She held my gaze for a beat, then looked away, out toward the ocean. "Figure of speech."

The beers arrived, cold and sweating in their bottles. Rio took a long pull from hers, then set it down carefully. Her fingers remained wrapped around the glass, as if she needed something to hold onto.

"You ride well," I said.

She shrugged. "Bikes make sense. Clear rules. You fuck up, you pay for it right away."

"Not like people."

She glanced at me, something flickering in her blue eyes. "Exactly. Not like people."

Our food arrived on a large metal tray lined with newspaper. Steam rose from the pile of shellfish, carrying the scent of garlic, butter, and salt. Small dishes of melted butter and cocktail sauce sat on either side. No plates, no utensils. Just food meant to be handled.

Rio considered the spread, then selected a shrimp. She peeled it with practiced movements, not a wasted motion. The meat disappeared between her very white, straight teeth.

"Good," she admitted.

I grabbed a crab leg and cracked it open, extracting a piece of meat and dipping it in butter. "Told you."

We ate in comfortable silence for a while, the sound of cracking shells and the distant crash of waves filling the space between us. With each bite, Rio's shoulders lowered a fraction. Her hands rested on the table between selections, no longer poised for immediate reaction. Small changes, barely noticeable if you weren't looking. But I was looking.

"How long you been riding?" I asked, keeping my tone casual.

She wiped her fingers on a napkin. "Started when I was fourteen. Uncle had a shop. Taught me everything he knew before..." She trailed off, then redirected. I already knew she didn't have family. From what Shade had found, first her uncle had died in a freak accident, then her mom had passed a little over a year later. "Been on and off since then."

"Army didn't let you ride?"

Her expression shuttered briefly. "Not the issue. Just didn't have the time. Or a bike." She cracked open a claw. "You?"

"Grew up on them. Father was a mechanic." I didn't elaborate. Some stories I liked to keep close to the heart.

Rio nodded, accepting the boundary. Another point in her favor.

She reached for her beer again, and this time her hand was steady, relaxed. The movement caught the light, highlighting a small tattoo on her inner wrist that I hadn't noticed before. Simple design -- just a lotus blossom.

I nodded toward it. "Meaning behind that?"

For a moment, I thought she wouldn't answer. Her fingers curled around her wrist, covering the mark.

"Had a sister once. Her name was Blossom," she finally said.

I nodded, not pushing for more. Some truths were like wild animals -- approach them too directly and they'd bolt. Shade hadn't mentioned a sister. I wasn't sure if it was a biological one, or maybe one she'd met in foster care after her mom died. It wouldn't do me any favors to tell her everything I'd learned about her through Shade's abilities. I needed to hear it all in her words in her own time.

We finished eating as the tide began to rise, waves creeping closer to the stilts beneath us. The rhythmic sound formed a backdrop to our silence, comfortable now rather than wary. Rio leaned back in her chair, one hand resting on the table while the other held her beer. It was the most relaxed I'd seen her.

The moment felt balanced -- not tense, but not fragile either. Like finding perfect equilibrium on a turn, that split second where everything aligns exactly right. Push too hard in any direction and you'd lose it. So I just let it be, storing the memory of her face in that rare moment of peace.

The old fishermen paid their tabs and left, nodding to us as they passed. The net-mender had vanished without me noticing.

"Thank you," Rio said suddenly, her voice quiet but clear. "For this." She gestured vaguely at the remains of our meal, but I understood she meant more than just the food.

I nodded once. "Anytime."

She smiled then, a real one that reached her eyes and transformed her face. It was brief -- there and gone -- but genuine. More valuable for its rarity.

We'd have to leave soon, head back before traffic got bad. But for now, I was content to sit across from this woman with her warrior's eyes and rare smile.

The last oyster shell sat empty between us, trails of butter and hot sauce drying on the newspaper. Rio had one hand on the table beside mine. Close enough that I could feel the heat from her skin, but not touching. That moment of almost-contact felt more intimate than if she'd grabbed my hand. Like a decision being weighed. Neither of us spoke. We didn't need to.

Rio's eyes had lost their constant vigilance, focused now on the water. Her breathing had slowed, matching the cadence of the surf.

My phone shattered it all.

The harsh electronic ring cut through our bubble of peace. Rio's hand jerked back instantly, her body tensing as if the sound itself might be a threat. I pulled the phone from my pocket, ready to silence it and deal with whoever it was later.

Then I saw Shade's name on the screen.

Shade didn't call unless it mattered. More importantly, he didn't call when I was off the grid unless something had gone seriously wrong. The relaxation of the past hour evaporated.

I met Rio's now-alert eyes. "Need to take this."

She nodded once, already scanning the room, the exits, the other patrons. Back to soldier mode in the space of a heartbeat.

I swiped to answer. "What's up?"

"Where are you?" Shade's voice had the clipped precision he used when time was a factor.

"Coastal road. That seafood place with the stilts." I kept my tone neutral, giving nothing away to Rio, who watched me with narrowed eyes.

"How fast can you get back?" Shade didn't waste words on niceties.

"Forty-five minutes if we push it. Why?"

The line went silent for a beat. Bad sign. Shade only paused when he was deciding how much to say over an open line.

"Those men Rio mentioned." His voice dropped

lower.

My fingers tightened around the phone. "What about them?"

"They're in town." Shade's typing created a backdrop to his words. "Showed up at *The Rusty Nail* about an hour ago, asking questions. Vince called it in."

"What kind of questions?" I turned slightly away from Rio, but I could feel her attention like a physical weight.

"About a strawberry blonde matching Rio's description. Said she was their friend, they'd lost touch after the Army." More typing. "Vince stalled them, said he might've seen her a few days ago, but she looked to be heading out of town."

"They armed?"

"Concealed. Vince caught a glimpse when one leaned over the bar." A pause. "That's not all. I ran their names through my system. And I mean a deeper dive than before. When it involves the military, it always takes more time. Lots of layers to peel back."

My jaw tightened. "And?"

"Three similar reports filed against them in the past. Sexual assault. All military women, different bases." Shade's voice held controlled rage. "All cases dropped due to 'insufficient evidence.' Last victim before Rio was hospitalized for two weeks. They have to be backed by someone high up to keep getting by with this shit."

Something cold settled in my chest. Not fear -- rage. The kind that sits like ice until it's time to act.

"Where are they now?" I kept my voice low, steady.

"Left *The Nail* twenty minutes ago. Heading toward the edge of town. I've got eyes on the traffic cams. They're in a black Dodge Ram, Georgia plates."

I glanced at Rio. Her body was coiled tight, ready to spring. She'd picked up on my tension even without hearing Shade's words.

"Keep tracking them. We're heading back now." I paused. "And, Shade? Get Java and Ripper on standby. We might need backup."

"Already done." The line went dead.

I lowered the phone slowly, my mind racing through options, scenarios, consequences. Rio didn't give me time to finish.

"What's wrong?" Her voice was sharp, all traces of relaxation gone. Her eyes had hardened into blue ice.

I met her gaze directly. "We've got a problem."

She didn't flinch, didn't blink. "What kind of problem?"

The words sat heavy on my tongue. I could lie, try to shield her. But one look at her face told me that would be both useless and insulting.

"The men from your unit. They're in town." I watched her reaction carefully. "Looking for you."

The color drained from her face, but her expression didn't change. Her knuckles went white where she gripped the edge of the table.

"How?"

I could tell there was something more she wanted to ask, or maybe something she knew. Was this more of a test to see how much we'd found out? "Don't know yet. They showed up at *The Rusty Nail* asking about a woman matching your description."

Rio's breathing changed, becoming deliberate and controlled. A technique to manage fear or anger -- maybe both. Her gaze never left mine, searching for any hint that I might be softening the truth.

"Names?" she demanded. "Are you sure it's them?"

I hesitated. "Shade confirmed it's them. The same ones you told me about. He hacked into the military files on them."

She stood abruptly, chair scraping against the wooden floor. "We need to go. Now."

I rose more slowly, dropping cash on the table to cover our meal. "We will. But first we need a plan."

"Plan is simple. I leave town." Her words were clipped, mechanical. "They're not your problem."

"They became my problem when they walked into my territory hunting one of mine." The words came out before I could consider them.

Rio's eyes flashed. "I'm not yours."

"You're under my club's protection," I clarified, though part of me wanted to challenge her statement. Not the time. "That makes them my problem."

She shook her head, already moving toward the door. I caught her arm, gentle but firm. She stiffened but didn't pull away.

"Rio. Stop." I kept my voice low. "Running blindly is exactly what they want. We need to be smart about this."

For a moment I thought she'd argue, but then her military training seemed to kick in. Tactical assessment overriding emotional response. She gave a short nod.

"What did Shade say?" she asked, her voice steadier now.

I guided her toward the door. "They're in a black Dodge Ram, heading toward the edge of town last he saw. He's tracking them on traffic cams."

Rio processed this, her mind visibly working through implications. "How many? Is it just the two of them?"

"Two. They didn't pick up any friends." I pushed the door open, scanning the area before stepping through. "Shade ran their names. Found three other reports filed against them. Similar to yours."

Her face hardened. "Charges?"

"Dropped." I didn't elaborate. Didn't need to.

Something shifted in her eyes then -- fear giving way to something darker, more dangerous. "They won't stop."

It wasn't a question, but I answered anyway. "No. They won't."

We reached the bikes, the gravel crunching beneath our boots. Rio grabbed her helmet but didn't put it on yet. "What's your plan?"

I pulled out my phone again, checking for updates from Shade. Nothing yet. "Get back to the clubhouse. Regroup. Figure out our next move with better intel."

"And then?"

"Then we make sure they never hurt anyone again." The promise came easily, cold certainty behind every word. Wasn't the first time I'd put someone in the ground. Wouldn't be the last.

She studied me for a long moment, assessing my sincerity. Whatever she saw must have satisfied her, because she nodded once.

"I need to make a call," I told her, already dialing. "Get ready to ride. We leave in two."

Rio put on her helmet, the visor hiding her expression. But her body told me everything I needed to know -- the precise, economical movements, the way she checked her bike with brisk efficiency. She'd switched fully into combat mode. Those men had awakened something lethal in the woman now straddling the Nightster.

I stepped away toward the shadows, phone pressed to my ear. Behind me, I heard the growl of the Nightster's engine coming to life, impatient and angry, just like its rider. It matched the feeling building in my chest -- a cold rage that would stay banked until it was time to let it burn.

These men had made two critical mistakes: they'd hurt a woman under my protection, and they'd followed her into my territory thinking they were the predators.

They were about to learn just how wrong they were.

Chapter Seven

Rio

Yesterday, we'd rushed back after getting word Ellis and Denton knew I was here. But then, a whole lot of nothing had happened. Shade had basically told me to hold off while he researched more. I didn't like sitting. It gave me too much time to think.

The compound was quiet this afternoon, with most of the members either sleeping off last night or handling club business elsewhere. I walked the familiar path between the buildings, trying to sort through the mess in my head. Rebel's face kept appearing in my thoughts -- his cocky smile, those eyes that saw right through me. I wanted him. I feared what it meant to be with him. Both feelings twisted inside me.

I kicked at a small rock, watching it skitter across the road. The Devil's Boneyard MC had become a strange sort of home to me in the past few days, but I still felt like an outsider looking in. Everyone had history here. Everyone except me.

"Rio?"

I turned at the sound of my name, finding Jordan standing there. Havoc's old lady was watching me with those perceptive eyes that didn't miss much. She was mature, strong, and completely comfortable in her skin.

"You look like you're trying to solve world hunger with that expression," she said, a half-smile crossing her face.

"Just thinking." I shrugged, trying to appear casual.

Jordan nodded toward a nearby picnic table. "Come sit. I've got coffee."

I hadn't planned on talking to anyone, but something about Jordan's steady presence drew me in. She wasn't like the club girls who gossiped and competed. I hadn't had to be around the club long to pick up on that bullshit. But Jordan had the kind of quiet confidence that only comes from living through hell and coming out the other side.

We sat, and she pushed a thermos toward me. I poured some coffee into the cup she offered.

"So," she said after a moment. "Rebel."

My head snapped up. "What about him?"

"I've seen how he looks at you. And how you look at him when you think nobody's watching."

When the hell had she had the time to watch us? Of course, we did venture out of his house frequently. It wasn't like I was holed up in a bedroom hiding. And the man did have a tendency to be nearby if not right by my side.

The coffee suddenly tasted bitter. "Is it that obvious?"

"Only to someone who's been there." She took a sip from her cup, eyes never leaving mine.

The words came tumbling out before I could stop them. "I'm scared of losing myself, but I'm drawn to him. And I'm worried that I may regret it if I decide to stay. It's not like we've known each other very long."

Jordan didn't react with surprise or judgment. She just nodded slowly. "That's how it goes with these men. They're like gravity."

"Did you feel that way with Havoc?"

A genuine smile crossed her face, softening the lines around her eyes. "Still do, after all these years."

"How did you two…" I let the question trail off.

"Meet?" She set her cup down. "He found me dying on the side of the road."

That wasn't what I expected. "What?"

"I'd been left for dead, essentially. Havoc was riding back from a run, saw me there, passed out. He could've kept going. Most people would have."

"But he didn't."

"No." Jordan's eyes grew distant. "He stopped. Brought me to the compound."

I tried to picture the intimidating Sergeant-at-Arms doing something so gentle. "Why here and not a hospital?"

"I begged him not to. Had my reasons." Her eyes met mine. "This club became my safe haven when I had nowhere else to go."

The wind picked up, rustling the leaves above us. In the distance, I could hear the rumble of motorcycles coming or going.

"The brotherhood looks rough on the outside," Jordan continued. "And it is. Make no mistake. But there's something else here too. Something most people never see. It's what we talked about the other day. Being a family."

I thought about Rebel and how he'd looked at me the first time we'd met. Like he could see every broken piece inside me and wanted to gather them up.

"You know," Jordan said, breaking the silence, "I'd just gotten out of prison when Havoc found me."

My eyebrows shot up. "Prison?"

"Got out and my own brother wanted nothing to do with me. The irony? He was a Prospect for this very club. He was supposed to pick me up and didn't. That's why I was passed out on the road."

"Shit."

"Yeah." She took another sip of coffee. "My own blood abandoned me, but strangers took me in. Havoc made sure I had a place to stay, food to eat."

"And you fell for him."

"Fast and hard." Jordan's face softened again. "Wasn't looking for it. Wasn't ready for it. But there it was."

I picked at a splinter in the wooden table. "Were you afraid?"

"Terrified." She looked me dead in the eye. "Thought I'd lose myself in him. In this life. At the same time, I knew I didn't want to be without him."

That hit close to home. "And did you? Lose yourself?"

"No. Found myself instead." She reached across and touched my hand briefly. "Never been happier than when I'm with him. It's not perfect. It's not easy. But it's real."

"How do you deal with... everything else? The club stuff?"

Jordan leaned back. "You find your place in it. Your boundaries. They respect that more than you'd think."

"You heard Rebel. He says he can be patient."

"And do you believe him?" she asked.

I thought about it. "Yeah. I do."

"Then trust your gut." She stood up. "These men aren't saints. But the good ones -- the ones worth keeping -- they love differently than other men. Completely. When they decide you're theirs, they'll move heaven and earth for you."

I nodded, absorbing her words. "Thanks, Jordan."

"Anytime." She picked up her thermos. "And, Rio? I meant what I said the other day. If you need to talk, about anything, you know where to find me."

I watched her walk away, her shoulders straight, her steps confident. Havoc was a lucky man.

I sat there a while longer, letting Jordan's story settle inside me. She'd gone from dying on the side of a road to finding a home, a family, a love that had lasted decades. I'd seen their kids around the compound. Pretty much grown-ass adults. It told me they'd been together a long while.

Maybe there was hope for someone like me too.

Standing, I continued my walk through the compound, feeling a strange new peace. The fear was still there. The doubts. But something else had taken root alongside them.

Hope.

* * *

I stood outside Rebel's house for a minute, gathering my courage. The porch light cast a warm glow against the gathering darkness.

I knocked once, quick and decisive before I could second-guess myself. The door opened almost immediately. Had he been waiting?

"Rio." My name sounded different on his lips. Softer. "You know you don't have to knock."

Rebel stood there in a black T-shirt and jeans, looking more approachable than the cocky guy he seemed to project around most people. Not that the danger had disappeared. It never did with him. It just simmered beneath the surface, controlled but present.

"Come in." He stepped aside, and I felt his eyes on me as I passed.

We walked into the dining area where he'd set the table. Two plates. Two glasses. A bottle of whiskey alongside a bottle of wine.

"Wasn't sure what you'd prefer," he explained, following my gaze.

"Whiskey," I answered. "Tonight feels like a whiskey night."

A small smile touched his lips. "Woman after my own heart."

He gestured for me to sit, then moved to the chair opposite mine. I sat with my back straight, shoulders tight. My hands found the edge of the table, fingers curling around it like I might fly away without something to anchor me. Across from me, Rebel leaned forward slightly, elbows on the table, gaze never leaving mine. He poured two fingers of whiskey into each glass, sliding one toward me.

"You look ready to bolt," he said, his voice low.

"I'm still here." I took a sip, welcoming the burn.

"Why is that, Rio?" His question cut straight to the chase. That was Rebel -- no bullshit, no games.

I set the glass down carefully. "Because I want to be."

"But?"

"But I'm still figuring things out." He nodded, taking a slow sip of his drink. "My talk with Jordan today helped."

His eyebrows raised slightly. "Jordan? You seem to have gotten friendly with Havoc's old lady. I didn't realize the two of you had met up again."

"She found me wandering the compound. We talked."

"About?"

I met his gaze. "About how it works. With men like you. The club."

Rebel leaned back slightly, studying me. "And what did she tell you?"

"That it's not easy." I took another sip. "But it can be worth it."

The corner of his mouth twitched up. "Smart woman."

"She is."

Silence stretched between us, not uncomfortable but full of unspoken things. The ice in our glasses clinked when we drank. The house creaked around us.

"I've been thinking about you," he said finally. "More than I should."

My heart kicked against my ribs. "Why's that?"

"Because you're different." He turned his glass slowly between his fingers. "You make me want things I haven't wanted in a long time. Possibly ever."

"What kind of things?"

His eyes darkened. "Stability. Connection." A pause. "Something real."

I'd known men like Rebel before. Women came and went without leaving a mark on his heart. But maybe he was different from those other guys.

"People wouldn't believe that coming from a guy like you," I said.

"I don't give a damn what people believe. They see what they want to."

"And what am I seeing?"

"The truth." He leaned forward again, his gaze so intense I nearly looked away. "Like I said before. I'll take things at your pace, Rio. Whatever you need."

Something inside me unclenched at his words. The promise in them.

"Why me?" I asked, the question that had been circling my mind since he first showed interest. "It's not like I'm the first woman to walk into your life."

A slight smile touched his lips. "Because you see through the bullshit. Because you don't flinch when things get ugly. Because when you look at me, I feel like you're actually seeing me, not just the cut or the reputation, or the mask I show the world."

His hand moved across the table, not grabbing mine, just resting close enough that our fingertips nearly touched. An invitation, not a demand.

"I don't want to be just another notch on your bedpost," I said, my voice steadier than I felt.

"You couldn't be if you tried."

I believed him. That was the scary part.

Slowly, I let my fingertips brush against his. The contact sent a jolt up my arm, like touching a live wire.

"The club comes first," I said. Not a question.

"The club is family," he corrected. "But that doesn't mean there isn't room for more."

"Jordan said something similar."

"She would know. She and Havoc have made it work for a long time."

I took another sip of whiskey, feeling the warmth spread through my chest. "I've been hurt before. And I don't just mean what happened in the Army."

"I know." His fingers lightly stroked mine. "I won't lie to you, Rio. This life isn't easy. But I can promise you won't face it alone."

"I'm not afraid of hard," I said. "I'm afraid of giving myself to someone and finding out I've disappeared in the process."

Understanding flashed in his eyes. "I don't want you to disappear. I want all of you -- the good, the bad, the broken parts, the strong parts. Everything. I happen to think you're one badass woman. I knew it the moment you walked into the clubhouse."

His words hit me like a physical touch. No man had ever wanted all of me before. They'd wanted pieces -- my body, my submission, my adoration. Never the whole, complicated mess.

"I'm not good at letting people in," I admitted.

"I've noticed." His smile was gentle. "But you're here. That's a start."

The distance between us felt too great suddenly.

I stood, moving around the table to his side. He watched me approach, his body going still like a predator sensing prey -- except I wasn't running away. I was walking straight toward him.

Rebel pushed his chair back slightly, making room. I stepped between his legs, looking down at him. This close, I could see the flecks of gray in his eyes, the small scar near his temple, the day's stubble darkening his jaw. He'd shaved his beard off the other morning, and I wondered if he'd decided to grow it back already.

"What are you doing, Rio?" His voice had dropped an octave.

"Taking what I want," I answered, surprising myself with my boldness.

His hands moved to my hips, strong but light, ready to let go if I pulled away. "And what's that?"

Instead of answering, I leaned down, bringing my face close to his. Our breaths mingled. For a heartbeat, we stayed like that, suspended in the moment before everything changed.

Then I kissed him.

It wasn't gentle. And that was fine. It was the last thing I wanted. I poured my fear, my desire, my hope into that kiss. His response was immediate, one hand sliding up my back to tangle in my hair, holding me to him as he took control of the kiss.

Rebel kissed like he did everything else -- with absolute confidence and skill. But there was something else there too. Something that felt like reverence.

When we finally broke apart, we were both breathing hard. His eyes had darkened to storm clouds.

"Been wanting to do that since the first time I saw you," he said, his voice rough.

"Why did you wait?"

"Told you. Your pace." His thumb traced my lower lip. "Worth the wait."

I smiled, feeling lighter than I had in months. Maybe years. "So what now?"

"Now we figure it out, day by day." He pulled me onto his lap, and I went willingly. I hadn't outright agreed to be his, but I'd implied it. Was that enough? "No pressure, no timeline."

I rested my forehead against his. "I can work with that."

His arms tightened around me. Safe. I felt safe with him, which was ironic given who he was, what he did. But maybe that was the point. The man most people would fear would move heaven and earth to make sure I never had reason to be afraid again.

"Stay with me," he said softly. Not a demand. A question.

"To sleep," I clarified.

He nodded. "Just sleep. I want to wake up with you."

The simplicity of it, the honesty, made my chest ache. This man, who could have anyone, wanted just to wake up beside me. The thought of sharing a bed with him both excited and terrified me. Was I really ready for that step? I liked to think I wasn't a coward.

"Yes," I said. "I'll stay."

His smile was slow and genuine, lacking the cockiness he showed the world. This smile was just for me.

Later, lying in his bed with his arm around me, I felt something I hadn't expected: resolution. Not an ending, but a beginning. The future stretched before us, uncertain but full of possibility.

Rebel's breathing had evened out, his body

relaxed in sleep. I studied his face in the moonlight filtering through the blinds. Peaceful. Human.

Mine, if I wanted him to be.

And I was starting to think I did.

Chapter Eight

Rebel

I leaned against the wall of the Church, which we'd turned into more of a war room, watching Charming pace the length of the space. The air hung heavy with cigarette smoke and tension, the kind you could cut with a knife. Maps spread out across the table showed our territory -- the roads we claimed, the places we protected.

"She's safe for now," Ashes said, his voice cutting through my thoughts. He stood at the head of the table, fingers splayed across the map like he was reading Braille. "We've got her covered here at the compound."

I nodded, but something in my gut twisted. Safety was always temporary in our world. How many times had this place been hit? We'd lost people from behind gates that should have been impenetrable. No matter how much we increased our security, it never seemed to be enough. At the same time, I couldn't lock her down in the house or the clubhouse. She needed the freedom to at least walk through the compound or go on a ride.

The door burst open, slamming against the wall hard enough to rattle the framed patches hanging there. Shade rushed in, his laptop balanced on one arm, his eyes wild behind his glasses.

"We're in deep shit," he announced, not bothering with greetings. His fingers flew across the keyboard the second he set it down, turning the screen to show us digital maps and security camera feeds. "Rio's attackers are pooling with the Moretti family for reinforcements. They've got at least fifteen men joining them from the east side of town."

"Fuck," I muttered, pushing off the wall. The room went silent.

I exchanged a look with Charming, his eyes narrowed, jaw set in that way that meant blood would spill before the night was over. He didn't need to speak. He'd always known when to listen first.

Ashes stepped forward, his weathered face grave. "Let's reach out to our Bratva contacts now. I don't think we need to sit and wait this time. Charming, your connection through your father might --"

"Waste of time," Rio interrupted, her voice cutting through the room. It was highly unusual for one of our women to be allowed in here, but with her background, Charming had made an exception.

She'd been in the corner, half-hidden by Renegade's broad frame. She stood with her arms crossed, her eyes hard as ice, but I caught the way her fingers dug into her own skin. She was scared, but damned if she'd let anyone see it.

"Those fuckers have a way to track me," she continued. "While I have no idea how they're pulling that off, what I do know is how they work. At least the military men. We can outmaneuver them."

"They drugged and raped you," I said bluntly. No point sugarcoating it. "And now they want to silence you."

Rio's chin lifted. "All the more reason to deal with this ourselves. The Bratva will want something in return, right?"

"They always do," Charming agreed, running a hand through his gray-streaked hair.

I began to pace, my boots heavy on the floor. Everyone watched me -- they knew my history before the club, the skills I'd brought with me. Despite the easygoing guy I appeared to be, I could handle myself.

"They'll expect us to fortify here," I said. "But that gives them time to surround us, cut off escape routes."

Renegade folded his arms, nodding slowly. "So we don't sit and wait."

"Exactly." I tapped the map sharply. "We split into three teams. First team creates a diversion at the north entrance. Second team circles around and cuts off their route back to the highway. Third team --" I looked directly at Rio, "-- extracts you to a secure location they don't know about."

"I'm not running," Rio said, stepping forward. The overhead light caught the strawberry tones in her hair, making it look like fire. "Those bastards already took enough from me. And if they're tracking me, won't they just find me anyway?"

Shade cleared his throat. "Not if I make sure you don't have bugs hidden in any of your shit. Clothes, shoes, vehicle. They could hide a transmitter anywhere really."

It made me wonder why he hadn't checked for that shit before now. For that matter, I should have asked him to the moment he said those fuckers had found her.

"Get your stuff to me, including your vehicle. I'll sweep everything. See what I can find," Shade said.

"Nobody's saying run away forever," I countered. "We're talking tactical retreat. Live to fight smarter."

Shade looked up from his laptop. "The Moretti family doesn't usually get involved in personal vendettas. These guys must have something the family wants."

"Or they're offering something in return," Ashes

added, gaze thoughtful.

I tapped my fingers against my thigh, thinking. "Those two men from Rio's unit -- they've got connections we don't know about. Military. Maybe even higher-level government. The fact they've remained free after all the shit they've done says plenty."

"They aren't just random soldiers," Rio said, her Georgia drawl thickening with emotion. "Denton -- his uncle runs some kind of security firm that contracts with three-letter agencies. But it never occurred to me he'd use that as a way to escape his fate. I should have. Rat bastard doesn't exactly play fair."

"Which means they've got resources." I resumed pacing, my mind racing through scenarios like flipping pages in a book. "Surveillance. Tracking. Maybe that's what they're offering Moretti. Intelligence."

"Weapons," Rio muttered. "What if they're leaking military secrets?"

"Like what?" I asked.

"Shipments." Her lips thinned. "What if he knows when and where weapons are being moved? If he sold that, or traded it to the Morettis…"

Charming's eyes met mine, and I saw the same realization dawn. That had to be it. And who knew what the hell kind of artillery we were talking about.

"Fucking hell." Renegade pinched the bridge of his nose. "If they know about that --"

"Then what else have those assholes shared," I finished.

Rio's face flushed red. "So I brought a shitstorm down on all of you by staying."

"No," I said firmly. "They did. And they're about to learn why that was their last mistake."

I turned back to the map, my finger tracing roads

and back alleys I knew blindfolded. "Shade, what's their current position?"

He typed rapidly, flipping through camera feeds. "Three vehicles approaching from the east. SUVs, tinted windows. Standard wannabe tough-guy bullshit."

"ETA?"

"Twenty minutes, tops. According to incoming messages on their phones, looks like they're planning to come here."

I locked eyes with Charming. "We need to move now. If we let them dictate the battlefield, we're already losing."

He nodded once, authority radiating from him like heat from a furnace. "She's your girl. What's the play, Rebel?"

I shook my head and pointed to Rio. "Let her take the lead. She needs this."

* * *

Rio

Everyone turned to me. Some clubs might balk at a woman calling the shots, but the Devil's Boneyard seemed to be different. Or at least, Rebel was. I'd been watching them since day one. Not just here at the clubhouse, but anytime I walked through the compound. Watching and listening. I'd picked up more about them than they probably realized.

"Azrael takes point on the diversion team," I said. "Rebel said he knows how to create chaos without leaving evidence. Renegade, you lead the blocking team here." I pointed to an intersection half a mile from the clubhouse. "Box them in, make it look like a traffic accident if civilians are around."

"And the extraction?" Ashes asked.

"Rebel," I said simply. "With Stripes as backup. I should be with the diversion team. I want those fuckers to see me."

"That's exactly what they want," Rebel countered. "You're the bait, remember? They see you, they call in whatever backup they've got waiting, and suddenly we're outgunned and outmanned."

"I'm some princess who needs rescuing?" I snapped. "Bait? Like I need to wait for you to swoop in and save me? Forget that shit."

"No, you're a strategic asset who needs protecting," he shot back. "And I don't mean just your body. Your testimony can put those rapist pieces of shit away. That's justice. That's power."

I held his gaze for a long moment before giving a curt nod.

Charming moved to the gun cabinet in the corner, unlocking it with practiced efficiency. "Everyone gear up. Standard armament plus comms."

"I've got something better than standard," Shade said, pulling a small black case from his backpack. He flipped it open to reveal earpieces smaller than the ones you typically saw. "These run on an encrypted frequency I set up last month. No chance of interception."

I took one, fitting it into my ear. "These are awesome."

Ashes distributed burner phones next. "One call, then destroy it. Emergency protocol if comms go down."

The room transformed as everyone moved with purpose. Weapons checked and loaded. Extra magazines distributed. Vests for those who wanted them. Through it all, I felt Rebel watching me. I took a Glock from Ashes, doing a quick check. I glanced over at Rebel and arched an eyebrow.

"I was military, remember? I can handle myself."

"Never doubted it," he replied. "But handling yourself and walking into whatever this is…"

"I'll say it again. Former military. Were you so worried you wanted to babysit me?"

He checked his weapons before answering. "No. It's because I'm the best shot in the club, and if those men get within fifty yards of you, I want to be the one putting bullets in their heads."

I could understand where he was coming from and gave him a quick nod.

Charming called for attention with a sharp whistle. "Listen up. This isn't just about protecting Rio, though that would be reason enough. These men aligned with Moretti are testing us, seeing if we're soft. We show them today that the Devil's Boneyard MC protects their own, and we do it with extreme prejudice."

Murmurs of agreement filled the room. Rebel glanced at his watch.

"Fifteen minutes until they reach our perimeter," he announced. "Everyone know their positions and routes?"

Nods all around. Charming made eye contact with each person in turn, a leader making sure his people were solid.

"Rebel," he said finally, "you're sure about this plan?"

"As sure as I can be without time for recon," he answered honestly. "I trust Rio. If something changes, we adapt."

"Good enough for me." He straightened, looking every inch the club President. "Let's move."

The energy changed instantly. Plans were one

thing; action was another. We filed out of the back room, and I fell into step beside Rebel.

"For what it's worth," I said quietly, just for his ears, "thanks for not treating me like I'm broken."

He glanced at me. "Being hurt and being broken aren't the same thing. Take it from someone who knows."

I didn't ask for details. Now wasn't the time for that sort of discussion. We needed to focus or we'd end up dead.

As we reached the door leading to the compound's yard, I caught Ashes looking our way.

"Watch her six," he said simply to Rebel.

He nodded. "With my life."

And I could tell he meant it.

* * *

Rebel

I stepped into the compound's open yard, the night air hitting my skin like a cold slap after the stuffy back room. Men were already moving with purpose, leather cuts and heavy boots, weapons prepped and ready. It was a beautiful, terrifying sight.

Rio stayed close to my right side, her steps matching mine. Her face had settled into something hard and focused -- the face of a soldier, not a victim. Good. We'd need that.

Across the yard, Azrael was already directing traffic, his features intense. He moved with the deadly grace of a man comfortable with violence, comfortable with death. They called him the angel of death for a reason.

"Gear up, we move in five!" I barked, watching small groups split off to secure the compound's exits. The pounding of heavy boots on concrete echoed off the surrounding buildings. I saw a few of our brothers gathering near the gate, not to leave with us, but to remain behind and protect the women and kids. Down the road a ways, I saw Jordan step out onto their porch, holding a shotgun.

"Perimeter team," Stripes called, his thick accent carrying across the yard. "You take the east approach first. No direct engagement unless you're compromised."

The designated men nodded, checking their weapons one last time before mounting their bikes. Engines roared to life, a familiar rumble that settled something in my chest. This was what we did -- we rode, we fought, we protected our own.

I led Rio toward a black SUV parked near the garage. "This is our transport. Tinted windows, reinforced panels. After the club's last fiasco, Charming had it ready for situations like this."

She ran her hand along the hood, assessing. "Bulletproof?"

"The doors and windows are. Not the whole thing."

"Better than nothing." She glanced back at the clubhouse. "You really think they'll come here? They aren't just faking us out to see what we do? Seems stupid to attack a compound full of armed bikers."

"Men like that -- men who drug and rape women -- they don't think like normal people," I said, checking the vehicle's supplies. Extra ammo, water, first aid kit. "They think they're untouchable. The Moretti connection makes them dangerous, but it also makes them cocky."

Rio studied my face. "You've dealt with men like this before."

It wasn't a question, but I answered anyway.

"Yes."

"Is that why you're so determined to be the one to extract me? Some personal vendetta?"

I closed the SUV's trunk with more force than necessary. "My reasons are my business."

"Not if they affect the plan," she countered. "Not if they put others at risk."

She had a point. I leaned against the vehicle, keeping my voice low. "A friend was attacked years ago, back when I was too young to know what the fuck to do. Men with connections, men who thought their money and their names would protect them. The cops did nothing. The courts did nothing."

"But you did something," she guessed.

I met her eyes. "Two months after the attack, one of them disappeared while boating. The other had a fatal accident with his motorcycle on a mountain road. Very tragic. I was twenty-two at the time. Before I came to the Devil's Boneyard."

Rio held my gaze, something shifting in her expression. Not judgment -- understanding.

"So this isn't just about protecting club interests."

"It's about justice," I said simply. "Sometimes the system works. Sometimes we need to be the system."

Before she could respond, Charming approached.

"Shade's got movement on the cameras," he said without preamble. "They've split up. Two vehicles heading for the front, one circling around back."

"They're trying to box us in," I muttered. "Expecting us to hunker down here."

"Which is why your girl's plan is already working." Charming nodded. "Azrael's team is in position for the diversion. Renegade's setting up the roadblock now."

I scanned the compound. The club had transformed from a group of hard-drinking bikers to a mercenary unit in minutes. This was why the Devil's Boneyard survived when other clubs folded. Discipline when it mattered.

Across the yard, Jackal was coaching a pair of younger members, showing them how to position themselves behind the concrete barriers at the entrance. His hands moved in sharp, precise gestures, demonstrating sight lines and cover positions. The men listened intently, nodding at his instructions.

"Remember," Azrael's voice carried to us through the comms. "Wait for my signal. Not before. We need them fully committed to the approach."

I checked my watch. "How long until they hit the perimeter?"

"Ten minutes, maybe less," Charming replied. "Shade's tracking their cell phones."

Stripes called me over with a sharp whistle. I joined him at the tactical map he'd brought outside, noting the new marks he'd added.

"They have set up here," he said, pointing to a spot a half-mile east. "Spotter with a rifle, most likely. You can't take the main road out." His finger traced an alternative route. "This service road connects to the highway five miles south. Not maintained, but passable. No streetlights, no cameras."

I studied the route. "That adds twenty minutes to our escape."

Stripes nodded. "*Da*. But adds zero bullets in your head. Fair trade, yes?"

Hard to argue with that logic. "We'll take it. Have you coordinated with the safe house?"

"*Da*. They expect you by midnight." He tapped another location on the map. "If your route is compromised, this is the backup location. Old hunting cabin owned by the Bratva. Stocked last month."

I committed both locations to memory, then glanced at Rio, who had joined us silently.

"Memorize these," I told her, pointing to the locations. "If we get separated --"

"We won't," she interrupted.

"If we get separated," I repeated firmly, "you need to know where to go. I've seen how these things play out. Have a plan A, B, and C."

Rio studied the map, her blue eyes scanning every detail. "Got it."

Stripes gave a curt nod, seemingly satisfied with her response. He folded the map, tucking it into an inside pocket of his cut. "Time to move. They will be here soon."

As if on cue, Ashes approached, distributing final equipment. "Comms check," he ordered, tapping his earpiece.

I adjusted mine, hearing the soft static as the channel opened. "Rebel, check."

One by one, each team leader confirmed their comms worked. The soft chatter in my ear was oddly comforting -- connection in the chaos.

"Two minutes to first contact," Shade's voice came through the earpiece. "First vehicle approaching the eastern checkpoint."

I turned to Rio. "Let's move."

She nodded, following me to the SUV. I opened the passenger door for her, scanning the compound one last time. Everyone was in position now.

Azrael caught my gaze from his location, giving me a single nod. We'd never been close -- he kept to himself mostly -- but there was a mutual respect between us. He understood what drove me tonight.

"Take care of your girl," he said through the comms.

"Count on it," I replied, sliding into the driver's seat.

I started the engine, its purr oddly subdued compared to the motorcycles I was used to. Rio buckled in beside me, her hands empty now -- the gun would be in her waistband or a holster, ready for access.

"You good?" I asked, pulling out of the parking space.

"No," she answered honestly. "But I'm ready."

I respected her candor. "That'll do."

As we approached the back exit, Stripes waved us down, approaching my window. I lowered it, waiting.

"You take first right after the bridge," he instructed. "The road looks blocked, but it's just brush. Push through."

"Understood," I said.

Through my earpiece, I heard Shade's urgent voice. "Contact! First vehicle stopped at checkpoint. Four men visible, armed."

"Showtime," I muttered, feeling the familiar rush of adrenaline flooding my system.

"Still time to turn back," Rio said, though her tone made it clear she didn't expect me to. "You could let me handle this alone. Less risk to the club."

I shifted the SUV into drive, easing toward the exit. "Two years before I joined the Devil's Boneyard, I was in a similar situation. Someone was gunning for me. A random stranger stood up for me when they didn't have to. I'm just paying it forward."

Her eyes widened slightly, but she didn't press for details. Instead, she checked her weapon one more time, the motion fluid and practiced.

"Then let's make sure we're both alive tomorrow to talk about it," she said.

I nodded, pressing the accelerator as the back gate opened. The night swallowed us, the compound's lights fading in the rearview mirror. Ahead, the road stretched dark and empty, but I knew better than to trust the apparent calm.

Behind us, I heard the first pop of gunfire, followed by shouts. The diversion had begun.

I pressed harder on the gas. "Hold on. This is where it gets interesting."

Rio braced herself against the dashboard. For a moment, she looked young -- too young for the hell she'd been through. Then her expression hardened again, and I saw the fighter beneath the trauma.

"Just drive," she said. "I've got your six."

And just like that, we were committed, racing through the night with nothing but determination, weapons, and the distant backup of a motorcycle club who'd decided this was a battle worth fighting.

Sometimes, that was all you needed.

Chapter Nine

Rebel

The road stretched ahead, my hands steady on the wheel as the SUV ate up the miles. Nothing but darkness surrounded us. Rio sat beside me, her fingers tapping an impatient rhythm against the door handle. We were making good time to the safe house, until the comm crackled to life with news that changed everything.

"-- repeat, Viper and Phantom are down." The voice broke through static, urgent and tight. "Hostiles have pulled back, but we need medical now."

I adjusted the volume, keeping one eye on the winding road. Trees crowded in from both sides.

"Status on the wounded?" I asked.

"Alive." The response was clipped. "Viper took a blade to the shoulder. Phantom caught a bullet in the thigh. We've got pressure on both, but it's messy."

Rio leaned forward, her blue eyes narrowed in the darkness. "Military or Moretti's?"

"Not your guys," came the quick response.

"Shit," I muttered, easing off the gas as we approached a sharp curve.

"We're securing the compound. Get to the safe house and stay put until we send the all-clear," Charming said.

The comm went silent. I glanced at Rio, who was already shaking her head.

"No fucking way," she said, her Georgia drawl thickening the way it always did when she was pissed. "We're not running to safety while our people are bleeding. I knew injuries were likely to happen, and we could possibly have even lost people, but they need us."

I didn't answer right away. The safe house was the smart play. But the thought of Viper and Phantom wounded while we sat on our asses didn't sit right.

"Rebel." Rio's voice cut through my thoughts. "They need us."

I'd known Rio for such a short time, but in this life, I'd learned it didn't matter how long you knew someone. Her presence had made me take immediate notice of her. But it was her loyalty that'd held my attention since then. It was evident in the way she talked to the club and the women, the way she seamlessly fit in, that she had our backs every bit as much as we had hers. That, and the fact that she didn't take shit from anyone. Just like now. She'd rather head back and face the danger head on than run and hide.

"President's orders were clear," I said, testing her. "Safe house."

"Fuck that noise." She crossed her arms over her chest. "Since when do you follow orders without question? I'm assuming you got the name Rebel for a reason. Those are your brothers back there."

The road curved again, moonlight flashing across Rio's face. The freckles scattered across her nose and cheeks stood out against her pale skin, but it was the determination in her eyes that caught me.

"Going back could make everything worse."

"Or it could save lives." She leaned in closer. "You really want to sit this one out? Hiding while others fight?"

I shot her a look. "I don't hide."

"Could've fooled me." A challenge glinted in her eyes. "Thought you were the one who told me the Devil's Boneyard never leaves its own behind."

The words stung because they were true. I'd said exactly that during one of our discussions. Looked like she'd been paying attention.

"We go back," she pressed, "or I'm jumping out at the next curve and walking my ass there myself."

"You're a real pain in the ass, you know that?" I muttered.

Her lips twitched. "Part of my charm."

I slowed the SUV, the engine humming lower as I eased to the shoulder. "If we go back, we're not rushing in half-cocked. We scout first, assess the situation."

"Fine." Rio nodded. "Smart."

"And if I say we pull back, we pull back. No arguments."

She hesitated. "If it makes tactical sense, sure."

"Rio."

"Fine." She raised her hands. "Your call. But I'm not sitting in the car if our people need help."

Our. I liked how she said that. Made me wonder if this meant she'd decided to stay, to be mine. She'd hinted at it when she'd decided to sleep in my bed, but we hadn't exactly clarified anything. With everything going on, Charming hadn't exactly asked us for an answer either.

I checked the mirror, the empty road behind us reflecting nothing but darkness. The decision was already made -- had been the moment we heard Viper and Phantom were hurt. But I needed Rio to understand this wasn't about heroics.

"We're not heroes," I said, echoing my thoughts. "We're smarter than that."

"Never wanted to be a hero." The edge in her voice was razor-sharp. "Just want to make sure the people who hurt ours bleed a whole lot more before this night's over."

I couldn't argue with that. If they thought hitting

our people would make us back down, they were dead wrong. Something told me they'd been prepared to either take Rio or hoped we'd just hand her over, deciding she was more trouble than she was worth.

"Comms silence from here on," I said, putting the SUV in gear. "Who knows if those assholes have the ability to monitor channels. Shade said they were in encrypted, but we honestly don't know what tech those guys might have access to."

Rio nodded, then reached into the glove compartment for the burner phones. She handed one to me.

I made a U-turn, the SUV's tires kicking up gravel as we spun around. The engine growled as I accelerated back the way we'd come, the night swallowing us once more.

"You know," Rio said after a minute of silence, "if we survive this, the President is gonna have both our asses."

I snorted. "Wouldn't be the first time. Not for me anyway."

"Won't be the last either." She grinned, all teeth and savage anticipation.

The miles ticked by faster now, urgency pushing my foot heavier on the gas. The curves came and went, the SUV hugging the road like it was made for it. We didn't talk much after that. There wasn't much to say. We both knew what waited for us back at the compound -- blood, chaos, and the very real possibility that things had gotten worse since that radio call.

Rio checked her weapon again, the *click-click* of the slide oddly reassuring in the quiet car. Her face was set, determined. I couldn't help but think that the assholes who'd hurt her had only made her more dangerous.

"You ever regret walking into our clubhouse that night?" I asked, breaking the silence.

She looked at me, surprise flickering across her features. "Random time for deep questions."

"Just curious."

She was quiet for a moment, her gaze drifting to the window. "No," she finally said. "Never. You all gave me something I'd thought I'd lost forever."

"What's that?"

Her voice was soft, but there was steel underneath. "People worth fighting for."

I nodded, understanding perfectly. The club wasn't perfect -- far from it -- but it was family. The kind that stood together when everything went to shit. The kind worth turning around for.

We crested a hill, and the first glimpse of the compound appeared in the distance. No flames, no smoke. A good sign, maybe. Or maybe just the calm before the next storm.

"Ready?" I asked, slowing as we approached.

Rio checked her weapon one last time, her blue eyes gleaming with determination in the dashboard light. "Born ready."

I pressed down on the gas, and the SUV surged forward, eating up the final stretch of road between us and whatever waited ahead. The night was still young, and the assholes who'd attacked us were about to learn a painful lesson about messing with the Boneyard.

* * *

The clubhouse was just ahead. I slowed the vehicle and scanned the area. Everything seemed quiet. Almost too quiet. I glanced at Rio and knew she was ready to charge ahead, damn the consequences, and right now, I felt the same way. I hit the gas and continued down the road.

The compound gate stood open when we arrived, which wasn't a good sign. Typically, after an attack, everything would be locked down tight. Especially since Charming had said they were going to fortify this place. I slowed the SUV, scanning for sentries, finding two armed men posted at the entrance. Their faces tightened when they recognized us, a mix of relief and wariness. I kept the engine running as we approached, one hand on my weapon. Better to be paranoid than dead.

"Thought you two were headed to the safe house," one of them said, voice low.

"Change of plans," I replied. "Status?"

"Just the two wounded. Viper and Phantom." He glanced over his shoulder. "They hit hard but ran when we returned fire and took out three of their men. Cowardly bastards."

Rio leaned across from the passenger seat. "They coming back?"

"Don't think so. Not tonight at least." He stepped back, waving us through. "President's gonna have questions."

"Let him ask," I muttered, rolling up the window and easing the SUV into the compound.

The main yard was lit with harsh floodlights, creating islands of brightness amid deep shadows. Men and a few women moved around the area, weapons visible on hips and shoulders of the men. Outside the clubhouse, a line of bikes stretched in either direction.

I parked next to the clubhouse and killed the engine. "Stay sharp," I said to Rio. "President's likely to shoot first, ask questions later when he sees us. To say he'll be pissed is an understatement."

She snorted. "Wouldn't be the first time someone

pointed a gun at me."

"Hopefully not the last either. Means you're still alive."

We exited the SUV simultaneously, scanning the yard. Three club members approached immediately, hands hovering near weapons. Scratch, Ripper, and Java.

"Got some balls coming back after a direct order," Scratch said.

I met his gaze evenly. "Never been good at following stupid orders."

His mouth twitched, almost a smile. "President's inside with the wounded. He's pissed."

"What else is new?" I started walking, Rio at my side.

Scratch fell into step beside us. "These assholes were definitely professionals. The Morettis didn't send their weakest links."

The clubhouse door was propped open, voices and the smell of antiseptic spilling out. Inside, the usual dim lighting had been replaced by bright portable lamps clustered around the pool table and a couple of couches. The tables and chairs had been pushed to the walls, creating a makeshift medical area in the center of the room.

Viper lay on the pool table, his cut and shirt removed, revealing a deep stab wound in his left shoulder. Doc had on surgical gloves and was stitching it closed while Viper gritted his teeth. His face was gray with pain, but his eyes were alert, tracking us as we entered.

On the nearest couch, Phantom sat with his pants cut away from a bandaged thigh. Blood had soaked through the white gauze, but someone -- most likely Doc -- had started an IV, the bag hanging from an improvised stand made from a pool cue and duct tape. Resourceful. Messy. Effective.

"Well, look what the cat dragged in," came a deep voice from the bar area.

I turned to face Charming. He stood with a glass of whiskey in one hand, his expression stormy.

"Sounded like you needed help," I said, keeping my voice neutral.

"Heard you needed to follow fucking orders," he shot back, but there was something beneath the anger. Relief, maybe.

"Figured you'd want your best fighters here, not sitting on their asses at a safe house," Rio said, her drawl more pronounced than usual.

Charming's gaze shifted to her. Few people spoke to him that directly, especially the women. He studied her for a long moment, then let out a rough laugh.

"You've got a mouth on you, Army girl." He drained his glass. "Lucky for you, I like people who speak their minds. Even when they're being insubordinate pains in my ass. As for toughest fighter… that remains to be seen."

He moved toward us. Up close, I could see the fatigue in his eyes, the tension in his shoulders. This attack had rattled him more than he was letting on.

"Report," he said, nodding to Scratch.

"Perimeter's secure. Doubled the guards on the south fence. Added more cameras out back. Got eyes on the road for a mile in each direction." Scratch shifted his weight. "No movement since they pulled back."

"They'll be back," Rio said. "This was too coordinated to be a one-off. Plus, they didn't get to me. Which means they won't stop until I'm in their grasp or dead."

Charming nodded. "My thoughts exactly."

Doc finished with Viper's shoulder, applying a clean bandage. Viper sat up slowly, his face tight with pain.

I moved closer to him, examining the bandage. "Clean cut?"

He nodded. "Blade went in smooth. No serrated edges. Missed anything important, according to Doc."

"You're lucky," he said, stripping off his gloves. "Two inches in the wrong direction, and you'd be bleeding out right now instead of just whining about the pain."

Viper grinned through clenched teeth. "Love you too, Doc."

Doc rolled his eyes and flipped him off.

Phantom tried to stand from the couch, wincing as he put weight on his injured leg. "They weren't aiming to kill," he said. "They had clean shots on both of us. Chose to wound instead."

"That's not their usual style," I said, frowning. The Morettis were known for their brutality, not their restraint.

"They wanted information most likely," Charming said. "Dead men don't talk."

Rio had moved to the window, peering out. When she turned back, I knew she hadn't spotted anything out of the ordinary. Didn't mean she wouldn't keep checking.

"If they're coming back, I want to be ready," Charming said. "This time we didn't move until they were on the attack already. We need to be smart. Go after them before they have a chance to regroup. Two teams, different entry points. Quick strike, maximum damage, then out before they can respond."

I studied him a moment. "When?"

"Dawn." Charming looked up, his gaze sweeping across the room. "They'll be at their weakest, and hopefully not expecting us to bring the fight to them."

"I want in," Rio said, her voice firm. It wasn't a request.

Charming assessed her for a moment, then nodded. "You'll go with Rebel's team. I already know I can't hold him back."

"What about Viper and Phantom?" I asked, glancing at the wounded men.

"They stay here with the men guarding the compound and our families," Charming said. "Along with anyone else not fit for combat."

The planning continued for another hour. Shade provided the intel on where the Morettis had moved, including a layout of the building. Charming went over every aspect of the attack -- entry points, escape routes, communications, weapons. I watched Rio throughout, noting how she contributed tactical suggestions that even the more experienced members hadn't considered. The woman knew her shit. By the time we finished, the plan was tight, with contingencies for every scenario we could think of.

"Get some rest," Charming ordered when we were done. "We move out at 0400."

The room emptied slowly, members breaking off to prepare in their own ways. Some headed to the homes, others to clean weapons or check gear. Rio and I remained at the table, studying the map one last time.

"You know this is probably exactly what they want," she said quietly. "Us charging in, angry and looking for payback."

"Probably," I agreed. "Doesn't mean we're not

going to give it to them."

She smiled, a cold, dangerous thing. "Never said we shouldn't go. Just said we should know what we're walking into."

I rolled up the map, tucking it into my jacket. "You having second thoughts?"

"About putting bullets in the people who hurt our friends?" She shook her head. "Not a chance. Just want to make sure we're the ones walking out afterward."

"We will be." I held her gaze. "I've got your back."

"And I've got yours." She checked her watch. "Five hours until we move. Enough time to gear up and maybe catch a power nap."

We walked together toward the SUV beside the clubhouse, the compound now humming with focused energy as everyone prepared for the coming fight. Rio's stride was confident, her back straight despite the exhaustion I knew she must be feeling. The woman had grit; I'd give her that.

"You know," I said as we reached the vehicle, "Charming could have had our asses for disobeying orders."

She grinned. "Knew he wouldn't. Man needs all hands on deck for this one."

I laughed softly. "Come on. Let's head to the house."

We got into the SUV and I drove us home. When we walked in, Rio stopped at the fridge and pulled out a cold beer. She took a long pull, then handed me a drink as well. She shut the fridge and leaned against the counter.

"Why don't you sleep with me again? We can set an alarm for two hours. That gives us plenty of time to prep."

She nodded. "Yeah. Not sure I can actually sleep right now though. I'm dead tired but wired at the same time."

I got it. Felt the same.

I held out my hand to her. "Only one way to find out."

She drained her beer and set the bottle on the counter before taking my hand. I finished mine as well, tossing it across the room into the trash. She shook her head when it went straight in.

"Show off," she muttered.

We went to the bedroom and toed off our boots. I shrugged out of my cut and set it aside then stretched out on the bed. Rio walked to the other side and lay beside me. I put my arm around her, tugging her closer. It didn't take long for her breathing to even out. I'd known she'd fall asleep once she allowed herself to relax. The beer had probably helped.

Dawn couldn't come soon enough. The Morettis had drawn first blood tonight, but we'd make damn sure they regretted it by sunrise. Didn't matter we'd already killed some of them. Far as I was concerned, they all needed to be six feet under. The fact they'd hurt my brothers infuriated me, and I knew the others felt the same. They were family, and family stood together, fought together, and if necessary, bled together. The Devil's Boneyard took care of its own, and heaven help anyone who forgot that lesson.

Chapter Ten

Rio

Glass shattered somewhere to my left as I ducked behind an overturned table. The roar of motorcycle engines, mixed with shouting and gunfire, created a symphony of chaos around me. Blood dripped from a cut above my eyebrow, but I ignored it. My focus narrowed to a single purpose -- finding the two Army pricks who'd attacked me. Somewhere in this hellhole, they were hiding, and the Devil's Boneyard assault gave me the perfect cover to hunt them down.

I peered over the edge of the table, taking in the carnage. The Moretti hideout had transformed from a nondescript industrial building into a war zone in less than ten minutes. Bodies littered the concrete floor, some moving, others eerily still. The sickly scent of blood and gunpowder filled my nostrils, a smell I'd grown unfortunately familiar with.

Not how I'd planned to spend my time, but here I was. At this rate, the battle with the Morettis would be never-ending. This made our third confrontation with them since the initial fight.

The attack had started with precision. Charming had received intel about the hideout's location from Shade, and he'd moved fast. At first, he'd intended to leave me out of the fight, but I'd insisted on going. I wasn't the type to sit at home and let the men go off to battle. No, if there was a chance at finding the assholes who'd hurt me, I wanted in on the action. They'd cheated by drugging me before. They'd also planted a tracker inside the heel of a boot and another under my truck. This time, I'd have the upper hand.

"Rio, three o'clock!" Chaos's voice cut through

the noise.

I spun right as a bearded man charged toward me, switchblade gleaming in his hand. I sidestepped, grabbed his extended arm, and used his momentum to slam him into the wall. His nose crunched against concrete, and he howled. Before he could recover, I spun him around, twisted the knife from his grip and drove my knee into his stomach. He doubled over, and I brought my elbow down hard between his shoulder blades. He crumpled to the floor, motionless.

"Thanks for the heads-up," I called to Chaos, who flashed me a wild grin before launching himself back into the fray.

I'd never seen the Devil's Boneyard in full attack mode before. It was terrifying and awe-inspiring. These men moved with practiced precision despite the apparent disorder around them. Chaos lived up to his name, spinning through the fight with unpredictable movements that left opponents disoriented. Three Moretti soldiers tried to corner him, but he laughed in their faces before putting two of them down with quick, brutal strikes. The third backed away, fear evident in his eyes.

I skirted the edge of a burning barrel, the heat singeing my arms as I passed. My eyes darted from face to face, searching for the men who'd made my life hell.

A bullet struck the wall inches from my head, showering me with plaster. I dropped to a crouch and scuttled behind a stack of wooden pallets. Fuck, that was close. My heart hammered against my ribs, but I forced my breathing to steady. Panic wouldn't help me now.

I spotted Rebel across the room, his movements fluid as he took on two men at once. His fists connected with sickening thuds, and I watched as he effortlessly dominated the fight. His confidence in battle was magnetic, drawing my eyes to him even amid this chaos. He caught my gaze for a split second, his lips quirking into that cocky smirk that both infuriated and thrilled me, before returning his attention to the men before him.

My momentary distraction cost me. A hand grabbed my hair from behind, yanking me backward. Pain exploded across my scalp as I stumbled, fighting to keep my balance. I twisted, driving my elbow blindly behind me, and felt it connect with something solid. The grip on my hair loosened slightly. I spun and found myself face-to-face with a woman I didn't recognize -- one of the Morettis' girlfriends, judging by the diamonds in her ears and around her throat. Her eyes blazed with hatred as she lunged at me again. What the fuck was this bitch doing in the middle of a fight?

"Biker whore," she snarled, aiming a knife at my stomach.

I caught her wrist, deflecting the blade away from my body. "Original," I replied, before headbutting her hard enough to make my own vision blur.

She staggered backward, blood gushing from her nose. I didn't give her time to recover. I swept her legs out from under her and watched as she crashed to the floor, the knife skittering away. She wouldn't be getting up anytime soon. Just to make sure, I stomped on her ankle, and she let out a shriek that would do a banshee proud.

I shook my head to clear it and continued my search. The back rooms. That's where they'd be. Cowards always hid while others fought their battles.

Same had been true in the Army. My unit had been sent in to deal with some skirmishes, and the two men who'd attacked me somehow managed to avoid most of the battle every damn time. I'd always found it odd how they could do that and get away with it. Now I knew. They were backed by someone powerful.

I navigated through the chaos, ducking under a flying chair and sidestepping a grappling pair of men who tumbled across my path. The din of the fight began to fade as I approached a corridor leading deeper into the building. I paused at the entrance, listening. The sound of low voices drifted from one of the rooms.

My fingers curled around a switchblade I'd taken earlier. The weight felt reassuring in my palm. I moved silently down the corridor, testing each door as I passed. The first two were locked. The third opened to an empty storage closet. The voices grew louder as I approached the fourth door. I pressed my ear against it.

"-- fuck's sake, we need to get out now!" The voice was panicked, frantic.

"Not until we grab the cash. I'm not leaving empty-handed. You saw how much these assholes brought with them." This voice was lower, calmer, but with an edge of frustration.

I recognized it immediately. My body tensed, anger coursing through me like electricity. *Found you, asshole.*

I didn't waste time on subtlety. I kicked the door open with enough force to send it slamming against the interior wall. Two men spun toward me, their expressions shifting from surprise to recognition to fear in the span of seconds.

"Remember me?" I asked, my voice deadly calm

despite the adrenaline surging through my veins.

Private Ellis made a break for the window. I intercepted him with a tackle that sent us both crashing into a desk. Papers scattered as we rolled across its surface and onto the floor. He outweighed me by at least sixty pounds, but I had rage on my side. I drove my knee between his legs, and he howled in pain, curling inward.

I barely had time to register Sergeant Denton lunging for me before something hard connected with the side of my head. Stars burst across my vision as I stumbled sideways, momentarily disoriented. I blinked away the dizziness in time to see him raising what looked like a metal paperweight for another strike.

I ducked beneath his arm and slammed my fist into his kidney. He grunted but didn't go down. Tougher than I remembered. He swung again, and I blocked the blow with my forearm, pain shooting up to my shoulder. I countered with a strike to his throat that had him gasping and staggering backward.

"You bitch," he wheezed. "Should've finished you when we had the chance."

"My thoughts exactly," I replied, before driving my foot into his knee. The crack was audible even over his scream.

Ellis had recovered enough to grab me from behind, his arm snaking around my neck in a chokehold. Spots danced before my eyes as he cut off my air supply. I struggled, clawing at his arm, but his grip was like iron. My lungs burned. The switchblade. I still had it clenched in my right hand. I flicked it open and stabbed backward, feeling the blade sink into flesh.

He screamed and released me. I gulped in precious air, spinning to face him. Blood stained his shirt where I'd caught him in the side. Not fatal, but enough to take the fight out of him. He stumbled back against the wall, clutching the wound.

Movement by the door caught my attention. Rebel. His knuckles were bloody and his eyes were wild. He took in the scene with a quick glance -- me standing, two Army boys down but alive.

"You good?" he asked, gaze lingering on the already-forming bruise on my temple.

I nodded, still catching my breath. "Found what I was looking for."

Denton tried to crawl toward the window. Rebel casually stepped on his injured leg, eliciting a howl of pain. "Friends of yours?" he asked me, raising an eyebrow.

"These are the bastards who hurt me. I had a score to settle."

Rebel's smile turned predatory as he looked down at the man beneath his boot. "Well, looks like the lady settled it." He increased the pressure, and Denton's face contorted in agony. "Want me to finish them off?"

I considered it for a moment. The rage inside me demanded their blood, but something else -- something colder and clearer -- held me back. "No. I want them to remember this. Remember that I found them." I knelt beside Denton, forcing him to look at me. "And I can find you again. Next time, I won't stop. I'd suggest you turn yourselves in."

Fear flashed in his eyes. Good. That's what I wanted -- them looking over their shoulders, wondering when I might appear. A fate worse than death for men like these. I didn't know how they'd escaped before, but maybe Shade could find the connection so we could sever it. If they went back to prison, maybe they'd stay there this time. As much as I wanted to end their lives, another part of me knew I wasn't a killer. Not when it came to this. If the military told me to point and shoot, I'd do it. I'd been following orders. This was different.

"Charming's calling a retreat," Rebel said, his hand resting casually on my shoulder. "Cops are inbound."

I nodded, stepping back from my attackers. They wouldn't be causing trouble anytime soon, and the Moretti hideout was thoroughly destroyed. Mission accomplished, even if the satisfaction I'd hoped for remained elusive.

As we headed back through the chaos of the main floor, I cast one last glance at the two men. They'd underestimated me not once but twice. They wouldn't make that mistake again.

If they came for me again, if they didn't turn themselves in and pay for their crimes, then I'd have to rethink things. I wouldn't play by the rules next time. Now that I was part of the Devil's Boneyard, it might be time to stop thinking like a law-abiding citizen. It hadn't done shit for me so far.

* * *

The Devil's Boneyard compound lay in darkness as we returned, the rumble of motorcycles cutting through the night before dying to silence in the lot. I slid off Rebel's bike, my body screaming in protest at every movement. He'd insisted I ride with him tonight instead of using the bike he'd given me.

Blood had dried in crusty patches along my forearms, and each breath sent sharp pains through my ribs where Ellis had landed a solid hit. The adrenaline that had carried me through the fight was fading fast, leaving behind bone-deep exhaustion and the dull throb of emerging bruises. But we'd won. I'd won. And that knowledge numbed the pain better than any painkiller.

The compound was eerily quiet after the chaos of the Moretti hideout. Most of the men had returned before us, having taken different routes to avoid drawing attention. A few members stood smoking near the entrance, nodding silently as we approached. Their faces showed the marks of battle -- split lips, swollen eyes, bloodied knuckles -- badges of honor in this world I was still learning to navigate.

Rebel's hand pressed lightly against my lower back as we entered, a small gesture of support that I was too tired to resist. "Medical supplies are at home, or there's some in a back room here at the clubhouse," he said, his voice gravelly from shouting during the fight. "Wouldn't hurt to patch up the worst of the spots now. Unless you want Doc to look at you."

I shook my head. "I can handle it." The club's medic would be busy with more serious injuries. Besides, I preferred to lick my wounds in private. Although, the small rooms down the clubhouse hallway *were* technically private. Or as close as anyone could get with so many people nearby.

The interior of the clubhouse smelled of leather, cigarettes, and now the metallic tang of blood. A few Prospects scurried about, distributing beer and bandages to the wounded men sprawled on couches and chairs. Chaos sat at the bar, animatedly recounting some moment from the fight to an attentive audience, his hands gesturing wildly despite the makeshift bandage wrapped around his left palm. His voice carried across the room, punctuated by bursts of laughter.

"-- swear the motherfucker pissed himself when I

came through that door!"

I didn't break stride as I passed them, following Rebel down a dimly lit hallway. My left ankle protested with each step, a subtle limp I tried to disguise. Show no weakness. That was a lesson I'd learned long before meeting the Devil's Boneyard.

Rebel led me into what looked like a bedroom. Except it had two sets of bunk beds on either wall. I wasn't sure what it was used for since all the men seemed to have their own houses.

"Bathroom's through there." Rebel nodded toward a door on the right. "Towels in the cabinet. Use whatever you need."

I stepped into the small bathroom, flipping on the light and immediately wincing at my reflection. A bruise was forming along my right temple, spreading into a purple stain beneath my eye. Dried blood crusted around a cut on my forehead. My bottom lip was split, and dirt smudged across my cheek like war paint. I looked like hell.

I turned on the tap and waited for the water to warm, propping myself against the sink as fatigue threatened to buckle my knees. The events of the night played through my mind like a fragmented movie. The initial assault. The sound of breaking glass and screams. The satisfaction of finding those Army bastards. The look in their eyes when they realized who I was.

Fear. They'd been afraid of me. Maybe that's why they'd drugged me before they'd raped me. They'd known I'd fight back, and the fuckers hadn't been sure they'd win.

Water steamed in the sink, and I plunged my hands into it, watching as blood and grime swirled into pink eddies. I'd fought before but never like tonight.

Never with such calculated violence. Never with the backing of men who treated brutality as just another Tuesday. In the Army, any battles had been more… methodical. Well, as much as they could be. This had felt wilder.

And I'd liked it. That was the truth I couldn't escape as I cleaned each scrape and cut. The power, the respect in Rebel's eyes when he'd found me standing over my attackers -- it had filled something empty inside me.

I soaked a washcloth and pressed it gently to my split lip, hissing at the sting. Over the last week, I'd gradually, inevitably, been pulled into his world. Into this world.

A soft knock at the door interrupted my thoughts.

"You alive in there?" Rebel's voice carried through the wood.

"Still breathing," I called back, wincing as the movement reopened my lip.

"Need help?"

I considered saying no. Independence was my default, a shield I'd carried for years. But tonight had shifted something fundamental between us. "Yeah," I admitted. "Could use an extra hand."

The door opened, and Rebel leaned against the frame, assessing me with those intense eyes of his. He'd removed his cut and T-shirt, revealing a torso marked with old scars and fresh bruises. A particularly nasty gash ran along his right bicep, hastily cleaned but still angry looking.

"Sit," he said, gesturing to the closed toilet lid.

I obeyed, too tired to maintain my usual defiance. He knelt before me, taking the cloth from my hand and wetting it again under the tap. His movements were surprisingly gentle as he cleaned the cut on my forehead, his other hand tilting my chin to get a better angle.

"That Army fucker do this?" he asked, his voice deceptively casual.

"Paperweight to the head," I confirmed. "Could've been worse."

His jaw tightened, but he continued his ministrations in silence. I studied his face as he worked -- the concentrated furrow of his brow, the tightness around his eyes that betrayed his anger, the three-day beard growth along his jaw. The man who'd upended my life and offered me something I hadn't known I wanted. There were still things we needed to discuss.

"You did good," he said finally, reaching past me for the antiseptic in the medicine cabinet. "Not many could take on two Army soldiers and walk away."

"I had motivation. Not to mention, I went through the same training as Ellis. Denton may have learned more with his higher rank, but at the end of the day, his balls could be crushed as easily as any other man's."

He huffed a laugh, dabbing antiseptic on my cut. I clenched my teeth against the burn. "Yeah. Remind me never to piss you off."

The silence stretched between us as he finished with my forehead and moved to my split lip, his thumb ghosting over the injury with uncharacteristic tenderness. Something shifted in his eyes -- a darkening that had nothing to do with anger.

"Anything else need attention?" he asked, his voice lower now.

I hesitated, then turned one hand palm up and the other palm down, revealing scraped knuckles on the left hand and a deep cut across my right palm. Not that I remembered where I'd gotten it. Without comment, he took my hands in his, cleaning each abrasion with careful precision.

"This will scar," he murmured, tracing the line across my palm.

"Add it to the collection," I replied.

His eyes met mine, and I saw understanding there. We all had scars -- visible and invisible. In the Devil's Boneyard, scars were currency, proof of survival.

"Your turn," I said, nodding to the gash on his arm.

He shook his head. "I'll get it later."

"Don't be stubborn." I took the cloth from him and gestured for him to sit on the edge of the bathtub. "Fair exchange."

A smile tugged at the corner of his mouth as he complied. "Yes, ma'am."

I focused on cleaning his wound, using the task to distract myself from the intimacy of the moment. Rebel wasn't just a hookup or casual fling. We'd been circling each other for days, the attraction undeniable but complicated.

"You're thinking too loud," he said, breaking into my thoughts.

I glanced up to find him watching me, that knowing look in his eyes that always made me feel transparent. "Just processing."

"Tonight?"

"Everything." I pressed a fresh bandage over his cut, securing it with tape. "Finding Ellis and Denton. The fight. Being here."

"Regrets?" His tone was neutral, but I caught the subtle tension in his shoulders.

Did I regret it? The violence, the danger, the

knowledge that I'd crossed lines I once thought immutable? I should. The Rio from before would have handed those men over to the police or Army. She'd have believed in justice. But that Rio hadn't known what it felt like to have a target on her back, to be hunted by men she'd thought she could trust. That Rio hadn't experienced the security and belonging the Devil's Boneyard offered, complicated as it was. Just the same, I hadn't been able to pull the trigger. I'd changed, but maybe not as much as I should.

"No," I said finally, the truth of it settling in my chest like a weight. "No regrets."

Rebel's expression remained unreadable, but something in his eyes softened. He caught my hand as I withdrew it from his arm, his thumb running over my battered knuckles. "Good."

We sat in silence for a moment, the small bathroom suddenly feeling too intimate, too charged. I broke away first, standing on legs that felt steadier than before.

"I should go home and shower," I said. "Get the rest of this off me."

He nodded, rising fluidly despite his injuries. "Let's head out."

I followed him back through the clubhouse to the lot out front. I climbed onto the back of his bike, my arms going around his waist. It didn't take long to reach the house. When we got inside, I went to the spare room to get a change of clothes. But before I could go into the bathroom, he reached out to take my arm.

"You should use my bathroom. It's bigger. You've been sleeping in my room anyway."

I stared at him, trying to see if there was some hidden meaning to his words. He just watched me, leaving the decision to me. I gave a quick nod and went into his room, then into the adjoining bathroom.

I shut the door and leaned against the sink. I'd chosen violence and vengeance. I'd chosen to stand with the Devil's Boneyard against their enemies. Against my enemies. And for the first time since I'd met Rebel, I found myself considering a future I'd been afraid to contemplate -- one where I fully embraced this life, with all its darkness and loyalty. One where I belonged at his side -- not just as a woman he protected, but as his equal.

His old lady.

The thought should have terrified me. Instead, it felt like coming home. Whether I wanted to fully admit it or not, I'd made my decision. I'd stay with Rebel.

Chapter Eleven
Rio

Steam followed me out of the bathroom, curling around my bare shoulders like phantom fingers. I'd scrubbed until my skin turned pink, washing away blood and grime until the water ran clear, but I couldn't erase the memory of tonight's violence so easily. Rebel's T-shirt hung loose on my frame, the worn fabric soft against my freshly cleaned skin. I'd swiped it the morning I'd woken up in his bed and hadn't given it back. Something about sleeping in it gave me comfort.

The bathroom mirror had shown me a woman I was still learning to recognize -- battered but not broken, eyes clear and determined despite the bruising. I stepped into Rebel's room, my hair damp against my neck, and found him sitting on the edge of the bed waiting for me.

He'd showered in the other bathroom while I'd taken my time under the hot spray. His hair was still wet, slicked back from his forehead, and he'd changed into clean sweatpants, his chest bare except for the tattoos that mapped his history across his skin. The Devil's Boneyard insignia dominated his right pectoral, a reminder of where his loyalties lay.

The room felt different now -- more intimate in the soft glow of the bedside lamp. What had seemed Spartan before now registered as intentionally minimal. No distractions, no sentimentality. Just the essentials and space to breathe. It suited him.

"Feel better?" he asked, tracking my movement as I padded barefoot across the floor.

"Cleaner, at least." My voice sounded rough even to my own ears. "Thank you. For having my back tonight."

He shrugged, the gesture dismissive but not unkind. "You didn't need me. You had those Army fuckers handled."

"Still. It's good to know someone's there."

A half-smile played across his lips. "Getting soft on me, Rio?"

"Maybe." I sank onto the bed beside him, close enough to feel the heat radiating from his skin but not quite touching. "Or maybe I'm just tired of pretending I don't care."

His eyes sharpened, that intense focus that always made me feel like I was the only person in his world. He didn't rush to fill the silence, just waited for me to continue. It was one of the things I'd first noticed about him -- how he could be still in a way few people managed, patient in his confidence.

I drew a deep breath, gathering my courage. Tonight had shown me something about myself, about what I was capable of and what I wanted. The woman who'd walked into the Moretti hideout wasn't the same one sitting here now. The more time I spent with the club, the more I changed. I wouldn't run from anyone who hurt me. I'd face everything head on, and I knew I'd have the club at my back and Rebel by my side.

"When I found Ellis and Denton tonight," I began, my fingers tracing the edge of a bruise on my thigh, "I could have killed them. Part of me wanted to."

"Why didn't you?" No judgment in his tone, just curiosity.

I considered the question, searching for the truth beneath my actions. "Because death would have been too quick. Too easy." I looked up, meeting his gaze directly. "I wanted them to remember. To know I'm not just some random woman they can terrorize. I have people behind me now, and I belong to something stronger than they are."

Understanding dawned in his eyes, but he remained silent, letting me find my way, find the right words.

"I've been fighting my whole life, but especially since my discharge from the Army," I continued. "Fighting to survive, fighting to stay independent. Fighting against needing anyone. But tonight, standing in that room with you behind me, I realized something. Being part of something doesn't make me weaker. It makes me stronger."

I shifted to face him fully, forcing myself not to look away despite the vulnerability of the moment. "I'm ready to be your old lady."

The words hung between us, simple but profound. In the world of the Devil's Boneyard, they carried weight that went beyond typical relationship labels. Being an old lady meant belonging -- to a man, yes, but also to the club. To a family bound by loyalty stronger than blood.

Rebel's expression remained steady, but I caught the flash of something primal in his eyes before he controlled it. "You sure about that? Life with me, with the club -- it isn't always going to be pretty."

"Pretty's overrated," I replied. "I don't need pretty. I need real."

A slow smile spread across his face, satisfaction and something deeper warming his features. "All right, baby," he said, the endearment rolling off his tongue with newfound possession. Without breaking eye contact, he reached for his phone on the nightstand.

"What are you doing?" I asked.

"Messaging Charming," he replied, thumbs moving across the screen. "Requesting a property cut for you. Technically our three days are long up, but with everything going on, he hasn't pushed. Now that you've made up your mind, I'm letting him know."

The phrase made something in my stomach tighten -- not unpleasantly, but with the weight of significance. A property cut. The visible symbol that I belonged to Rebel, that I was under his and the club's protection. My independence balked momentarily before quieting. This wasn't about submission or control. It was about choice. My choice.

"That fast, huh?" I said, aiming for lightness despite the gravity of the moment.

Rebel set the phone aside and reached for me, his hand cupping my cheek with surprising gentleness. "Been waiting for you to be ready," he admitted. "Didn't want to push."

The confession shouldn't have surprised me, but it did. For all his cocky exterior, Rebel had never pressured me, never demanded more than I was willing to give. He'd let me set the pace.

"What happens now?" I asked.

"Now?" His thumb brushed over my bottom lip, careful of the split. "Now we make it official. Charming will approve the cut. You'll get my mark. The club becomes your family, for better or worse."

"And us?"

His eyes darkened. "We were always heading here, Rio. From the first day you walked into the clubhouse."

I laughed, wincing as the movement pulled at my bruised ribs. "Just as cocky as ever."

"I haven't made a secret you held my attention from the very first moment I saw you." His hand slid from my cheek to the back of my neck, fingers tangling in my damp hair. "You never flinched. Never looked away. Even when you saw what this life really is."

"Because I've seen worse," I admitted. "At least here, the monsters are honest about what they are."

Understanding passed between us -- the recognition of shared darkness, of choices made in shadows. Rebel pulled me closer, his forehead resting against mine, our breath mingling in the space between us.

"Being my old lady means you're mine," he said, his voice low and rough with promise. "But it also means I'm yours. Equal exchange. I protect what's mine, Rio. With everything I have."

In another life, such possessive words might have sent me running. But tonight, covered in battle wounds and surrounded by the trappings of this dangerous man's world, they felt like sanctuary.

"I can live with that," I whispered.

His phone buzzed, interrupting the moment. Rebel checked it without fully pulling away from me. "Charming says the cut should be ready tomorrow. Says it's about damn time."

I smiled, some of the tension easing from my shoulders. "He approves of me, then?"

"After tonight? Hell yes." Rebel's hand traced down my arm, finding my scraped knuckles and raising them to his lips. "Club respects strength. You've got that in spades."

The gesture, unexpectedly tender from a man like him, made my breath catch. "This changes things," I said, needing to acknowledge the shift.

"Only what needed changing." He drew me closer, until I was practically in his lap, his arms encircling me with careful pressure that avoided my worst bruises. "Everything important stays the same. You're still you. Still stubborn as hell. Still won't take my shit."

"Damn straight."

His smile turned predatory. "Except now you'll be doing it with my name on your back."

The possessiveness in his voice sent a shiver through me that had nothing to do with fear. This was Rebel -- cocky, dangerous, loyal to his core. The man who'd watched me take down two Army soldiers and looked at me with pride instead of concern. The man who cleaned my wounds with hands that had caused violence.

"I can live with that too," I said, leaning into his embrace.

Tomorrow would bring the official recognition from the club, the adjustments to a life I was still learning to navigate. But tonight, in this room with the man who'd seen both my strength and vulnerability and wanted all of it, I felt something I hadn't expected -- peace.

Not the peace of safety -- nothing about the Devil's Boneyard would ever be truly safe. But the peace of belonging. Of choosing my path instead of just surviving whatever life threw at me. Of finding my place in a world that made sense to the woman I'd become.

Rebel traced the line of my jaw with his fingertips, tilting my face up to his. "No going back now," he murmured, the words both warning and promise.

I met his gaze steadily, unflinching despite the bruises marking my skin. "I'm not looking back. Only ahead."

His smile was all the future I needed.

He claimed my lips with an unexpected gentleness, mindful of my split lip. The kiss was a seal on the promise we'd just made. When he pulled back, his eyes had darkened, intense and focused solely on me.

"I want you," he said, voice rough with desire. "But you're hurt."

I traced my fingers along his jaw, feeling the scratch of his beard against my skin. "I'm not made of glass."

"No." His thumb brushed over the bruise darkening my temple. "You're made of something much stronger."

I leaned into his touch, my body responding to his proximity despite the aches pulsing through it. "We don't have to rush," I said, surprising myself with the admission. "I'm not going anywhere now."

That predatory smile returned, sending heat pooling low in my belly. "Taking it slow, huh?"

"Just for tonight," I clarified, not wanting him to think I was having second thoughts.

He nodded, accepting the boundary without question. Another surprise from a man who seemed built for taking what he wanted. "Come here," he said, shifting to lie back against the pillows and drawing me with him.

I settled against his side, my head resting on his shoulder, his arm curled protectively around me. The position should have felt confining. Instead, it felt secure. I traced the outline of a tattoo on his chest -- an intricate design I hadn't noticed before.

"What's this one mean?" I asked, following the lines of what looked like a compass rose surrounded by storm clouds.

"Got that after my first year as a Prospect," he

explained, his voice a low rumble beneath my ear. "Rode through a hurricane in south Florida. Thought I was gonna die. Decided if I made it, I'd mark the occasion."

"You rode through a hurricane? On purpose?"

His chest shook with silent laughter. "Not on purpose. Got caught in it. Too stubborn to find shelter until it was almost too late."

"Why does that not surprise me?" I murmured, continuing my exploration of his inked skin. Each mark told a story -- of survival, of loyalty, of choices made and consequences accepted.

"You got any more ink?" he asked, his hand making lazy circles on my shoulder.

"Small one. On my hip."

His eyebrows raised in interest. "Yeah? What is it?"

"A phoenix. Got it after my discharge." I didn't elaborate further, but I didn't need to. Rebel understood rebirth from ashes better than most.

His fingers slipped beneath the hem of my borrowed T-shirt, seeking but not demanding. "Can I see it?"

I hesitated only briefly before shifting to push the shirt up just enough to reveal my right hip. There, in vivid reds and oranges, a small phoenix spread its wings.

Rebel traced the outline with his fingertip, touch feather light against my skin. The calluses on his hands created a delicious friction that sent goose bumps racing across my flesh.

"Beautiful," he murmured. "Suits you."

I lowered the shirt, suddenly self-conscious in a way I rarely allowed myself to be. "Got it after everything fell apart. When I was lost and wandering.

Needed to remember I could rise again."

His eyes met mine, intense and knowing. "And you did."

"Yeah." I settled back against him, the day's exhaustion finally catching up to me. "I did."

Silence stretched between us, comfortable in a way I hadn't experienced with another person in years. The steady rhythm of his heartbeat beneath my ear was hypnotic, lulling me toward sleep despite my desire to stay in this moment.

"You know," he said suddenly, his voice quiet in the dimly lit room, "first time I saw you, I thought you'd be trouble. The fun kind though."

I huffed a laugh against his chest. "You weren't wrong."

His fingers combed gently through my damp hair. "Thought you'd be entertaining for a bit. Didn't expect…" He trailed off.

"Didn't expect what?" I prompted, lifting my head to see his face.

Something vulnerable flickered in his eyes before he masked it with his usual confidence. "Didn't expect to want to keep you."

I swallowed hard, forcing myself to hold his gaze.

"Good," I whispered. "Because I'm staying."

His arm tightened around me, and I felt the tension drain from his body. Neither of us spoke after that. We didn't need to. In this moment, wrapped in each other's arms, our bruised bodies testament to the violence we'd survived together, words seemed unnecessary.

I drifted toward sleep, my mind replaying the events that had led me here. The attack that had nearly broken me. Meeting Rebel. The gradual pull into his world. The fight tonight that had shown me who I truly was -- and who I wanted to be.

Tomorrow would bring new challenges. The official recognition as Rebel's old lady. The continued war with the Morettis, unless by some miracle they backed down. The lingering threat of Ellis and Denton, who wouldn't stay down forever. Sure, I'd told them to turn themselves in, but would they? Tonight, though, I allowed myself to simply exist in this space of belonging.

As sleep claimed me, one final thought surfaced: I'd spent so long fighting against needing anyone that I'd forgotten what it felt like to be wanted. Not just for my body or what I could offer, but for my strength. My resilience. The very qualities that had kept me alone for so long were what had drawn Rebel to me. Being a strong woman in the Army wasn't necessarily a good thing. Not when the men in your unit didn't want to accept you. They tended to have an old school mentality and thought I had no place among them.

* * *

The sound of metal crashing against metal jerked me from sleep. I bolted upright, instantly alert, my hand already reaching for a weapon that wasn't there. Beside me, Rebel moved with similar precision, his body tensing for combat.

"What the fuck?" he growled, voice rough with sleep.

Footsteps thundered down the hallway. The bedroom door burst open without warning. Chaos stood in the doorway, chest heaving, eyes wild. Blood spattered his cut like abstract art.

"Morettis are hitting back," he panted. "They've got Java."

Rebel was already moving, grabbing jeans from

the floor. "When?"

"Found out ten minutes ago. Shade immediately started accessing the cameras around town. Last we heard, Java was making a coffee run to that twenty-four place in the next town. We think he was ambushed on the way there, or on his way back."

I slid from the bed, ignoring the protest of my bruised body. "Is he alive?"

Chaos's eyes flicked to me briefly. "Yeah. For now. They sent proof of life -- cut off part of his pinky finger."

My stomach lurched, but I kept my face neutral. This was the reality of the life I'd chosen. No room for squeamishness.

"Everyone's at the clubhouse waiting," Chaos said. "Charming wanted me to get you two."

"We'll be there. Just need a minute to get dressed." Rebel ran a hand over his face. I could tell the news had hit him hard.

Looked like my peaceful moment was over. Time to jump back into the war I'd brought down on the club.

Chapter Twelve
Rebel

The Devil's Boneyard clubhouse buzzed with the kind of quiet that made my skin crawl. Not silence -- never silence with this many bikers in one room -- but the low hum of voices pitched just above a whisper, of boot heels scuffing the floor as members paced, of knuckles rapping on tabletops and phones being checked for the hundredth time. Three days of nothing from Java. Three days where every ring of a phone had us all jerking our heads up, hoping for news, dreading news.

I leaned against the far wall, watching the makeshift command center they'd set up in the main room. Maps spread across the pool table. Laptops open, their screens casting blue glows on tense faces. A whiteboard stood in the center, covered in names, locations, and times -- data that meant something to someone, but looked like chaos to me. The chaos of desperate men trying to find their brother.

Ripper stood nearest to me, his fingers twitching against his thigh in a nervous rhythm. His eyes hadn't left the door in twenty minutes.

"Anything?" I asked.

He shook his head. "Fuck all."

Across the room, Stripes slammed his palm against the wall. "I'm telling you, we should've hit the Morettis three days ago. The second Java went missing."

"And I'm telling you," Viper countered, voice low but sharp, "that would've been suicide without intel. We don't know if the Morettis have him or if they've already killed him. But if he's alive, going in guns blazing could make them decide to cut any loose ends."

I watched their faces -- the tight lines around Viper's eyes, the vein pulsing in Stripes' temple. Java meant something to each of us. He'd impressed the hell out of everyone here when he'd rolled in on a customized bike. He'd been in the Army, like my Rio, except he'd lost both legs to an IED. I was also the reason he was here.

My stomach tightened. How the fuck could he have survived all that to be taken down by the Morettis now?

I also knew Viper made a good point. Didn't mean anyone would listen to him.

Doc approached me, offering a bottle of beer I hadn't asked for. I took it anyway.

"This waiting is killing us," he said, eyes on the knot of officers gathered around one of the laptops. "You good?"

I nodded, though "good" wasn't the word I'd use. Tense. Wired. Ready to explode. Those fit better.

"You know Java well," Doc said.

"Well enough," I said. Truth was, I didn't think anyone really knew him. He only let people get so close. "Watched him grow up. There were times we'd go shooting together, once he was older. Said my aim was shit."

Doc's laugh was brief, hollow. "Sounds like him."

The minutes stretched. I counted the weapons I could see. Counted the times Azrael checked his phone only to shake his head at whoever was watching him for reaction.

The front door swung open. We all tensed, but it was only Gator, returning from his recon. His face told us everything we needed to know before he even opened his mouth.

"Nothing," he said. "Warehouse is clean. If they had him there, they've moved him."

"Or he's dead," someone muttered from the back.

Scratch shot them a look that could've frozen hell. "We don't know that."

"We don't know shit," Gator said. "That's the problem."

Scratch started to respond when the rear door opened, and the energy in the room shifted instantly. Backs straightened. Conversations died. All eyes fixed on the man who entered with measured steps that conveyed more authority than any shouted command could.

Charming.

He wore the weight of three sleepless nights in the lines of his face, but his eyes were sharp, focused. His leather cut was pristine, the President's patch a silent reminder of who called the shots. He surveyed the room, nodded once, and moved toward the center of our makeshift command post.

No one spoke. No one needed to. We all knew what three days of silence meant. We all knew the odds were stacking higher against Java with every passing hour. But none of us would say it, not until Charming did.

He stood before the whiteboard, studying it like it might reveal some secret if he stared long enough. Then, without turning: "Any word from our friends on the north side?"

Scratch shook his head. "Nothing. Their places are locked down tight."

"The Russians?"

"Radio silence," Viper replied. "But that could be

good or bad. They're not exactly chatty on the best days."

Charming nodded once, a single dip of his chin that somehow made the room even tenser. He turned, faced us all, his gaze sweeping across everyone before landing on mine for just a second longer than the others. I felt the weight of that look -- assessing, calculating.

Then he said it: "I'm calling Anatoly."

The room went still. Completely still. Like someone had hit pause on everything except our breathing.

Anatoly. The Bratva connection. Charming's friend from back before he'd broken ties with the Bratva. The nuclear option.

Scratch was the first to move, shifting his weight from one foot to another. "You sure that's the play? Once the Bratva are in --"

"I'm sure Java doesn't have time for us to debate," Charming cut him off. His voice wasn't raised, but it carried an edge that made men back down. "Three days. If he's alive, it's because the Morettis are trying to get information, or possibly hoping to make a trade."

No one argued with that. We all knew what it meant if the Morettis were interrogating Java. It meant pain. It meant names. It meant all of us were at risk. Except I didn't think he'd crack.

"Get me the secure line," Charming said.

Gator moved quickly, retrieving a satellite phone from a locked cabinet behind the bar. He handed it to Charming with a nod of understanding.

Charming took the phone and stepped toward the back office. "Scratch, Viper -- with me. Everyone else, start gearing up. If Anatoly's in, we move fast."

I pushed off from the wall, my beer forgotten. Around me, the clubhouse came alive. The waiting was over. Whatever came next, it would at least be action.

Charming paused at the door to the office, his hand on the knob. He looked back, and this time his eyes found mine directly.

"Rebel," he said. "You're with us for this call."

I felt every eye in the room on me as I crossed the floor. Some curious, some envious, some concerned. I kept my face neutral, though my pulse quickened. Being called into Charming's inner circle for something this big wasn't normal for someone who wasn't an officer and hadn't been around as long as some of the others. Especially since I didn't have a special skillset that would make me an asset right now.

The office door closed behind us, sealing in a different kind of tension. Charming sat behind his desk, Scratch and Viper taking positions on either side. I remained standing, back to the wall, watching as Charming punched in a number from memory.

He put the phone on speaker and placed it in the center of the desk. The dial tone seemed to stretch forever before a click, followed by silence.

"Identify," a heavily accented voice demanded.

"Charming, for Anatoly. Priority one."

More silence. Then a different voice, deeper, smoother but with the same undercurrent of steel and ice.

"Halden. It has been some time."

Charming's jaw tightened at the use of his given name. "Anatoly. I need assistance."

"Business or family?"

"Both." Charming's eyes flicked to each of us before returning to the phone. "One of mine is missing. Three days. We have reason to believe the Morettis have him."

A long pause. I could almost hear the calculation happening on the other end.

"The Morettis," Anatoly finally said, "have been making moves that concern my associates. Expanding where they should not. Taking risks that invite attention."

"Then our interests align," Charming said. "We need to find Java and shut down whatever the Morettis are planning."

"You are asking for Bratva involvement in your American motorcycle club business. This is not a small request, Halden."

"I'm aware of the cost," Charming replied, and something in his tone made me glance at him sharply. "But Java is one of ours, and he lost enough defending this damn country."

The silence stretched longer this time.

"You have a location?" Anatoly finally asked.

"We have three potentials. Need manpower and hardware to hit them simultaneously."

Another pause. "I'll send Dmitri. He'll arrive tomorrow. You will provide details then."

"That's not soon enough," Charming pressed. "Java might not have until tomorrow."

"Then pray he is a strong man, *da*? Dmitri comes tomorrow. With a team. Equipment. This is the best I can do." The line went quiet for a moment. "Halden. If your man is already dead, what happens next will be war. Are you prepared for this?"

Charming's eyes met mine, then moved to Scratch and Viper. In them, I saw the weight of what he was about to commit us to.

"We're prepared," he said.

"Then we'll speak tomorrow." The line went

dead.

Charming sat back, running a hand over his face -- the first sign of fatigue he'd shown all night.

"You think Anatoly will come through?" Viper asked.

"Dmitri will," Charming replied. "And that's better. Anatoly sends Dmitri when he wants a message sent, not just a job done." He looked at each of us. "Get some rest. Tomorrow, we go to war."

As we filed out of the office, I felt the shift in the energy of the clubhouse. The quiet desperation had transformed into something harder, more focused. Men were checking weapons, reviewing maps, making calls. Preparing.

I watched them, these men I'd sworn brotherhood with, and knew that whatever happened next would change us all. Some wouldn't make it back. That was the reality of war. But we'd go anyway, because Java was one of us, and in the Devil's Boneyard, we never left our own behind.

Not while there was still a chance they were breathing. And sometimes, not even then.

* * *

I knew trouble had arrived when the ground beneath my feet trembled with the heavy approach of the military-issue truck. The massive vehicle growled outside our compound like a beast announcing its territory. Twenty-four hours. That's all it had taken for Dmitri to respond to Charming's call. I set my jaw, feeling the familiar weight of my gun against my hip as I moved toward the main hall, each step measured, each breath controlled.

The rumble cut through the usual background noise of the clubhouse. Conversations halted. Bottles stopped clinking. Even the air seemed to thicken, waiting. I'd heard that sound before -- the distinctive thunder of a Russian military transport.

"They're here," someone muttered unnecessarily.

I positioned myself near the wall, giving me clear sight lines to both the entrance and Charming. Our President stood with his feet planted wide, hands loose at his sides -- a casual stance that fooled no one. Every Devil's Boneyard member in the room knew what that posture really meant: ready for anything.

The engine died outside, followed by doors slamming. My pulse quickened, not from fear but anticipation. When Charming had announced we were calling in the Bratva, opinions had split. Some said we were desperate. Others said we were smart. Me? I thought we were finally getting serious about ending the Moretti problem once and for all.

The main door swung open hard enough to bang against the wall. A man I assumed was Dmitri stepped through the threshold and fuck me if he didn't command the room instantly. Six-foot-four of pure intimidation in a black leather jacket that probably cost more than my bike. His face was all sharp angles -- high cheekbones, straight nose, jaw that could cut glass. His gaze swept the room in one calculating glance, missing nothing.

"Charming," he said, voice deep and accented. Just that one word carried weight.

Behind him filed in six men, each one built like they ate small children for breakfast. They wore identical black coats, and I knew without needing to check that they all carried at least three weapons each. The Bratva didn't fuck around, and these weren't regular soldiers -- these were Dmitri's personal enforcers.

I watched Dmitri's movements closely. The way

he held himself screamed military training, but there was something else there too -- a predatory grace that couldn't be taught. He moved with absolute confidence, each step purposeful. His eyes -- cold blue, almost gray -- scanned faces, exits, positions. I'd met men who thought they were dangerous before. Dmitri didn't think it; he knew it. And so did everyone else.

"You made good time," Charming said, stepping forward to meet him.

"When you said Moretti has expanded operations into your territory, I decided time was critical," Dmitri replied, his accent thickening certain words. "Show me what you have."

Around me, our club members shifted positions. Hands moved toward weapons, not to draw but to reassure themselves the hardware was there if needed. The Russians noticed. Of course they did. Their eyes tracked every movement, assessing threats, calculating response times.

I caught Havoc's gaze across the room. He gave me the slightest nod -- our silent language for "stay alert." We'd fought alongside the Bratva before, but alliances in our world were as stable as nitroglycerin. Useful but volatile.

Charming gestured toward the meeting room. "Maps and intel are ready. My guys have been tracking their movements for three weeks now. Just didn't realize the shitstorm that was going to happen during that time."

"Your men are prepared?" Dmitri asked, his gaze sweeping over us again. When that cold gaze landed on me, I didn't flinch. I stared right back.

"My men are always prepared," Charming answered, steel in his voice. There was history between these two -- respect, but also boundaries that needed maintaining.

Dmitri nodded once, apparently satisfied. He followed Charming toward the back room, but paused to speak quietly to one of his men who immediately turned and stationed himself by the door, scanning us with flat, emotionless eyes.

The rest of us remained where we were, watching as Dmitri's men spread out through our space with practiced efficiency. No one said it, but we all felt it -- our clubhouse had just become shared territory, at least temporarily.

"Fucking Russians," Gator muttered beside me, low enough that only I could hear.

"Better the devil you know," I replied, keeping my voice equally quiet.

"That what we're calling it now?" Gator's hand twitched near his knife. "Because I'm counting at least six devils I don't know standing in our house."

"Relax. We need them."

"Need's a strong word, Rebel."

"You got a better idea how to hit the Morettis across all their locations simultaneously?" I asked.

Gator didn't answer. He didn't need to. We both knew the math. From what Shade had found, the Morettis had expanded aggressively in the last six months, pushing into territory that belonged to both us and the Bratva. Rio showing up on our doorstep had pushed up our timeline. I'd planned to take my time figuring this shit out when Charming had asked for my help. Separately, neither of us had the numbers to hit back effectively. Together? We could send a message written in blood.

Twenty minutes later, the door to the meeting room swung open. Charming emerged first, his expression grim but determined. Dmitri followed, immediately flanked by two of his men as if they'd been waiting for precisely this moment.

"We move out tonight," Dmitri announced, his voice cutting through the room. No preamble, no explanation. Just the directive, delivered with absolute authority.

Charming nodded. "Four targets, simultaneous hits. We split into teams -- mixed groups, our guys and theirs on each team."

"Four?" Ripper asked. "Thought there were three."

Charming sighed. "Anatoly put his tech people on the issue. Found another location in our area."

I noticed the slight twitch in Ripper's jaw at that. None of us liked the idea of splitting up our strength, but the strategy made sense. Keep the Russians divided so they couldn't turn on us, while ensuring each strike team had enough firepower.

"My men have the heavy weapons," Dmitri added. "Your local knowledge guides us to the targets."

Charming's eyes found mine. "Rebel, you're with Team Two -- the warehouse district. Havoc leads Team One at the docks. Jackal, you're on Team Three, hitting their distribution center. I'll take Team Four to their local headquarters."

I nodded, already mentally cataloging what I'd need. My AR-15, my Glock, two knives, extra ammunition, night vision if we had it to spare. The warehouse district was a maze of abandoned buildings and blind corners -- perfect for ambushes.

"Each team has four hours to prepare," Dmitri said. "My men will brief you on communication protocols. No phones once we leave. No messages that could be intercepted."

The reality of what we were about to do settled over the room. This wasn't a skirmish or a warning. This was a coordinated attack to eliminate the Moretti presence completely.

One of Dmitri's men approached me, tall and solid with a face that had taken more than a few hits in its time. His eyes were dark, assessing.

"You ride point with me," he said, his accent thicker than Dmitri's. "I am Alexei. You know the streets, yes?"

"Every pothole and blind alley," I confirmed.

He nodded once, apparently satisfied. "Good. You will need this." He handed me a small device that looked like a watch. "Communication. Secure channel. Press here for team, here for all teams."

I strapped it to my wrist, feeling the weight of it. More than just a device -- it was commitment. Once we started, there would be no backing out.

Around me, the clubhouse transformed into a staging area. Weapons appeared from hidden compartments. Maps were spread across tables. The Russians produced equipment I'd only seen in military documentaries -- thermal imaging, signal jammers, armor-piercing rounds.

Charming and Dmitri stood at the center of it all, two leaders with different styles but aligned purposes. Charming caught my gaze again and beckoned me over.

"You good with this?" he asked quietly when I reached him.

"All in," I replied. "The Morettis crossed lines they can't uncross."

"Once we start, we finish it completely," Charming said. "No survivors, no witnesses, no trace leading back to us."

I nodded. "Understood."

Dmitri's cold gaze assessed me. "Your President says you know the warehouse district better than anyone."

"Used to live there," I said. "Before I joined the club."

Something that might have been approval flickered in his expression. "Then you are valuable tonight. Do not waste yourself on unnecessary risks."

Coming from him, it was practically a warm embrace. I nodded again, more to Charming than to Dmitri. "I'll get it done."

As I turned to prep my gear, I felt the energy in the room shift. The usual club chaos had transformed into something focused and lethal. We were hunters now, gathering our weapons, checking our armor. Four hours to prepare. Then we'd paint the town red with Moretti blood.

I caught my reflection in a window -- eyes hard, mouth set in a grim line. I barely recognized myself. But then, nights like this weren't about who we were in the daylight. They were about who we needed to become in the darkness.

Chapter Thirteen
Rebel

The industrial park loomed ahead like a graveyard of concrete and steel. Moonlight caught on broken windows, casting jagged shadows across cracked pavement. I led our flank on my bike, the engine's rumble beneath me vibrating up through my bones. Ahead, Dmitri's transport rolled silent and dark, no headlights to announce our approach. I checked my watch -- the synchronized timepiece Alexei had given me. Two minutes to zero hour. My grip tightened on the handlebars. Tonight, the Morettis would learn what happens when you piss off both the Devil's Boneyard and the Bratva.

Alexei rode beside me, his massive frame somehow balanced perfectly on a club bike we'd provided. Behind us, four more riders -- two Russians, two of ours -- formed a tight V formation. The warehouse district sprawled around us, abandoned factories and storage facilities creating a maze of blind spots and choke points. Perfect for an ambush. From either side.

I tapped the comm unit at my wrist. "Team Two in position," I reported, voice low despite the privacy of our channel.

"Team One ready," came Havoc's clipped response.

"Team Three in position," Jackal confirmed.

A pause, then: "Team Four moving in sixty seconds." Charming's voice, steady as always. "Commence on my mark."

I signaled to Alexei, who nodded once. The Russians' military precision was unnerving but reassuring in equal measure. These men didn't fuck around with their operations, and tonight, that discipline would work in our favor.

The warehouse that served as the Morettis' processing center stood three stories tall, a hulking shadow against the night sky. Two guards patrolled the perimeter -- sloppy, predictable patterns. One smoked, the cherry of his cigarette a beacon in the darkness. Amateur hour.

"Northeast corner has a loading dock," I murmured to Alexei. "Secondary entrance through the office wing on the west side."

He assessed the building with cold efficiency. "How many inside?"

"Intel says fifteen to twenty. Mostly muscle, two lieutenants."

Alexei nodded, then spoke in Russian to his men. I didn't need to understand the words to get their meaning. They were dividing responsibilities, assigning kill zones.

I spotted movement at the main entrance -- a third guard emerging to talk with one of the patrolling men. A brief exchange, then laughter. They had no idea what was coming.

My comm unit buzzed. "All teams." Charming's voice was steel. "Execute."

Everything happened at once. The transport truck surged forward, smashing through the chain-link fence surrounding the facility. The guards spun, reaching for weapons, but they were already too late. Silenced shots dropped them before they could raise the alarm.

I revved my engine, leading our flank around to the loading dock as planned. Alexei and two others peeled off toward the office entrance. Two stayed with me. We abandoned the bikes fifty yards out, continuing on foot. The weight of my AR-15 felt good in my hands -- familiar, an extension of myself.

"Dock doors are down," I whispered, scanning the area. "Control panel there." I pointed to a box mounted beside the large metal door.

One of the Russians -- Ivan, I thought -- moved forward, attaching a small device to the panel. He pressed a sequence of buttons, and the box sparked. The dock door began to rise, grinding upward with a mechanical groan that seemed deafening in the night air.

"Move," I ordered, crouching low as I approached the widening gap. I had maybe three seconds before someone inside noticed the door's movement.

Two… the gap reached knee height.

Three… waist height now.

I dropped to my stomach and rolled under, coming up with my AR-15 raised and scanning. The loading area was dimly lit, pallets of packaged product stacked in precise rows. Two men stood near a forklift, heads turning toward the rising door, expressions shifting from confusion to alarm.

I squeezed the trigger twice. Two bodies dropped. Clean.

"Clear," I called softly as my teammates rolled in behind me.

From somewhere deeper in the warehouse came the muffled *pop* of silenced gunfire. Alexei's team making entry. Good.

We moved forward in a practiced formation, covering each other's blind spots. The processing area opened up ahead -- a vast space with assembly tables where workers would normally cut and package product. Tonight, it was staffed by a skeleton crew of armed men, their attention now focused on the commotion at the far end where Alexei had entered.

"Six targets," the Russian beside me counted. "High ground at the observation platform."

I nodded, spotting a seventh man on the metal walkway overlooking the floor. "I'll take the high man. You sweep left, your partner right."

No debate, no questions. Just three nods and we moved.

I slipped between pallets, using the cover to approach the stairs leading to the observation platform. A burst of gunfire erupted from the far side of the warehouse -- no longer silenced. The element of surprise was officially gone.

"Contact," crackled through my comm. "Heavy resistance at the north entrance."

The guard on the walkway shouted something in Italian, gesturing wildly to the men below. I aimed, exhaled half a breath, and squeezed. His head snapped back, body crumpling against the railing before sliding down in a heap.

"Moving up," I reported, then sprinted for the stairs.

The warehouse exploded into chaos. Gunfire echoed off concrete walls. Men shouted in three different languages. From my elevated position, I could see Alexei's team pushing through from the west, methodically dropping Moretti soldiers who scrambled for cover.

My teammates had split as planned, flanking the main floor from opposite sides. The Russians fought with ruthless efficiency -- two shots per target, no wasted ammunition. Our club members brought a more aggressive approach, but the results were the same. Bodies hitting concrete.

I tracked movement below -- a Moretti lieutenant I recognized from surveillance photos. Marco, Salvatore Moretti's nephew. He was shouting into a phone, presumably calling for backup.

Not today.

I lined up the shot, but a burst of gunfire forced me to duck behind a metal filing cabinet. Bullets pinged off the walkway around me. I rolled to a new position, came up firing, and caught a glimpse of my attacker dropping behind some equipment.

"Rebel, status?" Alexei's voice in my ear.

"Pinned on the walkway. Target is Marco Moretti, northeast corner."

A pause, then: "Moving to support."

I risked a glance over the railing and spotted Marco again, now trying to access what looked like a safe built into the wall. Whatever was in there, we couldn't let him retrieve it.

Ignoring the continued fire from my hidden attacker, I steadied my AR-15 and focused. Three breaths. In. Out. In.

I squeezed the trigger. Marco jerked, stumbled. But he wasn't down. My shot had caught his shoulder instead of center mass. Fuck.

He looked up, spotted me, and dove behind a concrete support pillar. The man was wounded but still dangerous.

Movement caught my attention -- Alexei appeared at the far end of the floor, moving with startling speed for someone his size. He fired twice as he advanced, dropping a Moretti soldier who popped up from behind a processing table.

My hidden attacker chose that moment to make another attempt. He rose from cover, assault rifle raised toward me. I twisted, brought my weapon to bear, but he had the advantage.

A single shot cracked through the warehouse. The man's chest exploded in a spray of red, his finger twitching on the trigger and sending a harmless burst into the ceiling as he fell.

I glanced toward the source of the shot. One of our guys -- Chaos -- nodded once from his position by the loading dock before turning to engage another target.

"Thanks," I muttered, though he couldn't hear me.

Below, Alexei had reached Marco's position. The wounded Moretti lieutenant fired wildly with a handgun, forcing Alexei into cover. I used the distraction to descend the stairs, moving quickly but carefully, keeping my rifle trained on Marco's last position.

"He's trying to access the safe," I called to Alexei as I reached the bottom of the stairs.

Alexei nodded once. "Important?"

"Must be. Documentation, maybe cash, perhaps client lists."

"We take it," he decided.

Marco chose that moment to make a desperate move. He lunged from behind the pillar, firing rapidly as he tried to reach a door marked "EXIT." Two shots went wide. The third caught one of the Russians in the leg. He went down with a grunt but continued firing from his kneeling position.

I stepped out, planted my feet, and put multiple shots center mass into Marco's chest. He staggered, looked at me with genuine surprise, then collapsed face-first onto the concrete floor.

"Clear this section," Alexei ordered, moving toward the safe.

The warehouse had gone quiet except for the methodical sound of our team checking bodies and securing rooms. I approached the safe, examining it while Alexei covered me.

"Electronic lock," I noted. "Beyond my skill set."

Alexei pulled a small device from his tactical vest and attached it to the keypad. "Step back."

I didn't need to be told twice. I moved behind a pillar as the device hummed to life. A soft beep, then a click as the safe door swung open.

Inside were stacks of cash, several thumb drives, and a leather-bound ledger.

"Jackpot," I murmured, collecting the items and stuffing them into my backpack.

"Team Two secure," I reported into my comm. "Primary target eliminated, secondary objective acquired."

The responses came in rapid succession:

"Team One secure."

"Team Three secure."

"Team Four engaged. Five minutes to completion."

I checked my watch. Twelve minutes since we'd breached the warehouse. Efficient.

Alexei surveyed the carnage with clinical detachment. "Cleanup?"

I nodded toward the center of the warehouse floor where gallons of accelerant were being positioned by our teammates. "Fire solves many problems."

He nodded, apparently satisfied with the solution.

We worked quickly, gathering our wounded -- just the one Russian with a leg wound, thankfully -- and confirming each Moretti soldier was dead. No survivors, as ordered. The intel we'd recovered went into a secure bag that Alexei handed to one of his men.

"Your club President will want copies," he said. It wasn't a question.

"Only seems fair to receive shared intelligence," I reminded him.

A thin smile crossed his face. "Of course. Dmitri will honor the request."

I didn't completely believe him, but now wasn't the time to press the issue. We had minutes before the fire would draw attention, and we needed to be gone.

"Move out," I ordered our team, helping support the wounded Russian as we headed toward the loading dock.

Behind us, flames began to lick at the processing tables, consuming evidence and bodies alike. By the time emergency services arrived, there would be nothing left but ash.

Outside, the night air felt clean compared to the gunpowder-thick atmosphere of the warehouse. I inhaled deeply, feeling the familiar post-battle surge of adrenaline beginning to ebb.

"Good work," Alexei said as we reached our bikes.

Coming from him, it felt like high praise. I nodded once, then tapped my comm. "Team Two heading out. Rendezvous at point Alpha in twenty."

As we rode away, I glanced back once at the warehouse. Orange light glowed from inside, the fire growing hungry. Smoke billowed from broken windows, carrying with it the message we'd come to deliver:

This was what happened when you crossed the Devil's Boneyard and the Bratva.

And it was just the beginning.

Point Alpha was the abandoned barn ten miles

outside of town. It had been decided we'd rendezvous there on the off chance we were followed. No sense having a tail back to the compound.

We arrived to find Havoc's team already there, their faces grim but satisfied in the harsh glow of tactical flashlights. Blood spattered across their cuts told its own story.

"How'd it go?" I asked, dismounting my bike with muscles that had started to stiffen. The post-adrenaline crash was coming, but I pushed it back.

"Clean," Havoc replied, lighting a cigarette. The flame briefly illuminated the fresh cut above his eye. "Fifteen Moretti soldiers down, plus one of their captains. Found their shipping manifests. They've been moving product through three states."

I nodded. "We got their ledger and some drives. And Marco."

Havoc's eyebrows shot up. "Salvatore's nephew? Fuck, that's a statement."

"That was the point." I scanned the gathering. The Russians clustered near their transport, speaking in low tones. Our guys mingled nearby, weapons still visible, bodies still humming with battle energy.

I spotted Alexei conferring with another Bratva soldier, their expressions intense. Their conversation ended abruptly when Alexei caught me watching. He said something to his companion, then approached me with measured steps.

"Your club fights well," he said, his accent thicker now that the adrenaline was wearing off. "Disciplined. Not what I expected."

I wasn't sure if I should be insulted or flattered. "We're not just weekend warriors playing dress-up."

His lips twitched -- almost a smile. "No. You are soldiers. Different uniform, same heart."

Before I could respond, engines rumbled in the distance. We all tensed, hands moving to weapons until we recognized the distinctive sound of Harley-Davidsons approaching. Team Three rolled in moments later, their formation tight despite the darkness.

Jackal dismounted first, blood streaking one side of his face. His gaze found mine across the barn. "Warehouse?"

"Burning," I confirmed. "Yours?"

"Same. Six Morettis down, plus we found three civilians." Something dark crossed his face. "Workers. Girls. Young."

My stomach tightened. Human trafficking. We'd suspected the Morettis were branching out. If there was one thing we didn't tolerate in our town, it was the sale of women and children.

"The girls?" I asked, already dreading the answer.

"Alive. We got them out before we torched the place. Rooster and Irish took them to a safe house." Jackal's fingers drummed against his thigh -- a nervous habit he only showed when truly disturbed. "They'll need medical attention. Psychological help. One of them can't be more than sixteen."

"Jesus," Havoc muttered, grinding out his cigarette beneath his boot.

I'd seen a lot of ugly shit in my years with the club, but trafficking always hit different. Made the violence we'd just unleashed feel not just necessary but righteous.

Alexei's face hardened as he listened. He said something in Russian to his men, the words sharp and cold. Their expressions shifted, a collective darkening that made my skin prickle. The Bratva might be ruthless criminals by most standards, but even they had lines. Children were one of them. Well, at least that was true for Anatoly's men. I couldn't speak for all of the Bratva.

"This changes priorities," Alexei said. "Dmitri will want to know."

I nodded. "Charming too."

As if summoned by his name, my comm unit crackled to life. "Team Four en route."

Looked like the plan had been a success.

Chapter Fourteen

Rebel

I kicked the door shut behind me and stood in the dark for a moment, listening to my own breathing. The metallic scent of blood -- some of it mine, most of it not -- filled my nostrils as I flipped on the light. The raid had gone exactly as planned, except for one important thing -- Java was still missing.

The lock clicked into place with a satisfying *thunk*. I knew it didn't mean shit in a dangerous situation. If someone wanted into the damn house, they'd find a way in. A deadbolt wouldn't stop them.

My boots left dirty tracks on the wooden floor. I didn't care. Floors could be cleaned.

I shrugged out of my cut. Thankfully, I'd kept my distance and hadn't ended up bloody. I tossed the cut over the back of a chair.

"Fuck," I muttered, running my hands through my hair. If they didn't have Java at any of the locations we'd hit, where the fuck was he? What if they'd already killed him? I pushed that thought away. No use thinking about that right now.

I peeled off my shirt and toed off my boots. Right now, I needed a shower. The hot water might help clear my head.

My jeans were next. I left them in a heap on the floor with my boots and socks. Standing there in just my boxers, I took a deep breath, held it, then let it out again.

I padded barefoot to the bathroom, flipping on the light. I hadn't spotted Rio, which meant she was likely with Jordan or one of the other old ladies. She hadn't had a chance to get to know everyone well yet, but I knew she'd settle in.

I turned the shower knob all the way to hot and waited. The pipes shuddered and groaned in protest before spitting out a stream of lukewarm water. I stepped under it without waiting for it to heat up. The shock of it against my skin made me hiss through clenched teeth.

Gradually, the water warmed. Steam began to fill the small space, fogging the mirror over the sink. I closed my eyes and let it pound against my shoulders, my back, the top of my head. Water swirled at my feet. Usually after a fight, it would have been pink from blood. This time, I'd come home unscathed.

I reached for the bar of soap and scrubbed until my skin was raw. The others would be getting cleaned up too. As much as I'd wanted to immediately come up with a new plan, I knew we all needed to rest. Tomorrow, we'd hopefully figure out a way to get Java back.

I'd known him since he was just a kid, roughly fifteen years younger than me. Been there the day he graduated high school. Congratulated him when he joined the Army.

And now he was gone.

I slammed my palm against the shower wall. The sharp sting snapped me back to the present. Water continued to beat down on me, hot now, turning my skin red. I reached for the shampoo and worked it into my hair roughly, scrubbing at my scalp like I could wash away the memories too.

I rinsed my hair and shut off the water. For a moment, I just stood there, dripping, listening to the pipes settle. The house was quiet. Too quiet. Like a tomb.

Java could still be alive. I had to hold onto the hope he'd come home. We *had* to find him.

I grabbed a towel from the hook and dried off. The mirror had cleared enough to show my reflection. I barely recognized the man staring back at me. Hollow eyes. Tight jaw. The Devil's Boneyard colors tattooed over my heart.

It had seemed so simple once. The club was family. The only real family I'd ever known after my own had fallen apart. But family didn't leave each other behind. Family didn't retreat when one of their own was still in enemy territory. And yet, there hadn't been anything else we could do. Java hadn't been there.

I wiped the rest of the steam from the mirror with my palm and leaned closer, studying my face. I usually looked at least a decade younger than my fifty years. Not tonight. No, now I looked older. Harder.

If Java was still alive, tomorrow might be his last day. I couldn't imagine they'd keep him alive much longer. Assuming he wasn't already in a shallow grave somewhere. We hadn't had any word on him since they'd sent proof they had him.

I wrapped the towel around my waist and padded back to the living room. My phone lay on the table next to my gun. No messages. No calls. The club would be regrouping, licking their wounds, planning their next move. But would that move include rescuing Java? Or would they write him off as a casualty of war? Going against the Morettis had been a strategic move for multiple reasons. But a rescue mission was another matter. Although, things were different with Charming as the president. When Cinder had been in charge, there had been a time we'd nearly lost Ashes because he refused to go get him or negotiate with the men who'd taken him.

I pulled on clean boxers and a pair of sweatpants,

then rummaged through my drawer for a T-shirt that wasn't ripped or stained. As I tugged it over my head, I heard the front door open and the soft tread of boots. Rio.

I steeled myself for what came next. If Java was gone, Rio was the only family I had left. He'd been like a kid brother to me.

"You look like shit," she said, her Georgia drawl making the insult sound almost sweet.

Rio stood in the center of the room, arms crossed over her chest. The stance made her look tough, but I knew better. Knew the way her fingers dug into her own arms meant she was holding herself together.

"The others?" she asked.

"Either at home or the clubhouse. No casualties on our side."

She nodded once, sharp. Her eyes never left mine. "And Java?"

There it was. The question I'd been dreading. I walked past her to the kitchen, pulled out two beers from the fridge. Handed her one without asking if she wanted it. The cold glass against my palm was grounding. Real. Unlike the nightmare playing on repeat in my head.

"Rebel." Her voice had hardened. "Did you find Java?"

I popped the cap off my beer, took a long pull. "We couldn't find him," I said finally. "He's either gone or dead."

The words hung in the air between us. Just saying them nearly gutted me.

"What happened?"

"We went in, wiped the fuckers out, but Java wasn't at any of the locations. If they didn't move him elsewhere, then they've already killed him." I pressed the cold bottle to my forehead.

Rio set her untouched beer on the table. She moved toward me slowly, like approaching a wounded animal. In the harsh overhead light, I could see the freckles scattered across her nose and cheeks. Made her look younger. She stepped closer, the space between us charged with something I couldn't name.

I sank into a chair, the leather creaking under my weight. "We grew up in the same neighborhood, but I was much older," I said, surprising myself with the words. I didn't talk about the past. Ever. But Rio deserved to know. "Same block. His dad was gone. Mom worked nights. I'd help him with his homework, made sure he was safe."

Rio turned from the window, leaned against the wall. Listening.

"My dad was a mechanic. Good one, when he was sober. After my mom died, he crawled into a bottle and never really came out. Java's mom tried to help. Invited me for dinner. Made sure I knew how to cook, wash clothes. The basics. But she had three jobs and her own issues to worry about."

"Was Java already born?" Rio asked.

"He was a baby. His mom gave him little sisters over the next few years. They died. Car accident. Drunk driver. Java was fifteen." I stared at my hands. My father's hands. "That's when everything really went to shit. His mom checked out -- mentally, I mean. Started taking pills. Java nearly dropped out of school, but I convinced him to stick it out."

Rio pushed off from the wall, came to stand in front of me. Close enough to touch, but she didn't. Just stood there, her presence like an anchor.

"My dad's drinking got worse before I turned eighteen," I continued. "Started getting mean with it.

I'd stay out as late as I could. I started running with a local crew. Nothing serious at first. Selling weed to rich kids from the suburbs. Boosting car stereos. Stupid shit."

"When did you join the Devils?" she asked.

"I was in my twenties." I reached for my beer again, swallowed the last of it. "Java joined much later. He was in the Army, like you. Except he'd been in a lot longer, until an IED took his legs."

"And your dad? He still alive?"

"Wrapped his truck around a tree two days after my eighteenth birthday." I said it flatly. No emotion. Ancient history. "Closed casket. I didn't cry. Java's mom was the only one who stood with me at the funeral. I'd seen her around the neighborhood, helped carrying groceries in for her a few times. Mowed her lawn a time or two. Dad didn't exactly have a lot of friends by then."

Rio moved then, closing the distance between us. She reached out, her fingers hovering over the bruise on my jaw. Not quite touching. "You look like him," she said. "Java. Around the eyes."

"We're not related."

"Doesn't matter. You're brothers."

Something in my chest cracked open. A fault line I'd been ignoring for years. "Yeah," I managed. "We are. He's the kid brother I never had."

Her hand finally made contact, cool fingers against my hot skin. I had to fight not to lean into it like a starving man.

"We're going after him," she said. Not a question.

"Club may have to take a vote. Or Charming may decide we've risked enough already."

Her eyes hardened. "Fuck the vote."

"Rio --"

"No." She stepped back, and I felt the loss of her touch like a physical thing. "You know what they'll decide. They'll say it's too risky. That one man isn't worth endangering the whole club. They'll say we should hit the Morettis again another way, another time. You know as well as I do, there's no way that hit was all about getting Java back. Charming is focused on more than our brother. And I get it. To some extent."

She wasn't wrong. I'd sat through enough church meetings to know exactly how it would go. Devil's Boneyard protected their own -- but sometimes the cost got too high. Like when Ashes went missing.

"He'd come for you," she said. Her voice had dropped, that Georgia drawl thickening with emotion she'd never admit to. "If it was you they had, Java would go in guns blazing."

Also true. Java was loyal to a fault.

"I don't know where they'd take him," I said quietly.

Rio's eyes locked on mine. "What about the old mill? I saw it on my way into town. Even then, I thought it looked like a bad guy hideout you'd see in old cartoons. They may not have taken him out of the area. Just away from their known locations."

I nodded. It was isolated. Easily secured. I could see that being an option.

"I can't ask you to go against the club," she said. "But at the same time, I don't think you can live with yourself if you don't do everything you can to get him back."

Something passed between us. Understanding. A decision made without words.

Rio's posture changed subtly. Military precision

returning to her spine, her shoulders. Planning mode. "Two of us isn't enough. We need at least four for a solid team. Two to create a diversion, two to extract."

"Chaos might come," I said. "Possibly Azrael."

I stood, and moved to the closet, pulling out my go-bag. Always packed. Always ready. Another habit learned young: be prepared to run at a moment's notice.

Rio watched me. "We're really doing this?"

I unzipped the bag, checked its contents. Extra ammo. First aid kit. Cash. Burner phones. "Like you said, Java would do the same for me. Yeah. We're doing this."

She nodded once, decision made. Moved toward the door, then paused with her hand on the knob. Turned back to me. "I'm with you until the end. No matter what happens."

I crossed to her in three strides, stood close enough that she had to tilt her head to maintain eye contact. "You know if Charming finds out, I'm in not only for one hell of a monetary punishment, but possibly a beating."

"Some risks are worth taking." She reached up to touch my cheek, and I couldn't hold back.

Leaning down, my lips brushed against hers. It was like striking a match in a room full of gasoline. One moment, just a simple touch of lips. The next, we were burning alive.

Rio's hands were in my hair, gripping hard enough to hurt. I backed her against the wall, my body pressing into hers. She tasted like coffee and mint. Like salvation.

I broke away first. Rested my forehead against hers, breathing hard. "This is a bad idea."

"Yeah." Her voice was rough. "The worst."

But neither of us moved. Her heart hammered against mine, our pulses racing in tandem. This wasn't supposed to happen. Not right now anyway. Not with everything at stake.

"Java needs us," I said, stepping back. The space between us felt like miles. "We can't --"

"I know." She straightened her shirt, cleared her throat. "We should call Chaos. See if he's in."

I nodded, grateful for the change of subject. "I should reach out to Azrael too."

"Right."

And yet neither of us moved. As much as I wanted to rush off to save Java, I had to wonder, could I really do any better than the entire club and the Bratva? I stared at Rio, my beautiful, fierce woman. Even though she was mine, we hadn't done more than kiss. Java would give me shit if he knew.

"What if we're making a mistake?" she asked.

I nodded. "Thinking the same thing. For one, we don't know for sure that's where he is. For another, how the hell are we supposed to pull off something the club and the Brava couldn't? But we can let Charming know about our idea."

She licked her lips. "So, text him. He'll need time to look into it, right?"

"Yeah. Most likely have Shade check it out or send a recon team."

She came closer, pressing against me. "Then, we have the rest of the night to ourselves."

I swallowed hard. "Are you saying what I think you are?"

"I think I am. I know you won't hurt me, Rebel. It's time."

I pressed my forehead to hers. "Call me Dixon. But only when we're alone."

She smiled a little. "Nice to meet you, Dixon."

I picked up my phone and shot off a message to Charming about the old mill, then I took Rio by the hand and led her to the bedroom.

The bedroom was dark, just a sliver of moonlight cutting through a gap in the curtains. I fumbled for the lamp, but Rio caught my wrist.

"Leave it off," she whispered.

I understood. Sometimes darkness made it easier to be vulnerable. I'd lived enough years to know that.

Her hands found my chest in the darkness, palms flat against my T-shirt. I stood perfectly still, letting her set the pace. This wasn't just sex. This was Rio trusting me with her body after what she'd been through.

"You sure about this?" My voice came out rougher than I intended.

She answered by pulling my shirt over my head, her fingers tracing the tattoos that mapped my life across my skin. The Devil's Boneyard colors over my heart. The dates commemorating fallen brothers on my ribs. The half-sleeve that told the story of where I'd come from.

When her lips pressed against my collarbone, I couldn't hold back the groan that escaped me. I cupped her face, tilting it up toward mine. Even in the darkness, I could see the intensity in her eyes.

"Rio," I breathed.

"Shhh."

Her mouth found mine again, urgent this time. I slid my hands under her shirt, fingers tracing the warm skin of her back. She shivered against me, and I paused.

"Cold?"

"No." She pressed closer. "Don't stop."

I pulled her shirt over her head, revealing a simple black bra. My breath caught. Even in the dim light, she was beautiful. Scars and all. Each mark told a story of survival.

"You can touch me," she whispered.

I traced the outline of a scar that curved along her rib cage. "Tell me if I do something you don't like."

"I will."

We moved toward the bed, stumbling slightly in the darkness. I hit the mattress with the back of my knees and I sat, pulling her between my legs. Eye level with her stomach now, I pressed my lips to the soft skin just above her navel. She trembled.

"Dixon," she breathed.

My name in her mouth was like a prayer. I unfastened her jeans, sliding them down her hips as she stepped out of them. The moonlight caught the curve of her hip, the dip of her waist.

I stood up slowly, letting my hands skim up her sides until I was standing over her. She reached behind her back and unhooked her bra, letting it slide down her arms. My throat went dry.

"You're gorgeous," I murmured.

She hooked her fingers into the waistband of my sweatpants. "These need to go."

I stepped out of them, standing before her in just my boxers. We were equals now, nearly bare in the darkness, vulnerable in ways that had nothing to do with our lack of clothing.

"Last chance to back out," I said.

Rio answered by pushing me back onto the bed. She followed, straddling my hips, her hair falling around us like a curtain. I could feel her heart hammering against mine.

"I trust you," she whispered.

Those three words hit me harder than any "I love you" ever could. Trust was rare in our world. Precious. I cupped the back of her neck and pulled her down for a kiss that was almost reverent.

Her body melted against mine, curves fitting perfectly against the hard planes of my chest. I rolled us carefully, pinning her beneath me, my weight braced on my forearms.

"Tell me what you want," I said against her throat.

"You." Her hands slid down my back, nails digging in slightly. "Just you."

I took my time, exploring her body with my hands and mouth. Found the places that made her gasp, the spots that made her arch against me. I tugged her panties down her legs then teased her wet pussy. She let out a little moan as my fingers rubbed against her clit.

"This still okay?" I kissed her neck, then her lips as she nodded in affirmation, giving me the green light to keep going. I eased a finger inside her, testing how tight she was. The last thing I wanted was to hurt her.

"Dixon, I need more."

"You can have all of me, but I don't want to rush through our first time together."

She smiled and nipped at my shoulder. "Such a gentleman."

"Only with you."

I took my time teasing her, kissing her. I savored every second. When I finally slid my dick into her, she clung to me, her face buried against my neck.

"Dixon," she breathed, my name a plea on her lips.

We moved together in the darkness, finding a rhythm that built and crashed like waves on the sand. I watched her face as she came apart beneath me, her gaze locked on mine, trusting me to catch her as she fell. Feeling her squeeze my cock was enough to make me follow her over the edge, her name on my lips like a prayer as I came inside her.

Afterward, we lay tangled together, her head on my chest, my fingers tracing lazy patterns on her back. The world outside still existed -- Java still missing -- but for now, in this room, there was only us.

"You okay?" I asked quietly.

She nodded against my chest. "Better than okay."

I pressed my lips to the top of her head. "Get some sleep. Tomorrow's going to be rough."

"I know." Her voice was already heavy with exhaustion. "We'll find him, Dixon."

"Yeah," I said, staring at the ceiling. "We will."

I didn't sleep much that night. Just watched the shadows move across the ceiling, listened to Rio's steady breathing, and planned our next move. If Java was at the old mill, we'd need to be smart about this. No rushing in half-cocked. Too much at stake.

But for now, I'd enjoy this time with Rio and see what Charming could find out about the old mill.

Chapter Fifteen

Rio

The back room of the Devil's Boneyard clubhouse smelled like old leather and cigarettes. I sat in the corner, trying to make myself invisible while keeping my ears open. Rebel had insisted it was okay for me to be here, but I didn't know why. None of the other old ladies were here. In fact, Jordan had told me they pretty much were never allowed in these meetings.

Charming sat across from the Bratva man, his face a mask that gave nothing away. This wasn't a social call. This was business -- dangerous business.

The overhead light was dim, casting shadows across the wooden table. Charming's fingers tapped an irregular rhythm against his whiskey glass. The Bratva emissary -- a compact man with ice for eyes -- hadn't touched his drink.

"So," Charming finally said, breaking the silence. "You've come a long way just to talk."

The Bratva man's lips barely moved when he spoke. "We don't waste trips, Halden."

I fought to keep my expression neutral. Rebel had explained that all the men here used their road names. Only their families were supposed to use their real name. Halden Roberts was the man before the cut, before the presidency.

"Then let's not waste time," Charming replied, his voice deceptively casual. He had presence that men half his age would kill for. The gray streaking his hair only added to it. I'd never admit it to Rebel, or his wife, but the man was still sexy. "You've got information on Java."

It wasn't a question. It was the only reason any of

us would be sitting here with a Bratva emissary, sipping whiskey in a back room while the party raged on the other side of the wall.

"We know where he is being held." The man's accent was barely perceptible, which somehow made him more unsettling. "And who holds him."

I shifted in my chair, earning a quick glance from Charming that told me to be still. I forced myself to breathe evenly. Java had been missing for ten days. The club had been turned upside down searching for him. Every connection tapped, every favor called in. And nothing. Until now.

The emissary placed his hands flat on the table. "Your brother has managed to anger some very dangerous people, Mr. President."

"He tends to do that," Charming said, his tone dry. "But he's still one of mine."

"Of course." The man inclined his head slightly. "Family is everything. This is something we understand."

A patched member -- I thought they called him Gator -- stood by the door, arms crossed. His face was impassive, but his eyes never left the Bratva man's hands. Smart.

"Who has him?" Charming asked, cutting through the bullshit.

The emissary's mouth curved into what might have been a smile on anyone else. On him, it looked like a warning.

"The Albanians. Specifically, Besnik Vata's crew. The Moretti family handed him off within twenty-four hours of sending you that finger."

Charming didn't react, but his fingers stopped their tapping. I had no idea who Besnik Vata was, but the stillness that fell over the room told me everything

I needed to know.

"That makes things complicated," Charming finally said.

"Yes." The emissary leaned forward. "But not impossible. We have mutual interests regarding Vata."

"Which means you want something." Charming's voice had hardened. "Spit it out."

The Bratva man's eyes flicked to me for the first time since he'd entered the room. I stared back, refusing to look away first. After a moment, he turned back to Charming.

"We need specific skills for this extraction. The location is… challenging."

"You need Devil's Boneyard muscle," Charming translated.

"We need Ripper and Samurai."

The name sent a chill through me. Samurai. I'd seen him around, always quiet, always watching. There was something in his eyes that told you he'd seen hell and brought some back with him. And Ripper… even the club members spoke his name differently.

"You're asking a lot," Charming said, his voice even.

"We're offering a lot. Your brother, alive." The emissary's eyes narrowed. "Vata doesn't typically return his hostages in one piece."

My stomach turned. I'd only met Java twice, but he had kind eyes and an easy laugh. The thought of him in the hands of someone who'd make the Bratva send an emissary made my throat tight.

Charming took a measured sip of his whiskey. "What's your stake in this? Bratva doesn't do charity work."

"Vata has something that belongs to us.

Something valuable." The emissary's face remained expressionless. "The operation to recover your brother would create… an opportunity for us to recover our property as well."

"A two-for-one deal," Charming said.

"Precisely."

The music from the main room swelled as someone opened the door to the hallway. The bass thumped, a counterpoint to my heartbeat. I could hear laughter, glasses clinking, the sounds of normal life while in here, we discussed what sounded like a suicide mission.

"Why Ripper and Samurai specifically?" Charming asked, his eyes never leaving the emissary's face.

The man gave another non-smile. "Ripper because he can get into places others can't. And Samurai because of his past. Did I mention Vata has also started trading in boys?"

I frowned. What did that have to do with Samurai's past?

"Samurai's not as active in missions anymore," Charming said. "He has a family now."

"We are aware. But…" The emissary shrugged slightly. "Of course, if you prefer to leave your brother with Vata, we understand. Family obligations can be complicated."

The bastard was playing Charming, and we all knew it. But that didn't make the play any less effective.

Charming's jaw tightened. "When would this happen?"

"Three days from now. The location requires careful timing. Tides. Guard rotations." The emissary reached inside his jacket, causing Gator to tense, but he only removed a small flash drive. "All details are here. I suggest you review them quickly."

"And if I refuse?" Charming asked, though we all knew he wouldn't.

The emissary stood. "Then we pursue our own interests alone, and you continue searching for your brother with the same success you've had for the past ten days." He straightened his perfectly tailored jacket. "Which is to say, none at all."

The silence that followed felt like a physical presence in the room. Charming looked at the flash drive, then back at the emissary.

"We'll need both Ripper and Samurai with us," he finally said, his voice leaving no room for negotiation. "But I'm coming too."

The emissary raised an eyebrow. "That wasn't part of the arrangement."

"It is now." Charming stood, suddenly seeming taller, his presence filling the room. "Java is part of this club. Samurai and Ripper are my men as well. I don't send family into the fire without walking in myself. Take it or leave it."

For a long moment, no one spoke. The emissary studied Charming, reassessing. Finally, he nodded.

"Acceptable. But only you. No other additions."

"Agreed." Charming didn't offer his hand to shake. Neither did the emissary. Some deals weren't sealed with handshakes.

"We will contact you tomorrow with the meeting point." The emissary moved toward the door, then paused. "Mr. Roberts. If you are planning anything… creative, I should warn you that my organization has contingencies in place."

"I'd expect nothing less," Charming replied.

After Gator opened the door and closed it behind

the departing emissary, the room fell silent again. Charming stared at the flash drive in his hand, his expression unreadable.

"Get Shade," he told Gator without looking up. "And find Samurai."

"I know where Shade is," Rebel said. "I'll go get him."

I watched as my man walked out of the room, leaving me behind.

"What about Ripper?" Bones asked.

Charming's mouth twisted into something that wasn't quite a smile. "I know exactly where Ripper is. That's not the problem."

As Gator left the room, Charming finally looked at me. "You didn't hear any of this."

I nodded. "I was never here."

"Smart girl." He downed the rest of his whiskey in one swallow. "I'm sure Rebel is pissed."

"Because you're going?" I asked.

"Because he's not." Charming set his glass down with a sharp *click*. "And because I'm about to ruin Samurai's fucking day."

He seemed older suddenly, the weight of the decision visible in the set of his shoulders. I hadn't been with the club very long, and I had no idea what Samurai had been through, but if I had to guess, he'd lived in hell before coming to the club. It seemed he'd finally found peace. Taking that away, even temporarily, wasn't something Charming would do lightly.

"But you'll get Java back," I said softly.

Charming's eyes met mine. "Yes. We will." He stood up. "Now go find your man."

I walked out, letting the door click shut behind me. In the hallway, the music was louder, the bass pounding through the floor into my bones. Normal life, oblivious to what had just happened. In three days, Charming, Ripper, and Samurai would be walking into what sounded like hell to get Java back. And Rebel would be here, furious at being left out of the action, and wanting to go save the boy he'd watched over.

As I moved toward the main room, I caught sight of Rebel leaning against the bar, his cocky smile in place as he joked with one of the Prospects. He hadn't noticed me yet. I took a moment to watch him. Since Shade brushed past me, it seemed he'd been found. And for whatever reason, Rebel had remained out here. Maybe he really *was* pissed about being left out.

But part of me was glad he would be here with me. All we could do was stand on the sidelines and hope they all came back alive. And that's why I was glad he wasn't going. If I got the news he hadn't made it, it would gut me.

* * *

The main hall of the Devil's Boneyard clubhouse pulsed with energy, a living thing fueled by music, booze, and bad decisions. I worked the bar with practiced efficiency, mixing drinks and handing out beers without missing a beat. Charming had said the Prospects always manned the bar, but I'd wanted to do it on the nights I came here with Rebel. Since we'd met here, it seemed appropriate. Unlike the other old ladies, I wouldn't avoid this place. I belonged here more than the club girls did.

None of the old ladies liked coming here during a party. I could understand why. The mostly naked women roaming around and trying to latch onto any man in a cut wasn't a pleasant sight. Not that I begrudged them the chance at finding a moment of fun or happiness with one of the guys. As long that man was single.

"Two shots of Jack," barked a Prospect. His cut was still too new, the leather not yet softened by time and road grime.

I poured without looking, sliding the glasses across the bar top. "Ten bucks."

"Put it on my tab." He grinned. The brothers drank for free, but Charming had said I could charge the Prospects if they asked for anything other than beer.

"Don't have tabs. Have cash?" I raised an eyebrow, daring him to challenge me.

The Prospect's smile faltered. Another patched member -- Magnus -- clapped a heavy hand on the Prospect's shoulder.

"Pay the lady, dipshit. She ain't here for your broke ass to practice flirting." Magnus's voice was gravel and whiskey.

The Prospect fumbled for his wallet, dropping a crumpled ten on the bar. I snagged it and turned to my next customer without acknowledging him further. That was the trick with these guys. Never let them think for a second that you were impressed.

The music switched to something with a heavier beat that vibrated through the floor and up into my bones. The lighting was all wrong -- too bright in some places, too dark in others. Bodies moved on the makeshift dance floor, leather cuts mingling with tight dresses and worn jeans. Club girls circled like vultures, their eyes constantly scanning for the highest-ranking member not currently occupied.

I grabbed a beer from the ice-filled trough behind me, popped the cap against the edge of the bar, and handed it to a gray-haired member I'd seen several times but never spoken to. Even though I'd been around the club a while now, and interacted with most of them, I was still learning everyone's names and faces. The club was larger than most people probably realized.

"Thanks, darlin'." He nodded, eyes appraising me like I was merchandise. "You're Rebel's woman, right?"

I stared him down. "I'm Rio."

He laughed, a phlegmy sound that suggested decades of cigarettes. "Got some bite to you. Good. He needs that."

I didn't respond, just moved to the next customer. I wasn't here to discuss my relationship with anyone, especially not some old man who thought he had the right to comment on it.

From the corner of my eye, I tracked Rebel as he lounged against the far wall, one boot propped against it, his posture relaxed but his eyes alert. That was Rebel -- always looking casual while missing nothing. His dark hair fell across his forehead, and even from here I could see the cocky half-smile that seemed permanently etched on his face. Dixon Morreli, aka Rebel, had earned his road name a hundred times over. He answered to no one but Charming and even that was questionable on some days.

And somehow, against all odds, he was mine.

"Earth to Rio," a woman's voice cut through my thoughts. "You gonna serve me or just stare at your man all night?"

I refocused on Clarity, one of the old ladies who'd actually been decent to me since I arrived. She was Scratch's woman, had been for years from what I gathered.

"Sorry," I said, not meaning it. "What can I get

you?"

"Tequila. The good stuff, not that paint thinner you're serving the Prospects." Her lipstick was perfect despite the late hour, her eyes sharp and knowing. Scratch sat at a corner table, and I knew she'd only come because he was here. She couldn't stand the club girls.

Jordan had talked about Clarity in a few chats we'd had over the phone since I'd decided to stay. The woman I saw now didn't seem to fit with how she'd described her. I wondered if she was trying on a new look or attitude, or if I was just misremembering. I hadn't really interacted with Clarity much, other than a brief hello when we passed each other.

I reached under the bar for the bottle we kept hidden from the general crowd. As I poured her shot, she leaned in.

"Word is Charming had a visitor earlier. Bratva?" Her question was casual, but her eyes were intent. Why did I get the feeling she was testing me?

I shrugged. "Didn't see anything."

She studied me for a moment, then nodded slightly. "Smart girl. But if you hear anything about Java…"

"I'll find you," I promised, though I had no intention of sharing what I'd overheard. Charming had made it clear the meeting was confidential, and I wasn't about to betray that trust three hours later.

Clarity knocked back her shot, then placed a twenty on the bar. I noticed her grimace and realized that wasn't the type of drink she usually ordered. Yep. She'd been testing me. "Consider that a tip for putting up with all this crap."

She smiled and disappeared back into the crowd. I pocketed the cash.

As the night progressed, I kept up with the orders, pouring drinks with increasing speed, exchanging barbs with patrons, and earning respect one smart retort at a time. The buzz of alcohol in my system -- just enough to take the edge off -- made everything seem sharper and duller simultaneously. The noise, the smells, the constant movement swirled around me like I was standing in the eye of a storm.

Rebel hadn't moved much, though different members had stopped to talk with him throughout the night. His position in the club was solid -- not leadership but respected enough that even senior members sought his opinion. I watched as he laughed at something Gator said, his eyes crinkling at the corners, his whole face transformed by genuine amusement.

Then I saw her.

The club girl wasn't particularly remarkable -- bleached blonde hair, only wearing a bra and panties, makeup that had started sliding south hours ago. But the way she moved, weaving drunkenly through the crowd with singular focus, her eyes fixed on Rebel, set off every alarm in my head.

I tracked her progress while mechanically filling a beer glass from the tap. She stumbled slightly, caught herself against a chair, and continued her determined path toward my man. The possessiveness that surged through me was primal and immediate. I didn't think -- I reacted.

"Hey." I shoved the half-filled beer at the waiting brother and vaulted over the bar in one fluid motion. The man shouted something, but I was already moving through the crowd, shoving bodies aside without apology.

The girl reached Rebel before I could intercept

her. I watched her press herself against him, one hand on his chest, the other sliding up to touch his face. Her lips moved, saying something I couldn't hear over the music. Rebel's expression didn't change, but he didn't move away either.

Red filled my vision. I grabbed the girl's shoulder, spinning her around to face me.

"What the fuck?" she slurred, eyes struggling to focus.

I didn't waste time with words. My fist connected with her jaw, sending her staggering backward into a table. Glasses crashed to the floor. The music kept playing but conversations around us died as heads turned toward the commotion.

The girl touched her face, shock momentarily overriding her drunkenness. "You crazy bitch!"

I grabbed her arm, my fingers digging in hard enough to bruise, and dragged her toward the exit. She tried to resist, her feet scrabbling against the sticky floor, but she was too drunk and I was too angry for her to stand a chance.

"Rio." Rebel's voice behind me, a question and a warning all at once.

I didn't stop or look back. "Got this."

No one moved to intervene as I hauled the struggling girl through the door and onto the clubhouse porch. The cool night air hit me like a slap but did nothing to dampen the rage pounding through my veins.

I slammed her against the wall, her head bouncing off it with a dull *thud*. She tried to claw at my face, but her movements were sluggish and uncoordinated. I stepped back just enough to give myself room, then swung again, harder this time. My knuckles crunched against her cheekbone. Her eyes rolled back, and she slid down the wall, unconscious before she hit the ground.

I stood over her, breathing hard, my hand throbbing. Part of me wanted to kick her while she was down, but I reined it in. She'd gotten the message. No need to overdo it.

I used the bottom of my shirt to wipe blood off my knuckles, unsure if it was hers or mine. Didn't matter. What mattered was that everyone in that clubhouse was about to understand exactly where things stood.

I left her crumpled where she lay and walked back inside. The music was still playing but had been turned down a notch. Every eye tracked me as I strode through the room, past Rebel, and back behind the bar. I could feel him watching me, could sense his tension without having to look.

I grabbed a bottle of whiskey, took a long pull straight from it, then slammed it down on the bar top. The sound cracked through the relative quiet.

"Rebel is hands off," I announced, my voice carrying easily in the hushed room. "Next bitch who touches him loses more than consciousness. We clear?"

The silence held for one beat, two. Then someone -- Gator, I think -- chuckled. It broke the tension, and the room gradually returned to normal volume as conversations resumed and attention shifted away from me.

I busied myself cleaning up the area behind the bar, not looking up when I sensed Rebel's approach. He leaned against the counter, waiting until I finally met his eyes.

"That was interesting," he said, his voice neutral, but his eyes dancing with something that looked suspiciously like pride.

I shrugged. "She was drunk."

"So are half the people here."

"She touched what's mine."

A slow smile spread across his face. "That right?"

"Don't act surprised." I reached for another bottle, needing something to do with my hands. "I don't share."

Rebel caught my wrist, turning it to examine my bruised knuckles. His thumb gently traced the broken skin.

"Should get some ice on this," he said.

"It's fine."

"Didn't say it wasn't." He released my wrist but stayed where he was. "You know you didn't have to do that, right?"

I finally looked at him directly. "Yes, I did."

His expression softened almost imperceptibly. To anyone else, he would have looked the same -- cocky, slightly amused, untouchable. But I could see the shift, the acknowledgment of what I'd just done and why.

"Finish up whatever you're doing," he said, straightening up. "Then we're going home."

The promise in his voice sent heat curling through me, a different kind of fire than the anger that had driven me minutes before.

"Could leave now," I suggested.

Rebel's smile turned wicked. "Nah. Let 'em all sit here thinking about what I'm gonna do to you later. Build the anticipation."

He walked away before I could respond, returning to his spot against the wall. But something had changed. Clarity was looking at me differently -- with newfound respect. The club girls kept their distance from both me and Rebel. And the patch members nodded to me as they approached the bar, acknowledgment in their eyes that hadn't been there before.

I'd crossed a line tonight, made a public declaration of territory and relationship. In the strange, tribal world of the MC, I'd staked my claim and backed it with violence. It wasn't how normal relationships worked. But then again, nothing about life with the Devil's Boneyard was normal.

As I poured shots and opened beers, I felt a new kind of power thrumming under my skin. I belonged here. I'd earned my place. And everyone in this room now knew exactly where I stood.

With every passing minute, Rebel's eyes grew darker, his posture more tense. Anticipation built between us like an electrical charge. By the time I was ready to leave, the air between us was practically crackling with it.

I didn't say goodbye to anyone as I walked toward him. I didn't need to. He pushed off the wall as I approached, and without a word, we headed for the exit together, his hand possessive on the small of my back.

Behind us, someone whistled. I didn't turn around. Let them talk. Let them wonder. I'd made my position crystal clear tonight, and that was all that mattered.

Chapter Sixteen

Rebel

The doors slammed open with a *bang* that echoed through the compound. Samurai and Ripper burst in, their faces streaked with sweat and grime, carrying Java between them on what looked like a piece of corrugated metal torn from a shed wall. Blood dripped steadily onto the concrete floor, marking their path with crimson droplets. I froze, my breath catching as I took in Java's mangled body, barely recognizable beneath the layers of dried blood and fresh wounds.

"Doc!" Samurai's voice cut through the sudden silence. "We need you now!"

I stepped closer, drawn by some morbid need to see, to understand what had been done to one of our own. Java's chest rose and fell in shallow, irregular movements. His shirt hung in tatters, revealing deep lacerations that crisscrossed his torso like a grotesque roadmap.

"Get him on the bar," Doc ordered, already pulling on latex gloves with practiced efficiency.

They laid Java down, and the metal stretcher scraped against the wood surface. The sound made my teeth ache. Java's body jerked, and a low moan escaped his split lips. He was conscious. Christ. After everything they'd done to him, he was still conscious.

"What happened?" I asked, my voice sounding strangely distant to my own ears.

Samurai's eyes met mine briefly. "Vata's crew tried to get information from him on our club. He held out."

I counted the visible injuries -- fingers bent at unnatural angles, burns that peeled back skin to reveal raw flesh beneath, what looked like drill holes in his right arm. Days of that. My stomach twisted.

Doc moved methodically, cutting away what remained of Java's clothes. Each new inch of exposed skin revealed another horror. Cigarette burns dotted his chest, and purple bruises bloomed across his ribs. Someone had carved something into his thigh -- letters that spelled out a message I couldn't read through the dried blood.

"Is he going to make it?" The question came from somewhere behind me -- one of the Prospects, his voice cracking.

Doc didn't look up from his work. His hands moved with practiced precision as he cleaned a particularly nasty wound near Java's collarbone. "If his will is strong enough, he can pull through."

Java's eye -- the one that could still open -- focused suddenly, finding mine. Recognition flashed there, followed by something else. Pride, maybe. Or relief. His lips moved, trying to form words.

I leaned closer.

"Didn't... tell them... shit." The words were barely audible, each one clearly causing pain.

"Save your strength," I told him, my throat tight. "You're home now."

Around us, the compound had erupted into controlled chaos. Prospects ran for supplies, fetching clean water and more bandages. The air filled with the sharp tang of antiseptic as Doc cleaned wound after wound. The rustling of fabric and the shifting weight of club members as they steadied themselves heightened my own unsettled energy.

"Rebel." Samurai's hand landed on my shoulder, solid and warm. "We need to talk."

I nodded, following him to a corner of the room, though my gaze kept drifting back to Java. Doc had started an IV, the clear liquid in the bag a stark contrast to the red-soaked gauze piling up beside the table.

"We hit them hard," Samurai said, his voice low. "But this isn't over."

"They'll retaliate."

"Maybe. But they're hurting. We took out eight of their men, burned their stash house to the ground." A grim smile crossed his face. "And we got what we went for, and then some."

He held up a flash drive, small enough to hide between two fingers. I wondered how he'd walked out with that. The Bratva would have surely snatched it if they'd known it was in his possession.

"What's on it?"

"Everything. Their distribution routes, client lists, dirty cops on the payroll. Enough to cripple their operation if we play it right."

"He was bait?" I asked, the anger rising hot and fast in my chest.

Samurai shook his head. "No. They bargained with the Morettis for him. Thought he knew enough about club business to take us down. He didn't tell them a damn thing." His eyes darkened. "But he held out long enough for us to track him down."

We both looked back at Java. Doc had sedated him now, and his face had relaxed into unconsciousness. Small mercy.

"The things they did to him…" I couldn't finish the thought.

"I know." Samurai's voice hardened. "They'll pay for every mark on his body. That's a promise."

Across the room, Charming walked in, assessing the situation with a sweeping glance. His eyes lingered on Java, then found Samurai and me in our corner. He'd intended to go with them, but for whatever reason, had pulled back at the last minute.

"Report," he said simply, joining us.

Samurai filled him in, his words clipped and precise. I watched Charming's face, the subtle shifts in his expression as he absorbed the severity of what had happened. His jaw tightened when Samurai described finding Java chained to a pipe in the basement of the Albanian compound.

"And the flash drive I saw you with just now?" Charming asked.

Samurai handed it over. "It has a lot of intel we can use, stuff we didn't know before, but they know we have it."

"Then we move fast." Charming pocketed the drive. "Shade needs to start working on this tonight. Before they can relocate their operations."

I glanced at the clock on the wall. Nearly midnight. Not that it mattered. Sleep wasn't an option, not after this.

Doc called out, his voice cutting through my thoughts. "Need another pair of hands here."

I moved before I could think about it, crossing the room and stepping up to the bar. "Tell me what to do."

"Hold this." He pressed a thick wad of gauze against a wound that was bleeding freely again. "Pressure, steady."

Blood seeped through immediately, warm against my fingers. I pressed harder, feeling the heat of Java's skin beneath the gauze. He was already running a fever. Infection setting in.

"We got antibiotics in him?" I asked.

Doc nodded, busy with another wound. "Triple dose. His system's going to be fighting on multiple fronts."

Around us, the club members moved with purpose. Some stood guard outside, weapons visible. Others helped Doc or spoke in low, urgent tones about security and next steps. The air felt charged, like the moment before a thunderstorm breaks.

I looked down at Java's face. Beneath the swelling and bruises, I could see the man I'd shared drinks with in what felt like just days ago but had sadly been longer. Who'd laughed at Samurai's terrible jokes and arm-wrestled Ripper for the last beer. Who'd once given me his jacket when we got caught in a sudden downpour during a supply run.

A surge of rage washed through me, so intense I had to focus on my breathing to control it. The Morettis had made this personal in a way that couldn't be forgiven or forgotten. And now the Albanians had put a target on their backs.

"BP's dropping," Doc announced, his voice tight. "Need O-neg now."

On the off chance we found Java and he'd be in rough shape, Doc had been preparing. Meds. Any equipment he may need. And a few bags of blood.

A Prospect ran forward with a blood bag. Doc worked quickly to set up the transfusion, his movements precise despite the pressure.

"Is he going to make it?" I asked again, softly this time.

Doc met my eyes across Java's broken body. "He's fighting. That's all I can tell you right now. Doing all this in a non-sterile environment isn't helping, but I know we can't take him to the hospital. Too many questions."

"Should have set up one of the rooms. You'd clearly known to expect all this," I said.

Doc grunted but didn't comment.

Fighting. That's what we did. Fought for our brothers, fought for our territory, fought for justice when the law failed us. Java had fought for days in that hellhole, refusing to break. Now we'd fight for him.

"The Morettis and Vata are going to regret this," I said, not caring who heard me. "Every single one of them."

Samurai appeared at my side, relieving me of my position holding the gauze. His fingers brushed mine, a brief moment of connection.

"Yes," he said simply. "They will."

Outside, I heard the rumble of more motorcycles arriving. Reinforcements coming in from nearby clubs, no doubt. Even though I wasn't privy to any calls Charming may have placed, it wouldn't surprise me at all if he had. An attack on one was an attack on all. Especially when you had family ties to other clubs. But in our case, the same could be said with the Bratva since both Stripes and Charming had ties to them.

Doc continued his methodical work, stitching, cleaning, assessing. I stepped back, giving him space, but couldn't make myself leave the room. Java was family. We stayed for family.

Hours passed. Java stabilized enough for Doc to pronounce him "not actively dying," which passed for good news on a night like this. I found myself on a worn couch against the wall, watching the rhythmic rise and fall of Java's chest from across the room. Proof of life. Small comfort, but I'd take it.

Samurai sat beside me, our shoulders touching. He smelled like smoke and blood and the night air. Neither of us spoke. Words seemed inadequate for what we'd seen tonight, for what still lay ahead.

The Morettis and Vata had opened a door they couldn't close. I had a feeling this was going to be a long, drawn-out war between us and them.

I looked around the room at the hardened faces of my brothers, at the weapons being cleaned and checked, at the grim determination in every set of shoulders. They thought they knew what they were dealing with. They had no idea.

"Get some rest," Samurai said, his voice rough with fatigue. "Tomorrow's going to be a long day."

I nodded, but didn't move. Rest could wait. Right now, I needed to be here, needed to witness Java's fight, needed to feed the cold fury building in my chest.

The Morettis and Vata had made their move. Now it was our turn -- again.

I knew Shade had been trying to track the men who had hurt Rio. After he'd found them, he'd tried to keep tabs on them, only for them to vanish overnight. Now he'd have even more work to do. Never a dull moment at the Devil's Boneyard.

* * *

Two Days Later

The fluorescent lights hummed overhead, casting a harsh glare across the wooden table where we'd gathered. I shifted in my seat, the hard chair digging into my back as I watched Charming pace at the head of the room. The air felt thick with anticipation and something darker -- a current of rage that had been building since we'd discovered who had hurt Rio. Faces around the table were set in grim lines, jaws tight, eyes focused. This wasn't just another strategy session. This was personal.

Charming slapped a manila folder onto the table. The sound cracked like a gunshot in the tense silence.

"Shade," he said, nodding toward the club's

hacker who sat with his laptop open, fingers hovering over the keys.

Shade cleared his throat. "Got confirmation on the targets. The two men who hurt Rio have been found once more. Private Ellis and Sergeant Denton. As of three days ago, both were dishonorably discharged. But considering they escaped the custody of MPs, this should have gone down a lot different. They definitely have higher ups behind them."

"So they turned themselves in?" I asked.

Shade rubbed a hand along his jaw. "That's the thing. The reports are all a bit… off. Nothing is clear on this one. All I know is that they're in the wind."

I studied their faces. Ordinary. Unremarkable. The kind you'd pass on the street without a second glance. Hard to reconcile these bland features with the monsters who'd drugged and raped Rio, leaving scars that went deeper than skin. Even when I'd seen them in person I'd had the same thought. Completely unremarkable in every way.

Rio, sitting directly across from me, leaned forward. Her strawberry-blonde hair fell in waves around her face but couldn't hide the steel in her blue eyes as she memorized every detail on the screen.

"Current location?" she asked, her Georgia drawl more pronounced than usual. A tell that she was affected, despite the calm veneer.

"Working as private security in the next town," Shade replied. "They live in an apartment complex three blocks away from their job location. Separate units, but same floor. I've got work schedules, regular haunts, the whole package."

"That seems fast," I said.

Shade snorted. "Remember what I said? It looks like they have help."

Charming nodded. "Good work." He turned to the group. "We need to decide how to approach this. Clean, quiet, and permanent. These fuckers hurt one of ours."

"I'm handling them myself." Rio's voice cut through the room, firm and unyielding. All eyes turned to her.

"Like hell you are," Ashes snapped from the end of the table. His fist came down hard enough to make his coffee mug jump. "This isn't a solo operation."

"Didn't ask for your permission," Rio replied, her tone flat.

Ashes leaned forward, scarred forearms pressed against the table. "We need caution -- acting alone could end badly. These aren't just some random assholes. They're trained. Military."

"So am I," Rio shot back.

"Yeah, and look how well that worked out for you," Ashes retorted, then immediately clamped his mouth shut, as if he knew he'd crossed a line. He cleared his throat. "I just meant because they're back now."

The room went deadly quiet. Rio's face drained of color before flushing bright red. I tensed, ready to intervene if she went for his throat.

Renegade broke the silence. "That was out of line." His voice was low, dangerous. "She's earned the right to get closure on her terms."

"Bullshit," Ashes countered. "I want these fuckers dead as much as anyone but sending her in alone is suicide. Or worse -- she gets caught. I understand she's tough and can handle herself, but there's an entire club here ready to lend a hand."

"I didn't survive what I did to sit on the sidelines now." Rio's voice had dropped to a near whisper, which somehow carried more weight than if she'd shouted. "I'm the one who suffered. The one whose life they destroyed. They're mine."

I watched her hands -- steady, not a tremor in sight. That controlled rage was more frightening than any outburst.

"You were drugged at the time," Samurai interjected, his tone measured. "Against two men with combat training. The odds weren't in your favor."

"And now they will be," Rio replied, meeting his gaze without flinching. "Because I know exactly what I'm walking into. I hurt those fuckers when I saw them in the warehouse. This time, I'll make sure they can't walk away. I'm not playing by civilian or military rules anymore. I've learned my lesson. It's time to handle this the way the Devil's Boneyard would do it."

The argument exploded around the table. Raised voices bounced off concrete walls as members took sides. I caught fragments of heated exchanges -- safety concerns versus Rio's right to vengeance, tactical discussions about surveillance and extraction plans, debates over club involvement versus personal vendetta.

My jaw tightened as I watched the scene unfold. I understood both sides. Rio deserved her revenge -- needed it, probably, to ever move forward. But Ashes wasn't wrong about the risks. These men had hurt her once. Given the chance, they'd do worse.

A sharp whistle cut through the chaos. Charming stood, his expression thunderous.

"Enough," he ordered. "This isn't a fucking democracy. Rio, what exactly do you have in mind?"

She straightened in her chair. "I approach the first target at his apartment. They're both arrogant, and they'll want revenge for me kicking their asses." Her lip curled with contempt. "I get inside, I handle him. Then I move to the second target before word can spread."

"And if something goes wrong?" Charming pressed. "What if there are repercussions?"

"It won't."

"Not good enough," Samurai cut in. "We need contingencies."

Rio's eyes narrowed. "I'm not asking for help."

"You don't have to ask," I found myself saying, surprising even myself. All eyes turned to me. "We're offering it anyway."

Rio studied me, weighing my words. I met her gaze steadily. This wasn't about questioning her capabilities. This was about having her back, the way we always did for family. And the simple fact I didn't like my woman walking into this situation on her own. Didn't matter if she could handle herself or not.

"Surveillance," Renegade suggested, breaking the tension. "We keep our distance, but we're there if shit goes sideways. Your play, your way, but with backup."

Rio considered this, then gave a tight nod. "I can live with that."

"I still think --" Ashes began.

"It's decided," Charming interrupted. "Rio takes point. Renegade and Rebel on surveillance. Samurai coordinates from here with Shade monitoring communications." He looked around the table. "Anyone got a problem with that?"

No one spoke, though Ashes' scowl deepened.

"Right." Charming nodded to Shade. "Walk us through the details."

For the next twenty minutes, Shade outlined everything we needed to know -- building layouts, security systems, daily routines of the targets. As he spoke, Rio began methodically checking her gear on the table beside her. A hunting knife with a serrated edge. A gun with a silencer. Zip ties. Duct tape. Each item placed with deliberate care, like a surgeon arranging instruments before an operation. I hadn't questioned her when she'd brought it with her today. She'd noticed me grabbing weapons and had done the same. We'd both wanted to be prepared for anything.

I watched her hands move with practiced efficiency, and a chill ran down my spine. This wasn't just revenge. This was justice. She'd made up her mind and now she was ready to act.

"You'll need this," Shade said, passing Rio a small electronic device. "Jams any cameras in a thirty-foot radius. Gives you a fifteen-minute window before the system registers a malfunction. I have reason to believe they've installed some around the complex."

She pocketed it without comment.

"When?" I asked.

"Tomorrow night," Charming replied. "Target One gets off work at midnight. Usually stops for a drink, then heads home alone. That's our window."

Rio nodded, continuing her preparations.

"I need to know you can keep a clear head," Samurai said, addressing Rio directly. "These men hurt you. While you handled them last time, you decided to let them go. Couldn't follow through with ending their lives. Seeing them again…"

"I'll be the last thing they ever see," she finished, her voice deadly calm.

I remembered what Java had looked like, broken and bleeding on that makeshift stretcher. The rage I'd felt then. The desire to inflict that same pain tenfold on those responsible. Rio had been carrying that same rage for a while now, letting it burn slow and hot, waiting for this moment.

"This isn't just about revenge," she said, as if reading my thoughts. "It's about making sure they never do to another woman what they did to me. I should have killed them when I had the chance."

The room fell silent again. Even Ashes couldn't argue with that.

"We roll out at 2300 hours tomorrow," Renegade said, breaking the silence. "Full tank of gas, comms checked and double-checked. Rio, you ride with me in a club truck. Rebel follows in the SUV with the extra supplies."

I nodded my agreement. The practical details helped ground the conversation, pulling us back from the emotional edge where we'd been teetering.

Rio stood, gathering her gear into a black duffel bag. "I need some air."

No one tried to stop her as she headed for the door. I caught her eye as she passed, trying to convey a silent message of support. Something in her expression softened for just a moment before the steel returned.

After she left, the room erupted again, voices lowered but no less intense.

"She's not stable enough for this," Ashes insisted.

"None of us would be," Samurai countered. "But she's focused. That's what matters."

"And if she decides to make them suffer?" Ashes pressed. "Gets caught up in it, takes too long, misses the window for the second target?"

"Then we adjust," I said firmly. "That's what backup is for."

Charming rubbed a hand over his face. "This isn't ideal. Honestly, other than Jordan, I'd never let one of our women do something like this. But Rio needs this. And we need her whole, not broken by what those men did."

The conversation continued, hammering out details, preparing for contingencies. I half listened, my mind already on tomorrow night. On what we might find in those apartments. On what Rio might become in the process of getting her justice.

Eventually, the meeting broke up. Members drifted away in twos and threes, talking in low voices. I remained seated, staring at the empty chair where Rio had been.

Samurai paused beside me. "You good with this?"

I considered the question. Was I? Could anyone be "good" with what we were about to do? But then I thought about Rio's face when she talked about her attack. The nightmares that still woke her screaming. The way she flinched sometimes when a man moved too quickly near her.

"Yeah," I finally answered. "I'm good with it."

He nodded, understanding the weight behind my words. "Keep her safe. From them and from herself."

"I will."

He squeezed my shoulder once, then followed the others out. I sat alone in the harsh fluorescent light, mentally preparing for what tomorrow would bring. Not just violence; we'd all seen enough of that to be numb to it. But witnessing Rio confront the men who'd shattered her world. Being there as she either found healing or lost herself completely in revenge.

I thought of her methodical preparations, the steady hands checking weapons, the cold determination in her eyes. Maybe this wasn't about healing at all. Maybe this was about restoring balance to a universe that had allowed such cruelty to go unpunished.

Outside, I heard the distinctive rumble of Rio's motorcycle starting up. Likely heading for a long ride to clear her head, to steel herself for tomorrow. I hoped she found whatever peace was possible before the storm broke. Any other man here would be out there telling his woman to get her ass back to the house and sit tight. I couldn't do that to Rio. Was it a risk? Sure. But I also hoped she'd just ride around the compound. If she did venture out, I had no doubt she was armed.

I gathered my notes from the meeting and stood, switching off the harsh overhead lights. In the sudden darkness, tomorrow's actions seemed both more real and distant. Twenty-four hours from now, two men would be facing judgment for crimes they thought they'd escaped. And Rio would either be free of their shadow or bound even tighter to the trauma they'd inflicted.

Either way, I'd be there. That's what family did.

Chapter Seventeen

Rio

The door to Ellis's apartment gave way with a single kick from Renegade. I stepped inside, knife already in hand, my heartbeat steady despite what I was about to do. The stench hit me first -- cigarettes, sweat, and fear. Ellis's eyes widened when he saw me, panic setting in. Good. The asshole remembered our previous conversation. I wanted him to know exactly why I was here.

"What the fuck?" Ellis backed up, his hand instinctively reaching toward the coffee table where a pistol lay.

Rebel moved faster, snatching the gun and tucking it into his waistband. "Nuh-uh. You won't be needing this."

I took in the cramped apartment. Dirty clothes piled in corners. Fast food containers stacked on every surface. The blinds drawn tight. A fitting hole for a rat like Ellis.

"Private Ellis," I said, my voice unnaturally calm.

He swallowed hard, Adam's apple bobbing in his skinny neck. "Look, Rio, I don't know what you think --"

"She thinks you drugged her, asshole," Renegade said from behind me. "She thinks you held her down while your buddy Denton took his turn. And then you took yours. You may have gotten a reprieve last time, but now it's time to pay the price for your crime. She let you go before, and yet here you are. You were supposed to be in prison. Not living a new life."

Ellis's eyes darted between the three of us. Me with my knife. Rebel leaning against the wall, looking bored but alert. And Renegade, blocking the door.

"That's… that's crazy talk," Ellis stammered. "I never touched you."

I took a step closer. This fucker! Was he really going to pretend none of it happened? What the hell! "You're right. You didn't touch me. You wore gloves, and a condom." Another step. "You didn't want to leave evidence."

"Look --"

I flipped the knife in my hand, the blade catching the dim light from the single lamp in the corner. "I gave you time to tidy up your life, make any preparations. I hope you used the time wisely."

"You got no proof," Ellis blustered, but his voice wavered. His eyes kept tracking the knife in my hand. "Didn't even show up for the hearing. So who's to say anything ever happened to you?"

"You think I don't know you were dishonorably discharged?" I asked.

He sneered. "What of it? Doesn't mean it was all about you. Like I said, you don't have any proof either of us touched you."

"Don't need proof," I said. "Not anymore."

His back hit the wall. Nowhere left to go. "Listen," he said, forcing a smile that looked more like a grimace. "There's been a misunderstanding. We can work this out."

"Work it out?" I laughed, a cold, hollow sound that surprised even me. "The way you 'worked out' what to do with me when I couldn't fight back?"

I saw the moment he realized talking wouldn't save him. Hadn't worked for him last time, but I'd already learned this one wasn't all that smart. His eyes hardened, and he lunged at me, trying to grab my wrist, to wrestle the knife away.

I sidestepped. Easy. He was nowhere near as

good as me. Without drugs in my system, I had the upper hand. I slashed, opening a line across his forearm.

He cried out, clutching the wound.

"That's just the beginning," I said.

He charged again, desperate now. I drove my knee into his stomach, doubling him over, then brought the handle of the knife down hard on the back of his head. He crashed into the coffee table, sending beer cans and an ashtray flying.

"You think you can just walk in here --" he started, scrambling to his feet.

I didn't let him finish. The knife found his shoulder, sinking in deep. I twisted, feeling muscles tear. His scream filled the small space.

"You can't win against me now that I'm not drugged," I hissed in his ear as I yanked the blade free. "I made a mistake last time. Shouldn't have let you go. How does it feel to be the helpless one?"

Blood bloomed across his shirt. He stumbled back, eyes wide with terror. "Please," he begged. "I'm sorry. I didn't -- it wasn't my idea --"

"Shut up." I slashed again, catching him across the chest. Not deep enough to kill. Not yet. "Every word out of your mouth is another cut."

He tried to run, to push past Renegade, but the biker clotheslined him, sending him crashing back into the room. Ellis landed hard on his back, the air rushing from his lungs in a pained whoosh.

I straddled him, pinning his arms with my knees. The knife hovered above his face.

"Remember how you laughed?" I asked, my voice trembling with rage. "How you and Denton high-fived over my body like I was nothing but a piece of meat?"

"No, I don't -- I can't --"

I pressed the tip of the blade against his cheek, just hard enough to dimple the skin without breaking it. "Liar."

Tears leaked from the corners of his eyes. "Please. I've got money. I can pay you."

"You think this is about money?" The knife sliced down, opening his cheek from eye to jaw. His screams turned to sobs. "You can't buy your way out of this."

Blood ran freely now, staining the dirty carpet beneath us. I felt nothing but cold determination as I worked. Another slash across his chest. A stab to his thigh. Non-fatal wounds, prolonging his suffering.

Behind me, I could hear Rebel whistling softly, the sound incongruously cheerful against Ellis's cries for mercy.

"She's good," he remarked to no one in particular. "But, baby, might not want to drag this out too much."

Ellis's pleas grew weaker as blood loss took its toll. His eyes, once bright with fear, began to dull.

I leaned close, my mouth near his ear. "I want you to know something before you die," I whispered. "You're not going to be the only one to die today."

His eyes widened at that, a flicker of understanding before resignation.

I stood up, wiping the knife clean on his shirt. Then I reached behind me, where Rebel already had my gun ready. He placed it in my hand with a nod of approval.

"Time's up," I said, aiming between Ellis's eyes.

He didn't beg anymore. Just stared, defeated.

I pulled the trigger, the sound muffled by the silencer. Ellis's head snapped back, then he went completely still.

For a moment, none of us moved. I stared at Ellis's body, not feeling the relief I thought I would. Maybe once Denton was gone too.

"You good?" Renegade asked, his hand on my shoulder.

I nodded, not trusting my voice.

Rebel stepped forward, checking Ellis's pulse out of habit rather than necessity. The hole in his forehead told us everything we needed to know.

"Clean," he pronounced. "One shot. No suffering."

"More than he deserved," I said, my voice steadier than I felt.

"Maybe." Rebel's gaze met mine. "But you're better than him. Remember that."

I handed the gun back to him, and he tucked it away with practiced ease.

"One down," Renegade said. "One to go."

I took a deep breath, steadying myself. "Then let's go find Denton."

As we left Ellis's apartment, I didn't look back. His body would be found eventually, but by then we'd be long gone. Hopefully the police would write it off as a drug deal gone wrong, or a gambling debt unpaid. I didn't really care right now. Fury was pulsing inside me, and I refused to stop. I'd deal with the consequences of my actions later.

Justice, in this case, wouldn't come from the law. It would come from me. And I wasn't finished yet.

* * *

Denton's apartment was the opposite of Ellis's -- spotless, organized, with harsh fluorescent lights that left nowhere to hide. The clinical precision of it made my skin crawl. This wasn't the lair of a disorganized predator like Ellis; this was the domain of someone who planned meticulously, who left no evidence, who thought himself untouchable. I stepped over the threshold, my clothes still damp with Ellis's blood and felt Rebel's reassuring presence at my back.

"Nice place," Rebel whispered, running a finger along a perfectly aligned row of books. "Psychopath neat."

He wasn't wrong. Everything had its place -- shoes lined up by the door, mail sorted in a metal basket, kitchen counters empty of all but a coffee maker that gleamed under the overhead lights. No photos. No personal touches. Just order for order's sake.

"He's here," Renegade said, nodding toward a sliver of light visible beneath a closed door.

I gripped my knife tighter, the handle still sticky from Ellis. My heart thundered against my ribs, but my hands remained steady. One more. One more and it would be over.

Renegade touched my shoulder. "You don't have to do this one," he said softly. "We can handle it."

I shook my head. "No. It has to be me."

He nodded, understanding in his eyes. This wasn't just about revenge; it was about reclaiming what they'd taken from me. My power. My choice.

I moved toward the door. Denton was different from Ellis, which meant sneaking up on him. And it had to be now. If he knew Ellis was dead, he'd be more on guard. Right now, Denton had no idea I'd found him.

I pushed the door open with my foot, staying to the side in case he started shooting immediately.

Sergeant Denton stood by his bedroom window, a gun already in his hand. Unlike Ellis, there was no fear in his eyes -- just cold calculation as he assessed the three of us. I didn't see a brace or cast on his leg. I'd thought for sure something had broken before. Maybe the damage hadn't been as severe as I'd thought.

"I was wondering when you'd show up," he said, his voice as empty of emotion as his apartment was of warmth.

"Sorry to keep you waiting," I said.

His eyes narrowed, taking in my bloodstained clothes, the knife in my hand. "You've got no idea what you're doing. I'm not like Ellis. I'm not some jumped-up private who pisses himself at the first sign of trouble."

"No," I agreed. "You're worse. You're the one who orchestrated it all. The one who picked the target. The one who taught Ellis what to do."

Something flickered across his face -- surprise that I figured it all out, perhaps.

"The drugs were supposed to make sure you didn't remember anything," he said, confirming my suspicions. "Most of them don't."

"Most of them," I repeated, bile rising in my throat. "How many?"

He shrugged, as if we were discussing the weather rather than his crimes. "Does it matter? You won't leave here alive to tell anyone."

"Confident for a man outnumbered three to one," Rebel remarked.

Denton's smile grew colder. "I wasn't just a sergeant. Grew up in a rough neighborhood. Learned a lot from the gangs in the area. I've killed better men than you with less effort than it takes to tie my shoes."

"But have you ever killed someone who's already dead inside?" I asked, taking a step toward him. "Because that's what you did to me that night.

You killed something in me. And now, there's nothing left to lose."

His eyes flickered -- the first sign of uncertainty. Good. I wanted him off-balance.

"Put the gun down," I said. "Face me. Or are you only brave when your victims are drugged and helpless?"

His jaw tightened at the taunt. Pride. His weakness.

"You want a fair fight?" he asked. "Fine." He placed the gun on the nightstand -- still within reach, but a gesture of confidence. "Let's see what you've got."

I moved into the room, aware of Renegade and Rebel spreading out behind me, blocking any escape. This was my fight, but they were my backup.

Denton lunged without warning, faster than Ellis had been, more coordinated. His fist caught my jaw, sending me stumbling back. Stars exploded across my vision.

"Rio!" Rebel stepped forward, but I held up a hand.

"No. I've got this."

Denton smirked. "Do you?"

I spat blood onto his pristine floor. "Yeah. I do."

He came at me again, but this time I was ready. I sidestepped, slashing with the knife as he passed. He hissed as the blade opened a cut along his ribs.

"I'm just getting started," I said.

His face contorted with rage. Gone was the cold calculation. Now he attacked with fury, throwing punches and kicks in quick succession. I blocked some, took others, giving ground strategically.

He was good -- better than Ellis by far. But he was older, slower. And I had rage fueling every move.

I ducked under a wild swing and drove my knee into his stomach. He doubled over, and I brought the knife down toward his exposed neck.

He caught my wrist at the last moment, twisting hard. Pain shot up my arm, and the knife clattered to the floor.

"Not so tough now," he growled, forcing me back against the wall.

I headbutted him, feeling his nose crunch under the impact. Blood gushed down his face.

He staggered back, cursing. I followed, landing a solid kick to his knee. Something popped, and he went down hard.

I scrambled for the knife, but he grabbed my ankle, yanking me off balance. I hit the floor, the impact knocking the wind from my lungs.

Denton crawled over me, his blood dripping onto my face as he wrapped his hands around my throat.

"I should have killed you that night," he snarled, squeezing. "Should have snapped your neck when we were done with you."

Black spots danced at the edges of my vision. Behind him, I saw Rebel step forward, ready to intervene.

No. This was my fight.

I drove my thumbs into Denton's eyes. He screamed, releasing my throat to protect his face. I bucked, throwing him off, then rolled away, gasping for air.

"Fucking bitch!" He lunged for his gun on the nightstand.

I wasn't fast enough to stop him. But Rebel was. He kicked the nightstand, sending the gun skittering across the floor.

Denton changed direction, diving for the weapon. I tackled him from behind, driving him into the floor. We wrestled for control, rolling across the room, leaving smears of blood on his perfect white walls.

My muscles burned with exertion. My lungs ached. But I wouldn't stop. Couldn't stop.

"You're dead," Denton panted, managing to flip me onto my back. He pinned my arms with his knees, exactly as I had done to Ellis. "You hear me? Dead."

I saw Renegade pick up the fallen gun. He didn't interfere, just stood ready, waiting for my signal.

"Throw it," I gasped.

He understood immediately, but instead of throwing it, he slid the gun across the floor toward me.

Denton's head turned at the sound, giving me the opening I needed. I bucked hard, throwing him off balance, then lunged for the weapon.

My fingers closed around the grip. I aimed and fired in one fluid motion.

The bullet caught Denton between the eyes, just like Ellis. His expression of rage froze, then slackened as his body collapsed beside me.

I lay there, gun still raised, staring at the ceiling. The pristine white was now splattered with red. Like everything Denton touched, it was ruined.

Then something broke inside me. A dam bursting after holding back too much for too long. I curled onto my side, still clutching the gun, and began to sob -- harsh, ugly sounds that tore from my throat like they were being ripped out.

"Rio." Rebel's voice, gentler than I'd ever heard it. He knelt beside me, carefully prying the gun from my fingers. "You did good. It's over."

I couldn't stop shaking. Couldn't stop the tears.

Months of pain and rage and fear poured out of me as I lay in a pool of my enemy's blood.

Renegade crouched on my other side, his hand warm on my shoulder. He didn't speak, just offered his silent strength as I fell apart. He stood after a moment and moved around the apartment, pulling blinds, checking outside. "We're clear. No one's called in a disturbance or found Ellis's body. If they had, Shade would have alerted us. But we need to move soon."

I tried to sit up, but my body wouldn't cooperate. Everything hurt -- inside and out.

"I can't," I whispered. "I can't move."

"You don't have to," Rebel said. "We've got you."

He lifted me easily, cradling me against his chest like I weighed nothing. I buried my face in his shoulder, breathing in his familiar scent.

"It's over," he murmured in my ear. "You got them both. No one will ever hurt you like that again."

Renegade gathered my knife, wiping it clean on Denton's shirt. "I'll sweep for prints and call in a cleaning crew," he said. "You get her to the car. If we run out of time, maybe we can make it look like they killed each other. Rivals. Bad blood. Or maybe they pissed off the same person. Just not Rio."

I could tell this was a scenario they'd dealt with before. Probably many times. Cleaning crew? I had a feeling if the police weren't notified anytime soon, Shade or someone else would find a way to make this whole issue disappear... or at least keep it from involving any of us.

Rebel nodded, carrying me toward the door. "We'll be waiting downstairs."

As we left Denton's apartment, I felt strangely hollow. The rage that had sustained me through both killings was gone, leaving only exhaustion in its wake.

"Did it help?" Rebel asked as he took the stairs down. "Killing them?"

I thought about it, about the momentary satisfaction when they realized they weren't getting away with what they'd done. About the emptiness that followed.

"No," I admitted. "But it needed to be done."

He kissed the top of my head. "That's why we did it together. Some burdens are too heavy to carry alone."

Outside, the night air was cool against my tear-streaked face. Rebel set me gently in the back seat of the waiting SUV, then slid in beside me, pulling me against him.

"Rest," he said. "By the time you wake up, this will all be behind us."

I closed my eyes, feeling the weight of what I'd done settling into my bones. Ellis and Denton were gone. They couldn't hurt anyone else. But the memories remained.

"It wasn't just about revenge," I whispered, needing him to understand.

"I know," Rebel said. "Sleep now. Tomorrow, we start our lives together without this dark cloud over our heads."

As the car pulled away from the curb, I let exhaustion claim me, knowing that when I awoke, my family -- my real family -- would still be there, standing guard against the darkness that had almost consumed me.

Chapter Eighteen

Rio

I stood in the dingy back room of the clubhouse, sweat beading at my temples despite the chill from the air conditioner. Shade hunched over his keyboard, his fingers moving with practiced precision across the keys. The blue glow from the bank of monitors cast harsh shadows across his face. I shifted my weight, the floorboard creaking beneath my boots, but Shade didn't look up -- too lost in his digital world to notice anything as mundane as another human being.

"How long?" I asked, my voice sounding rough even to my own ears.

Shade held up a finger, asking for silence without bothering to speak. Five screens surrounded him, each displaying different information -- maps, code windows, spreadsheets filled with numbers that meant nothing to me. The constant hum of cooling fans provided a mechanical backdrop to our mission. With everything going on, Charming had insisted he move everything to the clubhouse. And since Shade didn't want half the club at his house, he'd readily agreed.

I moved closer, gripping the edge of the table beside his workstation. My knuckles went white with tension. Three days had passed since I'd exacted justice, and we were running out of time. By some miracle, the assholes hadn't been missed yet.

"Almost there," Shade muttered, pushing his glasses higher on his nose. Despite being in his sixties, his fingers moved with the agility of someone half his age. I knew he'd been working on this issue off and on since I got back to the compound after dealing with Ellis and Denton. "Digital breadcrumbs. That's the key."

"In English, Shade."

He finally turned to face me, the screens reflecting in his hazel eyes. "We need to make it look like they left of their own accord. Ticket purchases. Hotel bookings. ATM withdrawals in strategic locations." He pointed to one screen showing a global map with red dots scattered across several countries. "Non-extradition countries where our targets supposedly fled."

The clubhouse walls seemed to close in around me. Somewhere in the main room, music played and people laughed, but back here, in Shade's digital cave, the world narrowed to just us and the problem we needed to solve.

"Show me again," I said, pulling up a chair.

Shade nodded and clicked on one of his spreadsheets. "These are the targets. Your two Army assholes. Ellis and Denton. If they show up dead, you're going to be at the top of the list of suspects. You have a connection with them, a rotten history, and you have military training. I don't think even the best lawyer in the country could get you out of this one."

I leaned closer, studying the name. "What's the timeline?"

"I've already started laying the groundwork." Shade clicked to another screen showing airline booking confirmations. "Twenty-four hours ago, Ellis supposedly bought a ticket to Venezuela. Used his own credit card too." He smirked, the closest thing to emotion I'd seen from him today. "But, there's a chance people will be watching for him. So I'm going to do a bit more work. We need them to think Denton paid someone under the table to use a private jet to leave the country. Anyone searching may assume Ellis went with him."

"Can they trace it back to you? Or what about security footage wherever this plane is supposedly located?"

Shade gave me a look that made me feel stupid for asking. "I've been doing this for decades, kid. Trust me, they'll find exactly what I want them to find. As for cameras, it's such a shame they won't be operational the day of the supposed flight."

I nodded, not entirely convinced but knowing I had no choice. "What about the bodies from the warehouse that first time we went up against the Morettis? Did you do something similar?"

His fingers flew across the keyboard, bringing up more booking confirmations. "Two to Thailand. One to Belize. Two to Morocco. And another to Montenegro." He pointed to the center screen. "Different departure times, different airlines. Some took connecting flights. Makes it harder to track. And by the time anyone goes looking, I'll have scrubbed any airport footage. And to answer your other question, I do this type of thing more often than you probably think."

"And these countries wouldn't send them back?"

"No." Shade paused his typing to take a sip from a mug of coffee that had probably been sitting there since morning. "But they won't need to, because these seven men aren't actually in those countries. We just need the law to believe they are."

I tightened my grip on the table edge. "And the evidence?"

Shade's eyes gleamed with something like pride. "I'm fabricating digital trails as we speak. Hotel check-ins. Restaurant charges. Even social media activity that looks like it's coming from those locations." He pulled up a program I didn't recognize. "This little beauty spoofs IP addresses. To anyone checking, it'll look like our guys are posting from Internet cafes in Caracas or Bangkok."

"What about CCTV? Airport cameras? How are you handling those? You said you'd scrub the footage, but I don't know what that means."

He gestured to a screen running what looked like facial recognition software. "I've got programs searching for people who look similar enough. They won't hold up to serious scrutiny, but it should be enough to create reasonable doubt. And where I can't find any, I'll just make sure the footage is damaged during those times."

The weight of what we were doing pressed down on me. "What if there are real criminals there?"

"I'm also checking for that while scanning faces. If anyone pops up who's on a wanted list somewhere, I'll know about it. Then I'll figure out something else."

"And what about..."

He held up a hand to stop me. "Go. I need to concentrate."

I stood to leave but hesitated. The thought of fabricating evidence made my stomach turn. But I also knew it was necessary. The men who'd died were all evil bastards. We had nothing to feel guilty about. Right?

"One more thing," he said before I could leave. "I've planted a few mistakes. Small ones. Intentional."

"Mistakes? Like shit that will come back to haunt us?" I asked.

He just stared for a moment not answering my question.

"Why the hell would you do that?" I pressed.

Shade leaned back in his chair, the springs creaking. "Perfect cover stories raise red flags. People make mistakes. They get drunk and use their credit card at the wrong place. They forget to turn off location services on their phone. These little errors make the story believable. These two, if they really did flee like this, might get sloppy along the way. Planting those *mistakes* makes it more believable."

I nodded, understanding his logic but not liking it. "How big are these mistakes?"

"Small enough to be written off as human error. Big enough to be found by someone looking." He turned back to his screens. "It's a balancing act."

Just as I reached the door, Shade called out, "Rio."

I turned. "Yeah?"

"If anyone asks, I've been teaching you poker strategies all afternoon. We never discussed this."

"What's my tell?" I asked.

His mouth twitched. "You touch your left ear when you're bluffing."

I fought the urge to reach for my ear. "Good to know."

Shade returned to his work, already forgetting my presence. I watched him for a moment longer before stepping back into the main part of the clubhouse.

"Wait," he called just as I opened the door. I turned back one last time.

Shade didn't look up from his screens, but his voice was deadly serious. "I'll rig it so they look like they've defected to non-extradition countries but remember -- if the feds dig deep enough, this house of cards could collapse."

I nodded, the gravity of his words settling on my shoulders like a physical weight. "How long will it hold?"

"Long enough," he said, his fingers already back

to dancing across the keyboard. "Sooner or later, they'll shuffle these off to a cold case file and focus on the next big thing."

The rhythmic clicking of Shade's typing followed me out the door. In the hallway, I paused to collect myself, straightened my shoulders and headed toward the main room. How the hell did these men do this? It was my first time and I was a nervous wreck. If I had to do this too many times, I'd likely have a heart attack.

* * *

I spotted Rebel, leaning against the wall near the hallway junction, his gaze finding mine with laser focus. Something in his expression made my breath catch -- a determination that hadn't been there this morning. Without a word, he pushed off the wall and jerked his head toward one of the rooms. I followed.

"What's going on?" I asked as we stepped into one of the rooms that had once been a bedroom. When I'd asked about them before, Rebel had told me there had been a time everyone stayed at the clubhouse. Back when the club was still new-ish.

"Something that can't wait," he said, his words clipped.

Rebel gestured for me to sit, but I shook my head. Whatever this was, I'd face it standing.

"Spit it out," I said, crossing my arms. "What's so urgent?"

He ran a hand through his hair -- a nervous gesture I'd rarely seen from him. Rebel didn't do nervous. He was cocky, borderline arrogant, with the fighting skills to back it up. Seeing him this way set my nerves on edge.

He opened his palm, revealing a small silver ring. It wasn't new or flashy -- the band was worn in places, with a simple design etched into the metal. It looked old, possibly vintage.

"What is that?" I asked, though I had my suspicions.

"It was my grandmother's," he said, turning it between his fingers. "One of the few things I have from before... everything. My mom wore it until the day she died. When Dad died, I found it in his dresser drawer."

He rarely talked about his past, but I knew the broad strokes -- enough to understand what this ring represented to him.

"Rebel --" I started, but he cut me off.

"Dixon," he corrected softly. "It's just us here."

"Dixon," I tried again. "What are you doing?"

He stepped closer, close enough that I could smell the leather of his cut and the faint scent of his soap. "What I should have done the moment you agreed to be my old lady."

My heart hammered against my ribs. "Are you doing what I think you're doing?"

A sardonic smile crossed his face. "You know how I take my coffee, which side of the bed I sleep on, and that I talk in my sleep sometimes."

"That's not --"

"You know I check my gun twice before I holster it. You know I can't stand the taste of cilantro." His voice dropped. "And I know you sleep with a knife under your pillow. I know you sing in the shower when you think no one can hear. I know you're braver than half the patched members in this club."

His words wrapped around me, uncomfortably accurate. The intimacy between us had crept in during our time together -- in shared meals, in quiet conversations in the early morning hours, in the way he always seemed to appear when my anxiety was spiking.

"This isn't about romance," he continued, though his eyes said otherwise. "But to be clear, I care about you a lot."

I glanced at the ring again. "And what exactly does that mean in club terms? Charming already ordered a property cut."

"It means you're officially mine. Not just in the eyes of the club. But also in the eyes of the law." The possessiveness in his voice should have bothered me, but instead, it sent a different kind of shiver down my spine.

I swallowed hard. "And what does the club think about this sort of thing?"

"Most of the couples are married. Although, to be fair, Shade learned a few bad habits from Wire and Lavender over at the Dixie Reapers. He has a tendency to hack into vital records and marry people without their knowledge."

That surprised me. Not so much Shade's hacking skills, but the fact most of the couples were actually married.

"There are other benefits," Rebel added. "Legal protections. If something happens to me, you'd be entitled to my share of club earnings, my bike, my place. And the life insurance money. Yes, I have a policy. It's not a million bucks, but it's enough."

"Don't." The word came out sharper than I intended. "Don't talk about you dying."

His expression softened. "It's the reality of this life, Rio. You know that."

I did know. Had known every time he'd left on club business with a gun tucked into his waistband. Had known when I'd stepped into the fray with him.

"What about what I want?" I asked, needing to assert some control over what felt like a runaway train.

His confidence faltered for the first time. "What do you want?"

That was the question, wasn't it? Once my dream had been a military career. Of course, that would have been easier if the men in charge of such things hadn't found ways to hold me back. Then I'd been discharged and decided to travel. Now I was living in a motorcycle club compound, helping in any way I could, and contemplating tying myself permanently to a man who walked the edge of the law daily.

And yet, the thought of a mundane law-abiding life seemed impossible. Hollow.

"I want..." I started, then stopped, searching for the right words. "I want to not be afraid anymore. To not be alone."

Rebel stepped closer, close enough that I had to tilt my head to maintain eye contact. "I promise to always keep you safe," he said, his voice low and intense. "To be by your side as long as I can. Whatever it takes."

The sincerity in his eyes made my chest ache. "You could go out on a mission tomorrow and not make it back."

"That's why I said for as long as I can." He took my hand, his calloused fingers warm against mine. "I'm not asking for forever, Rio. I'm asking for however long we're both alive. Forever is just a fairy tale. This is real life."

The ring caught the light again as he held it between us. It was nothing like I'd ever imagined for myself -- no diamond, no proposal on one knee, no romantic setting. Instead, it was a worn silver band, a promise of protection, and a man whose dangerous life had become intertwined with mine through circumstance and choice.

"Yes or no?" he asked, the confidence back in his voice but vulnerability in his eyes.

I looked at the ring, then at him. This was my reality now -- this club, these people, this man. Somewhere along the way, I'd started to fall in love with him. Even if I hadn't said the words yet. I'd not been the sentimental type since I'd lost my mom. I'd tell him one day. I held out my left hand. "Yes."

The relief that washed over his face was almost comical, like he'd genuinely expected me to say no. He slid the ring onto my finger -- it was slightly loose, but not enough to fall off.

"We can get it sized," he said, noticing.

I shook my head. "It's perfect."

He lifted my hand to his lips, pressing a kiss to my knuckles just above the ring. The gesture was surprisingly tender from a man I knew could break another man's jaw with a single punch.

"We should tell Charming," I said. "Isn't this the sort of thing he needs to know?"

Rebel nodded but didn't release my hand. "In a minute."

He pulled me closer, one arm sliding around my waist as his other hand cupped my cheek. His kiss was gentle at first, then deepened with a hunger that matched the urgency of everything else that seemed to happen to us, or around us.

When we finally broke apart, I rested my forehead against his chest, feeling the steady beat of his heart beneath his shirt.

"So," I said, trying to regain my composure. "Mrs. Rebel. That has a certain ring to it."

His laugh rumbled through his chest. He tilted my chin up. "It's Mrs. Morreli, but you already know that. Though if you want to keep your name, I won't stop you."

My fingers found the ring, turning it on my finger -- a new habit already forming. Mrs. Morreli. I liked it.

"Come on," Rebel said, taking my hand again. "Let's go find Charming."

As we headed back toward the stairs, the ring on my finger caught the light once more -- a small but significant weight, a tangible symbol of how completely my life had changed since I'd arrived here.

Rebel led me back to the main room, my hand firmly clasped in his. The noise hit us like a physical wall -- music cranked to eleven, laughter, the clash of bottles and glasses. He paused, his gaze searching mine. "Ready?"

I nodded, my fingers instinctively touching the silver band on my left hand. The celebration rolled over us like a wave. Judging by the smiles and knowing looks, someone had tipped them off. Of course they had. Nothing stayed secret in this clubhouse for long.

The main room of the Devil's Boneyard clubhouse pulsed with energy. Bodies pressed together, the smell of leather, whiskey, and cigarettes creating the distinctive scent I'd come to associate with safety. The speakers blared rock, though the melody was nearly drowned out by the roar of voices.

"There they are!" someone shouted, and suddenly all eyes turned our way.

Rebel's hand tightened around mine. For all his cockiness, I could feel the tension radiating from him. This was a big step for him too. In the club's world, what you loved could be used against you. And I could tell, without him saying anything, he loved me. It might not be the fairytale kind some women dreamed of, but I didn't need all that. All I needed was Rebel.

A path cleared through the crowd as Charming approached us. He stopped a few feet away, looking between us before his gaze dropped to my hand.

"So he finally did it," Charming said, his deep voice carrying even over the noise. "About damn time."

A cheer went up from the gathered members. Rebel's chest expanded beside me, pride straightening his spine.

"You got something to say to me about it?" Rebel challenged.

Charming's mouth twitched. "Yeah. Your taste in women is better than your taste in bikes." He turned to me. "You sure about this one, Rio? Not too late to upgrade to someone who doesn't snore like a chainsaw."

The laughter that followed eased some of the tension in my shoulders. This was how they showed acceptance -- rough humor and gentle ribbing.

"I'll take my chances," I replied, squeezing Rebel's hand.

Charming nodded, then his expression shifted to something more serious. "We got business to handle first," he said, glancing around the room. "Everyone's here?"

A chorus of affirmations rang out.

"Good." He turned back to us. "Shade filled me in on the timeline. We've got moves to make tonight, but before that --" He gestured to a table near the bar where something lay folded. "We've got a proper welcome to give."

Rebel guided me forward, his hand moving to the small of my back. The crowd parted again, giving us a clear path to the table. As we got closer, I saw what waited there -- a leather cut, smaller than the men's versions but unmistakably a Devil's Boneyard vest.

My breath caught. I hadn't expected this. Not today anyway. They'd said I'd have it quite a while ago, but one thing after another happened and it kept getting pushed off. I'd honestly forgotten about it. It made sense something like this would have been at the bottom of their to-do list.

Charming picked it up, holding it so I could see the front. *Devil's Boneyard MC*. And under that, my name. Then he turned it around. The club's emblem -- a stylized skull with horns -- was embroidered in the center. Unlike the men's cuts, this one said "Devil's Boneyard" on the top rocker and "Property of Rebel" on the bottom one.

In the recent past, I might have bristled at the word "property," but I understood the club culture enough now to know what it really meant -- protection, respect, belonging. It didn't mean he owned me. But it did mean I would be cherished by Rebel.

"In the years I've led this club, and the ones prior to that as a patched member," Charming said, his voice carrying across the now-quiet room, "I've seen members come and go. I've seen old ladies stand by their men through hell itself. But there's only ever been one that was close to the same fire as you." His eyes met mine. "You've proven yourself loyal. You've earned your place."

He extended the cut toward me. "This marks you as one of us. Anyone messes with you, they mess with the entire Devil's Boneyard MC. Welcome to the family."

My hands trembled slightly as I reached for the cut. The leather was soft, well-worked, with the weight of significance behind it. Rebel stepped back, giving me space for this moment.

I slipped the cut on over my T-shirt, feeling the leather settle on my shoulders. It fit perfectly -- someone had taken care to get my measurements right. The room erupted in cheers and whistles as I adjusted the front.

Rebel moved back to my side, his arm sliding around my waist, possessive and proud. "Looks good on you," he murmured in my ear.

The formality broken, members surged forward. Hands clapped Rebel on the back, voices called congratulations, bottles of beer and shots of whiskey were thrust toward us. The celebration hit full swing, raw and unfiltered.

"Never thought I'd see the day," said a gruff voice to my left. I turned to find Shade, who had apparently emerged from his digital cave for the occasion. "Rebel officially settling down. Hell must be freezing over."

Rebel flipped him off good-naturedly. "Just because you're married to your computers doesn't mean the rest of us can't find happiness with actual humans."

Shade raised his beer in acknowledgment, then locked eyes with me. "You need anything, electronic or otherwise, you come to me. You're family now."

The simple words hit harder than I expected. Family. I'd been alone for so long. Now things were different.

A throat cleared behind us, and I turned to find Samurai standing there. The Japanese member was one of the more intimidating figures in the club, not just for his physical presence but for his quiet intensity. His tattooed arms were folded across his chest, his expression as stoic as ever.

"Samurai," Rebel acknowledged with a respectful nod.

The man's gaze moved from Rebel to me, then to the ring on my finger, and finally to the property cut I now wore. Something shifted in his expression -- the barest softening around his eyes.

"You chose well," he said to Rebel, his voice measured. Then to me: "And so did you."

He raised his glass in a silent toast before drifting back toward the bar. From Samurai, those few words were equivalent to an hour-long speech from anyone else.

"Damn," Rebel whispered. "High praise."

Music surged louder as someone cranked it a few notches. The celebration shifted into higher gear, taking on the feeling of stolen time -- joy snatched in the midst of danger. Everyone in the room knew that after tonight, things would move fast. Shade might have thrown people off with his digital breadcrumbs, as he'd called them, for Ellis and Denton. But I had a feeling things with the Moretti and Vata weren't completely over. And who knew what else would head our way?

But for now, there was this moment.

Charming reappeared at my elbow, pressing a shot glass into my hand. "Club tradition," he explained. "New family drinks with the President."

I took the glass, sniffing it cautiously. Tequila.

"To family," Charming said, raising his glass. "And to outlasting our enemies."

Rebel and I echoed the toast, and we all downed our shots. The liquor burned a trail down my throat, settling warm in my stomach.

"Now," Charming said, all business again as he

set down his empty glass. "Shade tells me we have an hour before he should have things wrapped up with his latest trails for Ellis and Denton. After that, you should be in the clear."

I nodded. I leaned against Rebel's solid warmth.

His arm tightened around me. "Welcome to club life, babe. Never a dull moment."

A loud crash from the bar drew our attention as two younger members started wrestling, knocking over stools in their enthusiastic celebration. Their laughter rang out as others egged them on.

"Should we stop them?" I asked.

Rebel shook his head. "Let them blow off steam."

Another member approached, this one with a camera. "Gotta document the historic moment," he insisted. "Rebel finally claimed."

Rebel pulled me against his side, his hand possessively on my hip. I felt the eyes of the room on us -- some curious, some approving, some calculating. My left hand came up instinctively to rest on Rebel's chest, the silver ring catching the light.

The flash went off, immortalizing the moment.

"One for the wall," the photographer said, gesturing to the clubhouse wall where dozens of photos chronicled the club's history.

I looked at that wall -- fights won, brothers lost, celebrations and mourning captured in faded photographs. Soon our picture would join them, marking this night as significant enough to be remembered.

Rebel kissed my temple, his lips lingering. "No going back now."

I turned to face him fully, my hands coming up to rest on the leather of his cut, fingers tracing the patches that told his story in the club. "I don't want to go back. I'm right where I belong."

His eyes darkened, and he lowered his head to capture my lips in a kiss that drew whistles and catcalls from around the room. I didn't care. Let them watch. This was my family now, my world -- for better or worse.

Chapter Nineteen

Rebel

I leaned against the kitchen counter, beer in hand, watching Rio tear through my house like a force of nature. She'd been at it for less than two hours and already half my shit was stuffed in trash bags. Before I could ask what she planned to leave, the front door banged open and three of my brothers from the Devil's Boneyard MC piled in with boxes of what looked suspiciously like new furniture.

"What the hell is this?" I asked, straightening up.

Rio flashed me a grin that hit me right in the gut. "Reinforcements."

"You got yourself a woman who's too good for you," said Phantom, dropping a box with a *thud* that shook my floor. "Figured we'd help her whip this place into shape."

I shot Rio a look. "You called in the cavalry."

"Damn right I did." She tossed her strawberry-blonde hair over her shoulder, those blue eyes challenging me to argue. "You want me staying here, want me to make this place a home, then it's out with the old and in with the new."

"But…" I glanced around. If she was going to do this, why hadn't she done it sooner? Then again, we *had* been incredibly busy. With her issue, Java, and dealing with the Morettis and Vata, it hadn't exactly been quiet around here. Or had she been waiting on something more official showing she was mine, like her ring and property cut? Whatever the reason, she could do what she wanted with this place. It was her home too.

The guys laughed, and I couldn't help but smile. Rio had already carved out a place in my life that felt inevitable, like she'd always been meant to be there.

"Move your ass, Rebel," she commanded, pointing to a stack of flattened boxes. "Start packing up that disaster you call a bookshelf."

I saluted sarcastically but did as I was told. Within thirty minutes, my house had transformed into a war zone of activity. Chaos and a new Prospect, Andrew, showed up with an actual couch -- not just any couch, but a deep sectional that looked like it cost more than my bike. When I raised an eyebrow at Rio, she just shrugged.

"I saw an ad in the paper. A man's ex left it behind and he wanted it gone. Got it for a steal."

The music started next -- someone had hooked up a speaker, and the heavy bass of Metallica thrummed through my house. The sound bounced around the space, mixing with laughter and the scrape of furniture across my floor.

"Christ, brother, when's the last time you cleaned under this?" Chaos held up a dust bunny the size of a small animal that he'd discovered under my TV stand.

"That's been there so long it deserves squatter's rights," I shot back, but I felt a twinge of embarrassment as Rio glanced over, her nose wrinkling.

She didn't say anything, just tossed me a roll of trash bags and went back to organizing the kitchen cabinets. That was the thing about Rio -- she called me on my shit without making me feel like garbage. It was refreshing as hell.

More club members streamed in as the evening progressed. Someone ordered pizza -- the good kind, not the cheap shit I usually got. Beer flowed, and the work somehow continued despite the party atmosphere that had developed. My bachelor pad was steadily transforming into something that actually looked like a home.

I caught sight of Rio across the room as she directed two Prospects where to place a bookshelf that had appeared from nowhere. A lock of hair had fallen across her face, and she blew it away with a puff of air, hands on her hips as she surveyed her domain. Something warm expanded in my chest at the sight.

"She's something else," a voice rumbled beside me.

I turned to find Azrael beside me, watching Rio with an appreciative nod.

"Yeah," I agreed. "She is."

"Don't fuck it up," he advised, slapping me on the shoulder hard enough to make me stumble.

The party moved around us like a living thing. Bodies shifted from room to room, carrying boxes, furniture, bags of trash. The rhythm of it was hypnotic -- the thumping music, the constant movement, voices rising and falling in waves of conversation and laughter.

Rio appeared at my side, her shoulder brushing mine. "Stop standing around like a useless lump and help me with these curtains."

I put down my beer. "Yes, ma'am."

She rolled her eyes but smiled. We worked together hanging curtains that actually matched, her directing me where to place the rod while she held them up to check the length.

"Where'd all this stuff come from?" I asked, drilling into the wall above the window.

"Club family, garage sales, and newspaper ads," she said simply. "I mentioned we were fixing up your place, and everyone just... offered things or tracked stuff down."

I paused, drill hovering. "They did that for you?"

Her eyes flashed. "For us, dumbass."

The way she said "us" made something flip in my stomach. I bent to the task, hiding my expression. I'd never been an "us" before and I liked it more than I'd realized.

The door opened again, and the room went briefly quiet. I turned to see Cinder enter, his white beard and hair standing out like a beacon. His wife followed along with another new Prospect, Jaden, carrying something wrapped carefully in a thick blanket. Even at eighty-something, Cinder commanded respect without saying a word. His wife might've been the only person in the club who could boss him around, and she did it with a smile that still lit up his weathered face.

"Place is looking good," Cinder said, his blue eyes taking in the transformation.

"Thanks to Rio," I replied, setting down the drill. "My decorating skills start and end with thrift stores or one of those discount places."

Rio snorted beside me, but I could feel her tense slightly. Cinder intimidated most people, even his own men. I'd seen hardened bikers turn into stammering teenagers under his gaze. Rio, though, just tilted her chin up and met his eyes directly.

Cinder's wife, Meg, stepped forward, smiling. "We brought you something." She nodded to Cinder, who unwrapped the blanket to reveal a rocking chair made of dark, polished wood. It gleamed under the overhead lighting, the craftsmanship obvious even to my untrained eye.

"Holy shit," I breathed.

"Language," Cinder's wife chided, but she was

smiling.

Rio stepped forward, her hand reaching out to touch the smooth arm of the chair. "It's beautiful."

"Cinder made it," his wife said proudly. "Been working on it for weeks."

I looked at Cinder in surprise. His calloused hands hadn't seemed capable of creating something so delicate, so perfect. He shrugged, uncomfortable with the attention. When the fuck had he taken up woodworking?

"Where do you want it?" he asked gruffly.

Rio looked at me, a question in her eyes. It was my house, but we both knew it was becoming ours in every way that mattered.

"By the window," I suggested. "Gets good light in the morning."

Cinder nodded and carried the chair to the spot I'd indicated. He set it down carefully, then stepped back to examine it. The rocking chair looked right in the space, like it had been made specifically for that spot.

"Perfect," Rio said softly.

I caught Cinder's gaze over Rio's head. Something passed between us -- understanding, approval. The chair wasn't just furniture; it was a symbol. A rocking chair meant permanence, a future. It was the kind of thing you kept for generations, the kind of thing that became a family heirloom.

Cinder gave me a slight nod, and I returned it, feeling a quiet surge of something I couldn't quite name. Hope, maybe. Or peace. The chaotic energy of the room continued around us, but in that moment, everything felt still and certain.

Rio's hand found mine, her fingers intertwining with mine in a gesture so natural it felt like we'd been doing it for years instead of weeks. I squeezed gently, and she squeezed back.

By the time the last club member staggered out, my house was unrecognizable. Clean, organized, with nice furniture and decorations that matched. It looked like a place where real adults lived, not the crash pad of a biker.

"What do you think?" Rio asked, surveying our work with her hands on her hips.

I wrapped my arms around her from behind, resting my chin on her shoulder. "I think it looks like a home."

She leaned back against me, her body relaxing into mine. "Yeah," she agreed. "It does."

The rocking chair sat by the window, catching the last light of the evening. I couldn't take my eyes off it, this tangible symbol of the future Rio and I could build together. Something solid and lasting in a life that had always been defined by movement and change.

"Been a while since I had a real home," Rio admitted quietly, following my gaze to the chair.

"Same," I said. "Guess we'll figure it out together."

She turned in my arms, facing me. Her blue eyes searched mine, looking for something I hoped like hell she could find. Whatever she saw must have satisfied her, because she nodded once, decisive.

"Together," she agreed, and sealed it with a kiss that felt like a promise.

* * *

I clicked the deadbolt shut, turning to find Rio already heading toward the bedroom, her hips swaying in a silent invitation. The house -- our house now -- felt different. Quieter. Like it was holding its breath for whatever came next. I followed her, my boots soundless on the new hall rug someone had brought. Even in the dim light spilling from the bedside lamp, I could see the transformation extended to this room -- the mattress now sat on more than a bed frame, with sheets that matched and pillows that weren't flattened from years of use.

Rio stood by the bed, her back to me. The shadows carved her silhouette against the faint light -- strong shoulders, narrow waist, the curve of her hips. She'd changed my life, stormed in and rearranged everything from my furniture to my heart. I hadn't stood a chance.

"You gonna stand there all night?" she asked without turning.

I moved behind her, close enough to feel her warmth but not touching. Not yet. "Just admiring the view."

She glanced over her shoulder, those blue eyes reflecting the lamplight. "Smooth talker."

"Only stating facts." I reached out, fingers hovering just above her hip. "May I touch you?"

Something flickered across her face -- appreciation, trust. She nodded, and I placed my hand on her hip, feeling her lean back into me. We'd been together enough times now that I knew the rules -- ask first, move slow, let her lead. The reasons behind those rules lived in the shadows of her eyes sometimes, in the way she'd flinch at unexpected contact.

"You transformed this place," I said, lips close to her ear.

"We did." Her voice was softer now, the hardness she showed the world melting away in the privacy of our room.

"Never thought I'd have curtains that match the

bedspread." I snorted. "Fuck. Didn't think I'd have a bedspread for that matter."

She laughed, the sound vibrating through her back against my chest. "Low fucking bar, Dixon."

"What can I say? You're raising my standards."

She turned in my arms, face tilted up to mine. "Good."

I waited, watching her eyes. Then I bent to kiss her. The first touch was gentle -- a question more than a demand. Her lips parted beneath mine, and the kiss deepened, became something hungrier. She slid her hands under my cut, pushing it off my shoulders. It hit the floor with a soft *thud*. "Been waiting for this all night," she murmured against my mouth, fingers working on the buttons at the top of my shirt.

"Watching you boss everyone around was pretty hot," I admitted.

"Yeah?" Her smile turned wicked. "You like being bossed around?"

"By you? Maybe."

She pulled my shirt off, palms flat against my chest. "Let's test that theory."

Her touch was confident now, sure. Each time we were together, she grew bolder, more certain. I let her set the pace, responding to her cues. When her hands went to my belt, I covered them with mine. "You sure?" It was something I asked every time, not wanting to assume it was okay.

Her gaze met mine, clear and steady, as she climbed onto the bed. "I'm sure."

The urgency built between us as our clothes found their way to the floor. The dim light painted shadows across her skin, highlighting the scattered freckles that I'd come to memorize. I traced them with my fingertips, then my lips, mapping constellations across her body.

"Dixon," she breathed, her hands in my hair.

My name on her lips never failed to undo me. I moved slower, more deliberately, watching her responses. Her breath hitched when I found a sensitive spot, her back arching when I hit another. Learning her body felt like unlocking a complex puzzle -- infinitely rewarding, endlessly fascinating.

"Tell me what you want," I said against her collarbone.

Her fingers tightened in my hair, directing me. "Here," she whispered. Then, more urgently, "Here."

I followed her lead, letting her guide me. Her breathing grew more ragged, her commands less verbal and more physical -- a tug of my hair, the press of her hand. The world narrowed to just us, the soft sounds of her pleasure, the heat building between us.

I loved seeing her like this, so vulnerable and needy. My hand roamed down her stomach to tease at the entrance of her wet heat, watching as she squirmed under my touch.

"Tell me what you want," I repeated, my voice low and rough.

She gasped, arching her back as if offering herself up to me. "Please... take me."

I slid a finger inside her, feeling the tight grip of her pussy as I began to thrust slowly inside her welcoming warmth.

"Oh God... yes!" She cried out as I felt her nails dig into my shoulders. Thrusting her hips up to meet my movements, she kissed me hungrily. "Harder... please..." she begged between breaths, her words barely audible over the sounds of our passion.

"Not going to manage that with just a finger."

She blinked up at me. "Then use something

else."

I grinned and forced her legs wider apart with my own, making room for my cock at her entrance. I took a moment to admire the sight before me -- her beautiful body begging for my dominance.

"Look at you," I growled, slapping my hardened cock against her soaking wet pussy. "You're so fucking sexy asking for this." With that, I pushed inside her in one swift motion, claiming her tightness for myself.

Her whole body shuddered under my onslaught as I began to pound into her greedy pussy.

"Yes! Oh God yes!" She cried out beneath me, arching her back and meeting every thrust with equal force.

I grabbed her hair, tugging her head back to expose her long neck. I could feel the pulse beating wildly as I planted soft kisses along its length.

"You're mine," I growled into her neck before capturing her mouth once again in a fierce kiss that left us both breathless.

Our bodies moved together in perfect rhythm, the new bed frame creaking slightly under our weight. I could feel her getting closer, her inner walls clenching around me as her breathing became more erratic.

"That's it," I encouraged, my voice strained with the effort of holding back my own release. "Come for me, Rio."

She shattered beneath me, waves of pleasure washing over her. The sight of her coming undone pushed me over the edge, and I followed her into bliss, groaning her name as I emptied myself inside her.

We collapsed together, a tangle of sweaty limbs and ragged breathing. I rolled to the side, pulling her with me so she rested against my chest. Her strawberry-blonde hair tickled, stuck to my beard, and

I brushed it back, pressing a kiss to her forehead.

"Fuck," she mumbled against my skin.

"Yeah," I agreed eloquently, still trying to catch my breath.

We lay in comfortable silence for a while, the sweat cooling on our bodies. Rio's fingers traced patterns on my chest, circling the tattoo over my heart.

"I never thought I'd have this," she said quietly.

"Same."

I watched her face, caught in the raw vulnerability of the moment. Her gaze met mine, and something passed between us -- something deeper than the physical connection.

"Stay with me," she whispered, and I wasn't sure if she meant in that moment or forever.

"Always," I promised, meaning both.

For several minutes, we just breathed together, her head on my chest, my fingers tracing idle patterns on her back. The comfortable silence wrapped around us like a blanket. Outside our window, the sounds of the compound provided a backdrop to our private world -- motorcycle engines going by, occasional voices, the hum of life continuing while we existed in this suspended moment.

I pressed a kiss to the top of her head, inhaling the scent of her hair. She hummed contentedly, her breath warm against my skin.

"You okay?" I asked, the question part of our ritual now.

"More than okay." She propped herself up on an elbow, looking down at me. Her strawberry-blonde hair fell in waves around her face, and I reached up to tuck a strand behind her ear.

"I'll stock up on condoms," I said, the thought occurring to me suddenly. "Been running low."

Something flickered across her face -- uncertainty, maybe. She bit her lower lip, considering her response.

"I mean, we don't have to," I added quickly. "If they're uncomfortable or something…"

"It's not that," she said, sitting up fully now. The sheet pooled around her waist, but she didn't seem to notice or care about her nakedness. "I just…"

I waited, giving her space to find the words. Pushing Rio never worked -- she'd shut down faster than a motorcycle with sugar in the gas tank.

"I love you," I said, the words falling from my lips before I could catch them. I hadn't meant to say it now, like this, but there they were, hanging in the air between us.

Her eyes widened, but she didn't pull away. Progress.

"I love you," I repeated, more firmly this time. "And I want you to set the pace for our future. Whatever that looks like."

She studied me, her blue eyes searching mine like she was looking for the lie, the catch. Finding none, she nodded slowly.

"Maybe someday I'll want children," she said, the words careful, measured. "But I'm not ready yet. I have an implant."

I nodded, keeping my expression neutral despite the surge of emotion her words triggered. She was thinking about our future -- a future with children. Someday.

"I'll have it removed when the time comes," she continued, her voice steadier now. "When I'm ready. When we're ready."

I reached for her hand, threading our fingers together. "No rush. We've got time."

The tension in her shoulders eased slightly. "You don't mind waiting?"

"Rio, before you, I didn't even think about having kids. Ever. Then you tornadoed into my life, and suddenly I'm thinking about shit like what schools they'd go to."

A small smile tugged at her lips. "Tornadoed?"

"It's a word."

"It's really not."

I pulled her back down beside me, her head finding its place on my chest again. "The point is, I'm in no hurry. You decide when or if you're ready. I'm just happy you're considering a future with me in it."

She was quiet for a moment, her fingers tracing the tattoo on my ribs. "Since I have the implant, you don't have to use condoms."

"If you decide you want kids, but don't want to go through a pregnancy, we'll figure it out," I said. "Adoption, surrogacy, whatever. Or just us, with no kids, if that's what you want."

She nodded against my chest, and I felt something wet on my skin. A tear. I pretended not to notice, giving her the dignity of her private emotion.

"I never thought I'd meet someone who'd just… accept me," she said, her voice slightly rough. "All my shit, my damage."

"We've all got damage, darlin'. Mine's just different than yours."

She lifted her head, her eyes shining but fierce. "Don't minimize what I'm trying to say, asshole."

I grinned. "There's my girl."

She smacked my chest lightly but settled back against me. "I'm trying to tell you I love you too, dickhead."

The words hit me like a physical blow, stealing

my breath. I'd hoped but hearing her say it made everything real in a way it hadn't been before.

"Say it again," I murmured into her hair.

"I love you." Clearer this time, no hesitation. "God help me."

I laughed, the sound rumbling through my chest. "God help us both."

We lay there in the dim light, the newly transformed bedroom a cocoon around us. Rio's breathing gradually slowed, deepened as she drifted toward sleep. I stayed awake, my hand stroking her back in slow, gentle circles. The night wrapped around us, quiet and full of possibility. In the morning, we'd face the world -- her demons, my responsibilities to the club, the everyday challenges of building a life together. But for now, in this raw, vulnerable moment, there was just us. Just this.

Our shared journey had just begun.

Epilogue

My hands trembled as I smoothed down the front of my wedding dress. Not from fear, but from the weight of the moment. Outside, the rumble of motorcycles announced more arrivals to the compound. The Devil's Boneyard MC didn't do traditional weddings, but they did do family and today was about making official what we all already knew -- Rebel and I belonged to each other. I took a deep breath, the smell of the makeshift dressing room in the clubhouse strangely comforting as I prepared to walk out and bind my life to a man who lived as dangerously as his name suggested.

The dress wasn't white. That would've been a joke. Instead, I'd chosen a pale blue that hugged my curves before falling in elegant folds to my ankles. The back dipped low, exposing the tattoo spanning my shoulders -- the club's emblem intertwined with wildflowers, marking me as both fierce and feminine. Charming had given his permission before I'd gotten it. No veil, just my hair styled in loose waves that fell past my shoulders. My only concession to tradition was the pendant my mother had given me.

I stepped outside and squinted against the harsh sunlight. The compound had transformed. Rows of folding chairs faced a makeshift altar, all arranged in the open space where normally bikes were parked in haphazard formations. Today, dozens of motorcycles lined the perimeter instead, chrome gleaming in the sun, a steel fence protecting our gathering.

"Nervous?" a female voice asked behind me.

I didn't turn. Didn't need to. I knew it was Josie.

"Not about marrying him."

"Just about doing it in front of everyone?"

I nodded, surveying the guests. Club members stood in clusters, leather cuts emblazoned with the Devil's Boneyard patch on full display. Some had cleaned up -- trimmed beards and fresh T-shirts -- while others looked like they'd just rolled in from a week-long ride. Women in varying degrees of biker chic mingled among them, mostly old ladies, but two club girls had asked to attend after seeing the way I handled myself -- all part of this world that had become mine.

Allies from other clubs had shown up too. I recognized cuts from the Dixie Reapers, Devil's Fury, and even a few from the Reckless Kings. I'd met some of them briefly before. In our world, alliances meant survival, and their presence meant respect -- both for the club and for Rebel.

My eyes found Charming at the front of the gathering. He stood on a raised wooden platform, his posture commanding attention even before he spoke. His cut looked freshly cleaned, and I'd have sworn he'd gotten a haircut. In his hands, incongruously, he held a clipboard. I couldn't think of what he'd have on there except maybe a cheat sheet for presiding over this wedding. He'd gotten ordained online for the occasion. His eyes scanned the crowd, assessing, always the President even in celebration.

"Time to go," the voice behind me said, and this time I turned to see one of the club girls giving me a knowing smile. "Your man's waiting."

I took another deep breath and began the walk. No wedding march played. Instead, the ambient sounds of the compound -- distant engines, low conversations, the whisper of wind through the surrounding trees -- created a soundtrack more fitting for who we were.

Rebel stood waiting, and the sight of him stole my breath. His cut was, for once, paired with a button-down shirt instead of his usual worn T-shirt or henley. His dark hair had been slicked back, revealing the sharp angles of his face and the intensity of his gaze as he watched me approach. Dixon Morreli -- Rebel to everyone else -- looked dangerous and beautiful, and entirely mine.

Scratch and Havoc flanked him like sentinels, both men nodding with approval as I approached. The old guard, showing their support for this union. Behind them stood Shade.

The crowd parted for me, some nodding, others offering brief smiles. I wasn't just marrying Rebel; I was cementing my place in this family. The weight of that commitment pressed on me as heavily as the vows I was about to speak.

I reached Rebel, and his hand, warm and calloused, took mine. "You clean up nice," I whispered.

"Speak for yourself," he returned, his eyes darkening as they took in the dress. "Not sure I'll have the patience to get you out of that properly later."

"You'll manage. If you tear it, you'll spend our wedding night in the ER." Rebel only grinned at me in response.

Charming cleared his throat, and the murmur of conversations died. He looked down at his clipboard, then surveyed the gathered crowd, his expression serious but with the hint of satisfaction that came from seeing his club strong and united.

"We don't stand on ceremony here," he began, his voice carrying easily across the compound. "But some things deserve marking. Today, we bind two warriors with a bond built on loyalty and the road we ride together."

His words resonated through me. Not the traditional "dearly beloved," but something that spoke to who we really were -- fighters who had found each other in a world that demanded strength.

"Rio," Charming continued, "came to us already carrying the spirit of the road. She proved herself worthy of our trust and our protection."

I felt Rebel's hand tighten around mine. We both knew what Charming meant. My path to the club hadn't been easy, and the trials I'd faced had left scars both visible and hidden. Those same trials had brought me to Rebel's attention, and eventually, to his side.

"Rebel has ridden with us through blood and fire. His loyalty has never wavered, his courage never faltered."

Around us, several members nodded in agreement, some raising fists in salute. Rebel's reputation in the club was solid -- not just for his fighting skills, but for his unwavering dedication to their brotherhood.

"Together," Charming said, looking pointedly at us both, "they form something stronger than either alone. A partnership built on respect and a shared understanding of what matters in this life."

Charming gestured for us to face each other. Rebel turned to me, his cockiness momentarily replaced by something deeper, more vulnerable. I saw in his eyes the same mixture of disbelief and certainty that I felt -- disbelief that we'd found each other, certainty that this was right.

"Your vows," Charming prompted.

Rebel spoke first, his voice low but steady. "Rio, I take you as my ride or die. In war and in peace. When the road is clear and when enemies close in. I pledge my protection, my loyalty, and my heart. No cage will ever hold us. No threat will ever separate us. You are my freedom and my home."

Simple words, but they hit me like a physical force. In our world, these promises carried life-or-death weight. I blinked back unexpected moisture in my eyes before responding. "Rebel, I choose you above all others. I pledge to ride by your side through whatever comes. To face our enemies without flinching. To guard your back as you guard mine. To find joy in the freedom we defend. You are my warrior and my peace."

Scratch stepped forward, producing two rings. Not gold bands, but silver rings engraved with the club's emblem intertwined with symbols unique to us -- a reflection of the tattoo across my back. Rebel had asked to have them custom made. I'd already moved his grandmother's ring to my right hand.

Rebel took one and slid it onto my finger, his touch lingering. I did the same for him, the metal warm from being carried close to Scratch's body.

"By the power vested in me as President of the Devil's Boneyard MC," Charming said, a hint of humor touching his voice at the formality of the words, "and with the witness of your brothers and sisters of the road, I pronounce you husband and wife." He paused, then added with a grin, "Kiss your woman, Rebel, before someone objects just to be an ass."

Rebel didn't need to be told twice. His hand came up to cup my face, and his kiss was both a claim and a promise. Around us, the compound erupted in cheers and catcalls, the solemnity of the moment giving way to the club's more typical rowdiness.

When we broke apart, I found myself laughing, a

release of tension I hadn't realized I'd been carrying. Rebel's eyes locked with mine, and in that glance passed a thousand unspoken words -- pride, possession, partnership, and something deeper that neither of us needed to name.

"Mrs. Morreli," he murmured, his thumb brushing across my lower lip.

"That's still Rio to you," I replied, but my smile betrayed my pleasure at hearing the name.

Havoc approached first, clapping Rebel on the shoulder before surprising me with a brief, fierce hug. "Welcome to the family," he said, though we both knew I'd been family long before the ceremony. "Officially," he added with a knowing look.

Scratch was next, his weathered face creasing in a rare smile. "You'll do," he said, which from him was high praise indeed.

All around us, club members and allies moved forward to offer congratulations and respect. But through it all, Rebel kept me anchored at his side, his hand at the small of my back or entwined with mine. We were tethered now, not just by choice but by oath, by the witnessed words that in our world carried the weight of blood promises.

As the crowd began to shift toward the clubhouse where the reception awaited, Rebel leaned close to my ear. "Any regrets?" he asked, his voice carrying a hint of vulnerability I rarely heard.

I turned to face him, taking in the man I'd just pledged my life to -- dangerous, complicated, and entirely mine. "Not one," I answered truthfully.

His smile, slow and predatory, sent a shiver through me that had nothing to do with fear and everything to do with anticipation. "Good," he said. "Because this is just the beginning." And as we walked toward the clubhouse, surrounded by leather-clad warriors who would kill or die for us as we would for them, I knew he was right. Whatever came next, we would face it together. Bound by choice, by vows, and by the road we rode together.

Harley Wylde

Harley Wylde is an accomplished author known for her captivating MC Romances. With an unwavering commitment to sensual storytelling, Wylde immerses her readers in an exciting world of fierce men and irresistible women. Her works exude passion, danger, and gritty realism, while still managing to end on a satisfying note each time.

When not crafting her tales, Wylde spends her time brainstorming new plotlines, indulging in a hot cup of Starbucks, or delving into a good book. She has a particular affinity for supernatural horror literature and movies. Visit Wylde's website to learn more about her works and upcoming events, and don't forget to sign up for her newsletter to receive exclusive discounts and other exciting perks.

Harley at Changeling: changelingpress.com/harley-wylde-a-196

Changeling Press LLC

Contemporary Action Adventure, Sci-Fi, Steampunk, Dark Fantasy, Urban Fantasy, Paranormal, and BDSM Romance available in e-book, audio, and print format at ChangelingPress.com – MC Romance, Werewolves, Vampires, Dragons, Shapeshifters and Horror -- Tales from the edge of your imagination.

Where can I get Changeling Press Books?

Changeling Press e-books are available at ChangelingPress.com, Amazon, Apple Books, Barnes & Noble, Kobo, Smashwords, and other online retailers, including Everand Subscription and Kobo Subscription Services. Print books are available at Amazon, Barnes and Noble, and by ISBN special order through your local bookstores.

Changeling Press LLC

ChangelingPress.com